THE LIVING MUMMY

THE LIVING MUMMY

Ambrose Pratt

RAMBLE HOUSE
2018

First American trade paperback edition

Ramble House
10329 Sheephead Drive
Vancleave MS 39565 USA

www.ramblehouse.com

Originally published in 1910 by
McLeod & Allen, Toronto
Frederick Stokes, New York
Ward, Lock & Co., London

ISBN 13: 978-1-60543-956-3

Preparation: Jim Weiler & Gavin L. O'Keefe
Cover design © 2018 Gavin L. O'Keefe

CHAPTER ONE

CONCERNING THE SON OF HAP

I WAS HARD at work in my tent. I had almost completed translating the inscription of a small stele of Amen-hotep III, dated B.C., 1382, which with my own efforts I had discovered, and I was feeling wonderfully self-satisfied in consequence, when of a sudden I heard a great commotion without. Almost immediately the tent flap was lifted, and Migdal Abu's black face appeared. He looked vastly excited for an Arab, and he rolled his eyes horribly. "What do you want?" I demanded irritably. "Did I not tell you I was not to be disturbed?"

He bent almost double. "Excellency—a white sheik has come riding on an ass, and with him a shameless female, also white."

"The dickens!" I exclaimed, for I had not seen a European for nine weeks.

Migdal Abu advanced with hand outstretched. "Excellency, he would have me give you this."

I took "this," and swore softly underbreath at the humourless pomposity of my unknown countryman. It was a pasteboard carte-de-visite. And we—in the heart of the Libyan desert!

With a laugh I looked at the thing and read his name—"Sir Robert Ottley."

"What!" I said, then sprang a-foot. Ottley the great Egyptologist. Ottley the famous explorer. Ottley the eminent decipherer of cuneiform inscriptions. Ottley the millionaire whose prodigality in the cause of learning had in ten short years more than doubled the common stock of knowledge of the history of the Shepherd kings of the Nile. I had been longing since a lad to meet him, and now he had come unasked to see me out on the burning sands of Yatibiri.

Trembling with excitement, I caught up a jacket, and hardly waiting to thrust my arms into the sleeves, rushed out of the tent.

Before me, sitting on an ass that was already sound asleep, despite a plague of flies that played about its eyes, was a little bronze-faced, grizzled old man attired from head to foot in glistening white duck and wearing on his head an enormous pith helmet. My Arabs, glad of an excuse to cease work, squatted round him in a semi-circle.

"Sir Robert Ottley!" I cried. "A thousand welcomes."

"You are very good," he drawled. "I presume you are Dr. Pinsent."

"At your service."

He stooped a little forward and offered me his hand.

"Will you not dismount?" I asked.

"Thank you, no. I have come to ask a favour." Then he glanced round him and began deliberately to count my Arabs.

I surveyed him in blank astonishment. He possessed a large hawk-like nose, a small thin-lipped mouth and little eyes twinkling under brows that beetled.

"Twelve, and two of them are good for nothing; mere weeds," said Sir Robert.

Then he turned to me with a smile. "You will forgive me?" he asked, adding quickly, "but then Arabs are cattle. There was no personal reflection."

"A cup of coffee," I suggested. "The sun is dreadful. It would refresh you."

"The sun is nothing," he replied, "and I have work to do. I am camped on the southern slope of the Hill of Rakh. It is twelve miles. I have found the tomb for which I have been searching seven years. I thought I had enough Arabs. I was mistaken."

"You may have the use of mine and welcome," I observed.

He gave a queer little bow. "He gives twice who gives quickly. The sarcophagus is in a rock hole forty feet beneath the level of the desert. I simply must have it up to-night."

"They shall start at once, and I shall go with them; I am as strong as six," I replied. Then I shouted some orders to Migdal Abu. When I turned it was to gasp. A woman had materialised from the sunbeams. I had completely forgotten that Sir Robert had a female companion. All my eyes had been for him. I swung off my hat and stammered some tardy words of welcome and invitation.

Sir Robert interrupted me. "My daughter—Dr. Pinsent," he drawled in slow, passionless tones. "My daughter does not require any refreshment, thank you, Doctor."

"I am too excited," said a singularly sweet voice. "Father's discovery has put me into a fever. I really could not eat, and coffee would choke me. But if you could give me a little water."

I rushed into my tent and returned with a brimming metal cup. "The Arabs have broken all my glass ware," I said apologetically.

She lifted her veil and our eyes met. She was lovely. She smiled and showed a set of dazzling teeth. The incisors were inlaid with gold. I remarked the fact in a sort of self-defensive panic, for the truth is I am a shy idiot with pretty women. Thank goodness she was thirsty and did not notice my confusion. Two minutes afterwards I was mounted on my donkey, and we were off on the long tramp to the Hill of Rakh, the Arabs trailing behind us in a thin ill-humoured line. We maintained the silence of bad temper and excessive heat until the sun sank into the sand. Then, however, we wiped our foreheads, said a cheerful goodbye to the flies that had been tormenting us, and woke up.

"I am immensely obliged to you, Dr. Pinsent," said Sir Robert.

"So am I," said Miss Ottley.

"The boot is on the other foot," I replied. "It's kind of you to permit me to be present at your triumph. Is it a king?"

"No," said Miss Ottley, "a priest of Amen of the eighteenth dynasty."

"Oh, a priest."

Miss Ottley bridled at my tone. "No king was ever half as interesting as *our* priest," she declared. "He was a wonderful man in every way, a prophet, a magician, and enormously powerful. Besides, he is believed to have committed suicide for the sake of principle, and he predicted his own resurrection after a sleep of two thousand years."

"He has been dead 3285 years," sighed Sir Robert.

"Is that his fault?" cried the girl.

"It falsifies his prophecy."

She shrugged her shoulders.

"Ptahmes was his name," said Sir Robert, turning to me. "He was the right-hand man of Amen-hotep IV; but when that king changed his religion and his name and became Akhenaten and a devotee of the old worship of Heliopolis, Ptahmes apparently killed himself as a protest against the deposition of Amen, his particular divinity."

"Read that," said Miss Ottley.

She handed me a page of type-written manuscript.

It ran as follows:

"Hearken to the orders which are put upon you by Ptahmes, named Tahutimes, son of Mery, son of Hap.

"All my ways were regulated even as the pace of an ibis. The Hawk-headed Horus was my protector like amulets upon my body. I trained the troops of my lord. I made his pylon 60 cubits long in the noble rock of quartzite, most great in height and firm as heaven. I did not imitate what had been done before. I was the royal scribe of the recruits. Mustering was done under me. I was appointed Judge of the Palace; overseer of all the prophets of the south and of the north. I was appointed High Priest of Amen in the Capital—King of all the Gods. I was made the eyes and ears of the king: keeper of my lord's heart and fan-bearer at the King's right hand. Great men have come from afar to bow themselves before me, bringing presents of ivory and gold, copper, silver and emery, lazuli, malachite, green felspar and vases of mern wood inlaid with white precious stones sometimes bearing gold at one time 1000 deben (200 pounds weight). For my fame was carried abroad even as the fame of the king, 'lord of the sweet wind.' And there was spoken of me by the son of Paapis that my wisdom was of a divine nature, because of my knowledge of futurities. Yet on the sixth day of the month of Pakhons in the 18th year I desire to rest. My lord, at the solicitation of the great royal wife and mother Nefertiti, has put off the worship of his predecessors. The name of Amen is proscribed from the country. Ra is proscribed from the country. Horus is proscribed from the country. Aten is set up in their place and worshipped in the land. My lord has even changed his name. Apiy is the high priest of the new God that is from the Mesopotamian wilderness. Amen, king of the Gods, dandled my lord and is forsaken and proscribed. I am an old man and would rest: although my lord has not forsaken me. He has appointed me overseer of all his works. Therefore, shall you carry me to the temple of Kak, and give my body to the hands of the priests of Amen who will wrap me in the linen sheets of Horus without removing my heart, my entrails or my lungs. Then you shall carry me to Khizebh and enclose me in the place prepared for me; and cover my tomb to a depth of five fathoms with the sand of the desert at that hour when no man looks or listens. Do this even as I command, and as royal scribe I trace the order with my pen. But you shall place my papyri and the sign by which I shall be known, and the stele of ivory engraved with the directions to the priests of Amen who are to wake me from my sleep at the distant hour, in the tomb that is prepared for my body in the temple of Merenptah and in such manner that I shall there appear to sleep. And all these things you shall do, or my curse shall pursue you and your children and their children for the space of four hundred lives. Nor shall you remove the endowment of my gifts nor touch them where they lie under a penalty of great moment."

I strained my eyes to catch the last words, for the darkness was already setting down upon the desert; and I was profoundly interested.

"Wonderful!" I said, as I returned her the document. "A papyrus, of course?"

"Yes, one of several. Father found it seven years ago at Dier el Batiri."

"I had not heard."

Sir Robert coughed. "No," said he, "nor anyone else. I have never published it. It did not come to me in the usual way. I bought it from an Arab who had rifled the tomb in which it was discovered."

"And the other papyri and the ivory stele?" I questioned.

"They are in my possession, too."

"They enabled you doubtless to locate the real tomb that holds the body?"

"They helped."

Then silence supervened. To me it was filled with wonder. I could not help asking myself what circumstances could possibly have induced Ottley to withhold so valuable an historic treasure for so many years from the world. Such a course of action was utterly opposed to all practice, and the unwritten but immutable laws of scientific research. It seemed strangely at odds, too, with the man's reputed character. It would have covered him with glory to have placed his discovery before the Society to which we both belonged. And a dozen incidents related of him far and wide, proved that he was not indifferent to praise and fame. He read my thoughts probably, for at length he cleared his throat and spoke.

"There were reasons why I should not blazon the find abroad," he said.

"No doubt," I observed, with unintentioned dryness.

"One papyrus speaks of a golden treasure," he went on quietly. "If published, it would have set thousands looking for the tomb. In that case the chances are that the body of Ptahmes would have been destroyed by some vandal intent solely on pillage."

"You assumed a great responsibility," I remarked. I simply had to say it, for I was angry, and his explanation appeared puerile to me.

"Do you dispute my right?" he demanded coldly.

I shrugged my shoulders. "It is not for me to say, Sir Robert. Doubtless when the time comes you will be able to satisfy the Society and the world that you have acted rightly."

"I admit no responsibility," he answered; "and permit me to observe that you are talking nonsense. I owe no duty to communicate the results of my purchases or discoveries to any Society or to the world."

"True, Sir Robert. An action for damages could not lie against you."

"Sir!" he cried.

"Father," said Miss Ottley, "how can Dr. Pinsent's foolish sarcasm affect you? Besides, we need his Arabs."

"Quite so," said Sir Robert. "We need his Arabs. How brightly the stars shine to-night, Dr. Pinsent."

The cool impudence of the pair struck me dumb. I shook with passion. For a moment I thought of calling a halt and returning the way we had come to my own camp with my Arabs. But for my curiosity to see the tomb of Ptahmes very probably I should have done so. In a few seconds, however, my rage cooled, and my uppermost feeling was admiration mixed with mirth. I had never been treated with such open and absurd contempt before. It was a refreshing experience. I burst of a sudden into a peal of laughter. Miss Ottley joined me in the exercise. But Sir Robert rode on like a hook-nosed sphinx.

"I knew I could not be mistaken," said Miss Ottley. "You should thank God for your sense of humour, Dr. Pinsent."

"And who is benefiting from it at this moment, I should like to know?" I retorted. "The thanks are due from you, I fancy."

"Deo gratias!" she flashed. "In sober truth, we need your Arabs sadly."

"I repeat, I am glad to be of use."

"We shall use you, but not necessarily in the cause of your Society. Understand that fully."

"You mean?"

"That you must not expect to share our secrets."

"In plain words, you will not let me help you open the sarcophagus."

"Your penetration is remarkable."

"And if—"

"And if," she interrupted quickly, "you require a reward for the courtesy we asked and you accorded or have promised to accord, you have but to name a sum in cash to have it paid."

"Or—" said I, stung to the quick.

"Or," she flashed, "return! You are at liberty to make your choice. Yours are not the only Arabs in Egypt. At a pinch we can wait a day or two. It is for you to say."

I tore off my hat. "Miss Ottley—my Arabs are yours for as long as you require them!" I furiously announced. "Good day to you. Sir Robert, good day!"

Then I dragged the head of my ass round and set his face to my camp. The beast, however, would hardly budge, and I had to be-labour him unmercifully to induce him to trot. Never did man make a more undignified exit from circumstances of indignity. And it did not need Miss Ottley's mocking laughter to assure me that I looked ridiculous. I could have strangled her with all the cheerfulness in life; and from that moment I have cherished an ineradicable hatred of donkeys. Sir Robert did not open his lips. He did not even return my angry salute. Almost choking with rage, I finally got out of range of Miss Ottley's laughter. Then I dismounted and told the desert just what I thought of her and her father. It was almost mid-night when I reached my camp, for, to crown all, I neglected the stars in my passion, and for two hours lost my way.

CHAPTER TWO

A PATIENT OF THE DESERT

I SPENT THE next two days in absolute solitude, and got through a tremendous quantity of toil. In fact, I added two whole chapters to my treatise on the Nile monuments and I arranged the details of a third. By the end of that time, however, I was ravenously hungry. I had been too engrossed in labour to think of eating anything but biscuits. And appetite at last turned me out of the tent. I looked around for my Arabs and saw sand and sky—no living thing—oh, yes, there was my donkey. The little beast had eaten his way through a truss of straw, and was asleep. Strolling over to the ruined pylon, I glanced down into the hole my Arabs had excavated. It was empty. "Gad!" I exclaimed. "They must still be working for Ottley." I had to build a fire and turn cook, willy nilly. Later, fortified with the pleasant conviction of a good dinner, I turned my telescope on the Hill of Rakh. An Arab stood on the treeless summit leaning on a rifle whose barrel glittered in the sunlight. I was puzzled. He was manifestly posted there as sentinel, but why? I watched him till dark, but he did not move. That night I shot a jackal—omen of disaster. It was long before I slept. Yet I seemed only to have slumbered a moment or two when I awoke. A voice called my name aloud. "Dr. Pinsent! Dr. Pinsent!" I started upright and listened, nerves on edge.

"Dr. Pinsent!"

"Who calls?" I shouted.

"I—May Ottley."

"Miss Ottley!" I hopped out of my bag bed like a cricket. "Just a moment." I struck a light and, grabbing at my clothes, proceeded to dress like mad. Thus for thirty seconds; then I remembered how I had been treated, and went slower. Then I thought —"Pinsent, you're a cad—she's a woman, and perhaps in trouble." So I got up steam again and called out, "Nothing wrong, I hope?"

"Yes," said Miss Ottley. Well, here was a woman of business, at any rate. She seemed to know the use of words, and valued them accordingly. Waste not, want not. I drew on my jacket and lifted the flap. An Arab rustled past me.

"Hello!" said I. "Not so fast, my man."

But it was Miss Ottley. I stepped back, bewildered. Her hair was tucked away in a sort of turban, and she was wrapped from head to heel in a burnous that had once been white—very long ago. But the costume, though dirty, was becoming. She sank upon a camp stool and asked at once for water. She seemed very tired. My bag was empty. I hurried off without a word to the barrel in the temple. When I returned she was asleep where she sat. I touched her shoulder and she started up, suppressing a scream. "Now," said I, as she put down the cup. Miss Ottley stood up. "A bad thing has happened," she began. "The sarcophagus was filled with treasure, gold and silver in bars, and other things. The Arabs went mad. My father fought like a paladin and held them off for a day and a half. But soon after dark this evening a caravan arrived. The fight was renewed and my father was wounded. The Arabs secured the treasure and fled into the desert. The dragoman only kept faith with us. He has gone by the river to Khonsu for troops. I hurried here for you. I ran almost all the way. Will you come? Father is very ill. He has lost a lot of blood. He was shot in the shoulder."

I nodded, caught up my revolver and surgical pack and rushed out of the tent. In two minutes I had saddled the donkey. Miss Ottley was standing by the door of the tent. I lifted her on the beast and we started off in silence. An hour later she spoke.

"There is one thing I like about you," she announced. "You haven't much to say for yourself, but you are a worker."

"Tu quoque," I replied. "You must have done that twelve miles in record time. It is not yet two o'clock."

"I made it in two hours, I think."

"You are an athlete, by Jove!"

"I am no bread-and-butter miss, at any rate. This donkey has a bad pace, don't you think?"

I kicked the brute into a trot and ran beside it. The Hill of Rakh soon began to loom large among the stars on the horizon. "I suppose you were pretty wild at our cavalier treatment of you the other evening," said Miss Ottley.

"Well, yes," I admitted.

"We were sorry when the fight came."

"No doubt," said I.

"It served us right, eh?"

"That is my opinion."

"Do you bear malice still?"

"I am thinking of your father's wound."

"That atones?"

"Your twelve-mile run helps."

"But you are still angry with us?"

"Does it matter? I am serving you."

"Be generous," said Miss Ottley. "We have been sufficiently punished. Not only have we lost the treasure, but there was no mummy in the sarcophagus.

"Be a lady and apologise," I retorted.

"No," said she, with a most spirited inflection. "It is not a woman's place."

"Then be silent or change the topic," I growled.

She was silent. We arrived an hour later at the mountain. I was bathed in perspiration and as tired as a dog. But Miss Ottley had no time to notice my condition. She slipped off the donkey and hurried away through the smaller of the three pylons that fronted a small temple hollowed out of the rock face of the hill. There was no sign of tent, so I concluded that Sir Robert had made his camp within the temple. I hitched the ass to a stake and cooled off, thanking Providence for a cool breeze that swept up from the placid surface of the Nile. Day was already showing signs of breaking, and a broad flight of long-legged flamingoes hurried its coming with a flash of scarlet just above the eastern horizon. The distant howling of a hyena was borne to me in fitful snatches on the wind. The earth was wrapped in mystery and melancholy. Oh, Egypt! Egypt, land of sun-lit spaces and illimitable shadows; of grandeur and of squalor without peer; of happy dreams and sad awakenings; of centuries ingloriously oblivious of glory; of sleep and sphinx-browed, age-bound silences; of darkly smiling and impotent despair. What a mistress for a man of curiosity and of imagination! Little wonder that since I had been caught in her magic and most jealous spell the face of no human being had possessed the power to threaten her supremacy or cancel my allegiance to the mystic desert queen.

"Dr. Pinsent!"

I awoke from my reverie with a start. "This way," said Miss Ottley. I bowed and followed her into the temple, through a broad but low stone doorway, past a row of broken granite columns. A light within showed us the path. The chamber was about eighteen feet square; there was another of equal size beyond it, in the heart of the hill. An immense sarcophagus composed entirely of lead almost blocked the door. The lid, carved to represent the figure and face of a tall grave-featured man, was propped up on end against a pillar. The sarcophagus was empty. Beyond stood a trestle cot, a table and a lamp. Sir Robert Ottley lay upon the cot. He was awake, but evidently unconscious, and in a high fever. I examined his wound and prepared for action. There was an oil stove in the room. I lighted it and set water to boil. Miss Ottley watched me with an expression I shall not forget easily. Her face was as wan as that of a ghost; and her big red-brown eyes glowed like coals, and were ringed with purple hollows. She was manifestly worn out and on the verge of a breakdown. But although I begged her to retire, she curtly refused. Judging by her eyes, she was my enemy, and a critical enemy at that. When everything was ready I walked over to her, picked her up in my arms and carried her struggling like a wildcat to the door. Then I put her out and blocked the entrance with the lid of the sarcophagus. She panted—"I hate you," from behind it. Then she began to cry. I said nothing. It seemed one of those occasions wherein silence was golden. I tied Sir Robert to the cot and set to work. Half an hour later I found the bullet under his clavicle, and then dressed the wound and bound him up. He came out of the influence of the anæsthetic in his sober senses; but he was so eager to tell me all his disappointment that I gave him a hypodermic dose of morphia, and he dropped asleep in the middle of a rabid diatribe against Arabs in general and our Arabs in particular.

I found Miss Ottley reclining against a ruined pillar in an angle of the pylon. She had cried herself to sleep and was breathing like a child. I slipped out and found the Arab's store-house and kitchen. Luckily the gold had exhausted their cupidity. The stores were untouched. I lighted a fire and prepared a meal—coffee and curry for Miss Ottley and myself; beef tea and arrowroot for the invalid. By that time the sun was riding high in the heavens, but Miss Ottley still slept. Willing to assist her rest I secured a cushion from the chamber and pushed it gently beneath her head. She sighed and turned over, allowing me to see her face. I examined it and found it good. The features were well-nigh perfect, from the little Grecian nose to the round chin. But it was a face instinct with pride, the pride of a female Lucifer. And her form was in keeping. "God save her husband," was my conclusion. And I ate a hearty breakfast, watching her and pitying him, whoever he should be.

Sir Robert woke about noon, and although a little feverish, I was quite satisfied with his progress. After eating a dish of what he feelingly described as "muck" he went to sleep again. I prepared a second meal and brought it on a box to where Miss Ottley still lay sleeping. Then I sat down and coughed. Her eyes opened at once and she looked at me. It is marvellous what a woman's glance can do. I became instantly conscious of a dirty face, unkempt hair, and a nine-weeks' growth of beard. In order to conceal my appreciation of my ugliness I grinned.

"Ugh!" murmured Miss Ottley, and she got up.

"Sir Robert is asleep," I observed. "I found the bullet. He has had lunch and is going on nicely. You had better eat something."

She gave me a glance of scorn and glided into the temple. I helped her to a plate of curry, poured out a cup of coffee and made myself scarce. Returning a quarter of an hour later, I found the plate bare, the cup empty and not a crumb left on the box. I took the things away and washed them, and my own face. Then I shaved with a pocket amputation knife, using for mirror a pot of soapy water; and I brushed my too abundant locks into something like order with a bunch of stubble which I converted into a hair brush with a tomahawk and a piece of twine. Feeling prodigiously civilised and almost respectable, I strolled back to the pylon, sat down on Miss Ottley's cushion, and lighted my pipe.

About two minutes later Miss Ottley appeared.

"Patient awake?" I asked.

"No," said Miss Ottley. "What an objectionable smell of tobacco!"

War to the knife evidently. I stood lip. "When you need me shout," I remarked, and strolled off, puffing stolidly. But I saw her face as I turned, and it was crimson, perhaps with surprise that I could be as rude as she, perhaps with mortification that I had dared. If ever a girl needed a dressing down it was she who stood in the pylon staring after me. I squatted in the shadow of a rock and spent the afternoon stupefying over-friendly flies with the fumes of prime Turkish. She shouted just before sundown. Her father was delirious, she said. I found him raving and tearing at his bandages. He was haunted with an hallucination of phantom cats. The whole cavern, he declared, was filled with cats; black as Erebus with flaming yellow eyes. I shooed them away and after some trouble calmed the poor old man. But it was going to be a bad case, that was plain. Luckily the cave temple was, comparatively speaking, cool. I spent the evening disinfecting every cranny, and quietly dispersing the suspicious dust of vanished centuries. When I had finished it smelt carbolically wholesome and was as clean as a London hospital, even to the ceiling. Miss Ottley sat all the while by her father's cot, and occasionally sneezed to relieve her feelings. I had very little sympathy for her distress. I said to her, "You will take first watch, I'll sleep in the pylon. Call me at midnight." Then I placed my watch on the edge of the sarcophagus and went out. She said nothing. I woke at dawn. She was sitting like a statue beside her father's bedside. Her face was grey. Sir Robert was asleep, but breathing stertorously. I beckoned her out to the pylon. "See here, Miss Ottley," I said, in a cold rage, "I'm not going to beat about the bush with you. I told you to call me at midnight. Kindly explain your disobedience."

"I am not your servant to obey your orders," she retorted icily.

"No," said I, "you prefer to serve your own prickly pride to behaving sensibly. But let me tell you this—your father's life depends on careful nursing. And that is impossible unless we apportion the work properly between us. You'll be fit for nothing today, and my task will be doubled in consequence. A little more of such folly and you'll break down altogether. You are strung up to more than concert pitch. As for me—I am not a machine, and though I am prepared to do my best out of mere humanity, I don't pretend to do the impossible. Nor shall I answer for your father's life if you force me to nurse two patients single-handed."

She looked me straight in the eye. "Very well, sir, I shall henceforth rigidly obey you."

"You must," I said and strode into the open. When I had prepared breakfast, she did not want to eat. But I had only to frown and she succumbed. Afterwards I made her lie down, and she slept through Sir Robert's groaning. It was a hideous day. The patient grew steadily worse, and so great was his strength, despite his diminutive size, that our struggles wore me out at last and I was obliged to strap him down. By nightfall he was a maniac, and his yells could be heard, I make no doubt, a mile around. And the worst of it was that my stock of bromide was gone. I had to dose him with morphia. But I had not to speak to Miss Ottley again. She woke me out of a delicious sleep at a quarter to the hour. She was quite composed, but as pale as a sheet.

"My father is going to die, I think," she whispered.

I went in and looked at him. He was straining like a tiger at his bonds. "Not to-night, at any rate," I observed. "He has the strength of six. You go straight to bed!"

She went off as meek as any lamb, and I began to talk to Sir Robert. Our conversation was somewhat entertaining. He was Ixion chained to the wheel. I was Sisyphus with a day off duty. We commiserated one another on our penalties, and bitterly assailed

King Pluto's unsympathetic government. Finally we conspired to dethrone him and give the crown of Hades to Proserpine, whose putatively tender heart might be reckoned on occasionally to mitigate the anguish of our punishment. He fell into a fitful doze at last with his hand in mine, but he soon awoke, and with a yell announced the return of the imaginary plague of cats. On the whole, the night was worse than the day. And morning was no blessing. Sir Robert had shed five and forty years. He was once again at college, and if his unwilling confessions are to be relied upon, and his language, he must have been a precious handful for his masters. But now he steadily lost strength, and the flame of fever ate him up before our eyes. As the shadows lengthened into afternoon I began to look for the crisis.

CHAPTER THREE

TWO LIES

SLEEP WAS NOT to be dreamed of that night for either of us well people. I had thought of a plan. Leaving Miss Ottley to watch the unconscious but ceaselessly babbling patient, I scoured out the sarcophagus, and then built an enormous fire before the pylon. Over this I hung the Arab's cauldron. By nightfall I had the sarcophagus nigh abrim with hot water. It formed a huge but most admirable bath. It was a heroic experiment to make; but the dark angel was in the cavern and I had little chance left. Kill or cure. It seemed a toss of the coin either way, for Sir Robert was dying fast. After the bath he slipped into a state of blank insensibility. Miss Ottley thought him asleep, and she took heart to hope. I did not deceive her. For four hours I waited, my finger continually on his pulse. It grew continually weaker. I administered nitro-glycerine every half hour, but at length even that spur failed.

"Miss Ottley," said I, "you must prepare for the worst."

She showed me a face of more than mortal courage. Pride is not always amiss in characters like hers. "I have felt it all along," she said quietly. "Will he regain his senses?"

"Yes. At least I think he will—before the end."

"Is there no hope?"

"None—unless he can be miraculously aroused. Pardon me—is he very much attached to you?"

"No—his heart and soul are wrapped up in his work. He died, to all intents and purposes, the hour he was shot. His terrible disappointment had deprived him of his best support."

"The robbery, you mean?"

"No—the knowledge of his failure. He made certain of finding the body of Ptahmes."

"Ah!" said I—and gave myself to thought. When I looked up next Miss Ottley was gazing at her father with a marble countenance, but tears were streaming from her eyes.

"You love him," I whispered.

19

"More than all the world," she answered simply. Her voice rang as true and unbroken as the chiming of a bell. I began in spite of myself to admire Miss Ottley.

Ten minutes passed; minutes of hideously oppressive silence. Then, without warning, Sir Robert's eyelids flickered and opened. There was the light of reason in them. I bent over him and his glance encountered mine. I pressed his hand and said in brisk, cheerful tones, "You must hurry up and get well, Sir Robert, or I shall not be able to restrain my curiosity. This Ptahmes of yours is the most extraordinary mummy I have ever seen; and I am simply dying to take him from his shroud."

The dim eyes of the dying man actually glowed. His fingers clutched at my wrist, and with a superhuman effort he gasped forth, "No—No."

"Be easy," I returned, "I'll not touch him till you are well. But you must hurry. Remember we are of a trade, you and I."

He smiled and very slowly his eyes closed. His breathing was absolutely imperceptible; but his pulse, though faint, was regular. I made sure and then put down his hand.

"He is dead," said Miss Ottley, and her voice thrilled me to the core.

"No," said I, "he is sleeping like a babe. The crisis is over. He will live."

"Oh! my God!" she cried, and fell on her knees beside the bed shaken with a storm of sobbing.

I sneaked out of the temple and smoked my first pipe in three days. I was only half through it when I felt her at my side.

"No, please continue smoking," she said, "I like it, really. I have come to try and thank you."

"You can't," I replied; "I'm not a man to overestimate his own services, but this is the sort of thing that cannot be repaid by either gold or words."

"Oh!" she said.

"You see," I went on, "I lied. It was to save his life—for your sake. The sight of your distress touched me. I am glad that he will live, of course. Glad to have served you. But the fact remains, I am a liar."

"Dr. Pinsent!" she cried.

"Oh, I daresay I'll grow used to it," I interrupted cheerfully. "Perhaps I have only shed a superstition, after all. I confess to an unwonted feeling of freedom, too. Undoubtedly I was shackled, in a sense. Yet a convict chained for years feels naked, I am told, when he gets, suddenly, his liberty. I can easily believe it. My own experience—but enough; we leave the patient too long alone."

She flitted off like a phantom and as noiselessly. I refilled my pipe. An hour later I found them both asleep, she seated on the camp-stool leaning back against the tomb. Nature had been too strong for her, poor girl. I felt towards her the brotherhood of vice. She, too, had lied—in pretending a little while before—a hatred of tobacco.

I took her quietly and gently in my arms and carried her to her own cot in the inner cabin. She did not wake.

CHAPTER FOUR

THE SARCOPHAGUS'S PERFUME

TOWARDS MORNING MY mind grew much easier. Sir Robert awoke and took a few mouthfuls of liquid nourishment. But although too weak to speak, he was sensible and the fever had left him. He fell asleep again immediately. Soon afterwards my eyes fell on the sarcophagus. Its great size affected me with wonder—and its construction. Why should imperishable treasures, gold, silver, and precious stones be enclosed in lead? Why not in stone? And the sarcophagus had been hermetically sealed too, witness the chisel and saw marks on the lid, of Ottley's making. I examined them attentively, then sat down and stared at the sarcophagus again. It was coffin shaped. Why? If it had been intended for a mere treasure chest surely—I was struck suddenly by a fact and a remembrance. The sarcophagus manifestly measured four feet high at least. And I remembered that in filling it with water for Sir Robert's bath I had only had to fill eighteen inches in depth. What if underneath the treasure it contained another chamber overlaid with lead? There was room. I got afoot and measured the depth of water on my arm. Eighteen, well, certainly not more than nineteen inches. I seized a bucket and began to bail the water out, having need to be noiseless for the sleepers' sake. The task occupied the better part of half an hour. By then morning had begun to pale the lamplight, and I was weary. But I kept on, and finally mopped the interior of the huge basin dry with a towel. Thereupon I examined the bottom with the lamp. It did not show a single crevice. The lead was in a solid and impervious sheet. Curious. But the difference between the eighteen inches and the four feet remained to be accounted for. Was the interspace filled with lead? If so—why such uneconomic expenditure of a valuable mineral? The mystery interested me so much that my weariness was forgotten. I felt that at any cost it must be solved forthwith. Casting about, I found a fine-pointed and razor-sharp chisel in the drawer of Sir Robert Ottley's camp table. With this, I set to work. Climbing into the sarcophagus, I selected a spot, and using the weight of my body in place of a hammer, I forced the chisel into the lead. It bit into the metal slowly but surely. One inch. One inch and a half. Suddenly it slipped. I fell forward and was brought up by the handle. The mystery was solved. I recovered my position and wiped my forehead. Instantly a thin but strangely overpowering perfume filled my nostrils. It resembled camphor, and violets, and lavender, and oil of almonds, and a hundred other scents, but was truly like none of them. It created and compelled, however, a confused train of untranslatable reflections which might have been memories. But God knows what they were. I experienced a mysterious sensation of immeasurable antiquity. And wildly absurd as the idea appears set forth in sober language, something assured me that I was thousands of years old or had lived before—so long—so very long ago. I saw lights—the sound of chanting voices and of rushing waters filled my ears. I seemed to be assisting at a solemn ritual. Ghostly forces and dim spirit figures filled the cave. The air was thick with incense fumes. My reason rocked and swung. Just in time I realised that I was becoming mysteriously anæsthetised. I held my breath and with a powerful effort leaped to the floor. Then I carefully blocked up the chisel hole with my kerchief and staggered into the open air. Very soon I was my own man again. Returning filled with apprehension for the patient, I found nothing to alarm me. The perfume had absolutely disappeared. Sir Robert was sleeping like a babe. I took a nip of brandy and. sitting down, gave myself to dreams watching the sarcophagus. What was its secret? And what the secret of Sir Robert Ottley's passionate interest in the corpse of Ptahmes that had been potent enough to call him back to life from the very brink of dissolution? But plainly I must wait to learn. For it would not do to trifle with the perfume in the cavern. In that confined space it might bring about the destruction of us all. Already it had affected me. My head ached fearfully, and I knew that my blood vessels were distended, and that my heart was still violently excited. My agitation was not all painful. There was an insidious pleasure mingled with it, an intangible titillation of the nerves; but that only alarmed me the more. The poisons that are most to be feared are those which captivate the senses; they convey no warning to the body, and betray the mind, however watchful, by effecting a paralysis of will. Perhaps—unwittingly—I had been very near death. The notion was disturbing. I began to regard the sarcophagus much in the light of an infernal machine possessing dangerous potentialities for ill. I determined as soon as possible—that is to say, as soon as help arrived—to have it removed from the sick room to the pylon. There at least it would be less manifestly perilous; having the play of the whole wide desert atmosphere in which to dissipate its noxious energies.

A rustling sound dissolved my meditations. I glanced up and saw Miss Ottley bending over her father. I slipped out and sought the Arab's quarters. Soon I had a good fire alight and water on to boil. I rather spread myself that morning. I cooked some tinned asparagus, boiled a tinned chicken, and opened a jar of prunes. Breakfast spread on the lid of a brandy box looked and smelled very good. I carried it up to the pylon and whistled "Come into the garden, Maude."

Miss Ottley appeared at once, round eyed with surprise.

"Your father has already eaten," I observed. "In all likelihood he will sleep for hours yet. Kindly sit down. You'll excuse my novel breakfast call. It is the only invitational air I am acquainted with."

She stared at me.

"May one not be light-hearted when all goes well?" I asked.

"One may," she answered. Then her eyes fell and she coloured painfully. "But not two. I slept at my post. Oh! how could I?" Her voice was quite despairing and bitterly contemptuous.

I bit at the leg of a chicken which I held in my fingers. "After all, you are a woman, you know," I commented, with my mouth full. "This chick's prime—done to a turn."

"How tired you must be!"

"I'm not complaining. Nor do I grudge you the extra rest. You look better. Hungry?"

"Y-yes," she admitted.

"Then don't be a ninny spending time in vain regrets. Fall to and repair your waste tissues. In plain English—eat."

She sat down on a ruined column and I handed her a plate.

"You look—positively merry!" she said. "You are nursing some—pleasant—or profitable reflection." She considered the words with care.

"I have discovered that I may have—told the truth to your father last night after all. By accident."

"I beg your pardon."

"I believe I have found your friend Ptahmes, Miss Ottley."

The plate slid off her lap and broke. Chicken and gravy littered the pavement. But she had no idea of it. "Impossible!" she cried.

I explained my examination of the sarcophagus and the result in detail. She sat gazing at me like a graven image. When she had finished she arose and vanished—without a word. I followed and found her standing beside the great lead coffin, my kerchief in her hand. She had reopened the chisel hole, and the cavern was already saturated with the infernal gas. I snatched my handkerchief away and once more blocked the vent. Then I exerted all my strength and with a prodigious effort placed the lid on the sarcophagus. With a woman's curiosity to reckon with, such a precaution seemed a vital safeguard, I found her standing in the pylon, breathing like a spent runner.

"You might have taken my word," I said coldly. "You'd have saved yourself an ugly headache at the least."

Her face was crimson; her eyes burned like stars. The fumes of that uncanny perfume had made her drunk. She swayed and leaned dizzily against a pillar. I went up and took her hand. The pulse was beating like a miniature steam hammer.

"Sit down," I said.

She laughed and sank at my feet in a heap. "Oh! Oh!" she cried and fell to sobbing half hysterically though tearlessly.

"Lord!" I said aloud. "What a bundle of hysterical humours it is, and how plain to look on when its resolution takes a holiday."

That is the way to treat hysteria.

Miss Ottley sat up and withered me with a glance. "I—I am. It—it's not hysteria," she stammered, between gasps. "Besides—you—confessed—it—overcame—you, too."

Then she fainted. I sprang up, but even as I moved I heard a loud sigh in the cavern. "The sick man first," I muttered, and let the girl lie. But at the door of the cavern chamber I stood transfixed. A dark shape bent over the patient's cot, hiding Sir Robert Ottley's face from view. It seemed to be a man, but its back was presented to my gaze. "What the deuce are you doing here, whoever you are?" I cried out, and started forward. The shape melted on the instant into thinnest air. "Nothing but a shadow," I said to myself. It was necessary to say something. I was shocked to my soul. I stood for a moment shaking and dismayed. The shadow had been so thick and bodily and had fled so like a spirit that I had work to do to readjust my scattered faculties. Of course a shadow—and my eyes, dazzled by the sunlight without, had momentarily failed to pierce it. A reasonable and quite ample scientific explanation. But what had cast the shadow? Pish—what but myself? And yet: and yet: I was shivering like a blancmange. Never had my nerves used me so ill. Perhaps, however, that accursed perfume had affected them. Ah! there was a reassuring solution of the puzzle. Reassuring to my reason, be it understood, for the fleshy part of me was taken with an ague and refused for many seconds to return to its subjection to my will. Sometimes now I doubt but that the flesh has an intelligence apart from the brain cells and nerve structures that usually control it. Indeed, I have never met a man of intellect whose memory does not register experience of some occasion in which his flesh took independent fright—like a startled hare—at some bogie which made his sober reason subsequently smile; nay, contemptuously at times. "Well, well," I said at length and pushed forward—to receive another shock. Sir Robert Ottley was almost nude. The bed clothes had been pushed down past his waist. His fingers convulsively gripped the paillasse. His face was livid. His eyes were open and upturned. His whole form was stiff and rigid. A fit? It seemed so. His pulse was still. He did not breathe. But a cataleptic fit then, for at a lance prick the blood flowed. I forced him to his right side and tried massage. No use. Strychnine and nitro-glycerine equally refused to act. Finally I saturated a cloth with amyl nitrate, placed it over his open mouth and tried artificial respiration. A whole hour had passed already, but I refused to give in. It was well. In another twenty minutes my efforts were rewarded with a sigh. I kept on and the man began to breathe. When it seemed safe to leave off, I disposed him easily and watched events. First his normal colouring returned. Then his mouth closed. Finally his eyes revolved. The lids closed and opened several times, then rested closed. His pulse beat feverishly, but in spite of that he slept. I walked to the door. Miss Ottley—whom I had completely forgotten—still lay insensible where she had fallen. I picked her up and brought her into the cavern. She awoke to consciousness in transit. I forced her to drink a stiff nobbler of brandy, and very soon she was in her old, cold, bright, proud, self-reliant state—armed cap-a-pie with insolence and egotism.

"Is your father subject to fits?" I asked.

"He has never had, till this, a day's illness in his life," she responded—with a touch of indignation.

I nodded. "Well, his period of disease indemnity has passed. While you swooned he had a fit. I use the expression colloquially. You would probably have so described his condition had you seen him. As for me I don't know. The symptoms were unique. I restored him by treating him as a drowned man. He was in a sort of trance. From this moment he must never be left, even for a second."

"He was insensible?"

"He was inanimate."

"That perfume!" she cried.

I shrugged my shoulders. "No doubt."

We glanced at the sarcophagus, then at each other.

"Was there need?" she asked, colouring. Then her eyes sparkled. "Oh, for such strength!" she cried. "It took six Arabs to lift that coffin lid. You must be a Samson."

"Fortunately," I observed.

Her brows drew together and her lips. "You treat me in a way that I resent," she said. "I am as reasonable a being as yourself."

I retired to a corner and stretched myself upon the floor without replying.

"When do you wish to be aroused?" she asked.

"An hour before sunset. We must eat—that is I. You appear to thrive on air."

She bit her lips and I stared at the ceiling. I was dog-tired, but could not sleep. I counted a thousand and then glanced at Miss Ottley. Her gaze was fixed on me.

"You are overtired," she said, and her tone was pure womanly.

It irritated and amused me to find she could so unaffectedly assume it. I smiled.

She interpreted the smile aloud. "What sound reason have you for despising- me?" she asked. "You pretend to be a scientist. Answer me as such, rejecting bias."

"I don't," said I.

"Then you dislike me; why?"

"I don't."

Her lip curled. "Oh, indeed." She arose and brought me a cushion. I took it and our hands touched. "I must conclude, then, that you like me?" She drew her hand swiftly away and returned to her seat.

I smiled again. "Undoubtedly, Miss Ottley."

"Thank you." The tone was instinct with sarcasm.

"Confess that you are craving for a little human sympathy."

"I!" she exclaimed and started haughtily.

"Being a woman and in a simply damnable position."

"Ah!" she cried, "you admit that."

"My dear girl, whenever I think of it your pluck amazes me."

To my astonishment her eyes closed and her bosom heaved. Then I saw such a struggle as I do not wish ever to witness again. Pride prevented her from raising her hand to hide her face. And pride put up a superhuman fight with human weakness. Her features were distorted. One could see that soul and body were engaged in mortal combat. That spectacle was poignantly fascinating. I thrilled to see it and yet hated myself for not being able to look away. Why—who knows? But at length I could stand it no longer. I got up and shook her gently. She stiffened into marble, but did not offer to resist me.

"Peace, peace," I said. "You foolish, foolish child, you are wasting forces that were given you for quite another purpose."

Suddenly her eyes opened and looked straight in mine. "What?" she questioned, and two great tears rolled down her cheeks.

"Why do you hate your sex?" I asked. "God knows it is more valuable than mine."

"Man," she muttered—and shuddered from me—bitterly defiant.

"Woman," I retorted. "And each of us with a fateful mission to fulfil, not to fight against."

"Yours to sting, to hurt, to crush."

"And yours to foster and create a better, finer-natured breed."

"Generous?" she sneered. "Is it possible?"

"My dear girl," said I, "I haven't a temper to lose; I am a sober, cold-blooded man of the world. Of thirty."

I laughed out heartily, then stopped, remembering the patient. He stirred and we both hurried to his side. But he did not wake.

I looked up and offered Miss Ottley my right hand.

"We started badly," I whispered, "but still we may be friends."

Her eyes darkened with anger. She stood like a statue regarding me, her expression sphinx-like and brooding. "Instinct says one thing and pride another!" I hazarded.

She coloured to her chin, but her firm glance did not falter.

"Ah, well," said I, and made off to my stone couch, convinced that a man who argues with a woman is a fool. And I was punished properly. She haunted my dreams.

CHAPTER FIVE

THE SHADOW IN THE CAVE

WE ATE HEARTILY, the pair of us, that evening. The effect on me was comforting and humanising. I felt well disposed to my fellow man—and woman, and inclined to sanguine expectations. Miss Ottley, however, was, as usual, impenetrable. She belonged of right to the age of iron. A female anachronism. To cheer her I suggested a game of chess. She consented, and mated me in fourteen moves. We played again, and once more she beat me. My outspoken admiration of her skill—I rather fancy my own play at chess—left her perfectly imperturbable. In the third game she predicted my defeat at the eleventh move on making her own fourth. I did my best, but her prophecy was fulfilled. "Enough!" said I, and retiring to the door way, I lighted a cigarette.

"Hassan Ali, our dragoman, should be here tomorrow," she presently remarked, "with troops."

"They will never catch our rascal Arabs," I replied. "With five clear days' start those beggars might be anywhere."

"Just so," said she, "but they will be of some use none the less—if only to drag that sarcophagus out of the temple."

"Eh!" I exclaimed—and looked at her sharply. "What is the matter with the thing—here?"

She shrugged her shoulders, then of a sudden smiled. "Do you wish to be amused?"

"Of all things."

"Then prepare to laugh at me. While you slept this afternoon—" She paused.

"Yes," I said.

"My father awoke."

"Oh!"

"And conversed."

"Good," I murmured. "He was sensible."

"I do not know. He seemed so. But he did not speak to me."

"You said that he conversed."

"Ay—but with a shadow."

Miss Ottley compressed her lips and looked at me defiantly.

"A shadow," she repeated. "I saw it distinctly. It moved across the room and stood beside the cot. It was the shadow of a man. But you are not laughing."

"Not yet," said I. "Had this shadow a voice?"

"No."

"What did your father say to it?"

"He implored it to be patient."

"And the shadow?"

"Vanished."

"And you?"

"I told myself I dreamed. I tried not to die of terror, and succeeded."

"Why did you not wake me?"

"I wished to, but the shadow intervened."

"It reappeared?"

"For a second that reduced me to a state of trembling imbecility."

"That infernal perfume has simply shattered your nerves," I commented cheerfully. "You'll be better after a good rest. Overstrain and anxiety of course are to a degree responsible. Indeed, they might be held accountable for the hallucination alone. But I blame the perfume to a great extent, because it similarly affected me."

"What!" she cried, "you saw a shadow, too?"

I laughed softly. "My own—no other. But its appearance shocked me horribly. In my opinion that coffin perfume works powerfully upon the optic nerve. How are you feeling now?"

"As well as ever in my life."

"No fears?"

"None. But I admit a distrust of that sarcophagus—or rather of the perfume it contains. Are you sure that you stopped up the chisel hole securely?"

"Quite. But pardon me, Miss Ottley, you are looking weary. Take my advice and retire now."

"Thanks. I shall," she said, and with a cool bow she went into the inner chamber. An hour later Sir Robert awoke. He was quite sensible and appeared much better. I fed him and we exchanged a few cheerful remarks. He declared that he had turned the corner and expressed a strong desire to be up and about his work again. He also asked after his daughter, and thanked me warmly for my services.

Soon afterwards he dropped off into a tranquil slumber, and I spent the remainder of my watch reading a *Review*. As I was not very tired I gave Miss Ottley grace, and it was a quarter to one when I awakened her. She came out looking as fresh as a rose, her cheeks scarlet from their plunge in cool water and consequent towelling. She invited me to use her couch, but I declined, and sought my accustomed corner. I slept like the dead—for (I subsequently discovered) just about an hour. But then I awoke choking and gasping for breath. I had an abominable sensation of strong fingers clutched about my throat. At first all was dark before me. But struggling afoot, the shadows receded from my eyes, and I saw the lamp—a second afterwards, Miss Ottley. She stood with her back against the further wall of the chamber, her hands outstretched as if to repel an impetuous opponent; and her face was cast in an expression of unutterable terror.

"Miss Ottley!" I cried.

She uttered a strangled scream, then staggered towards me. "Oh! thank God—you were too strong—for him," she gasped. "He tried to kill you—and I could not move nor cry."

"Who?" I demanded.

"The—the shadow." She caught my arms and gripped them with hysterical vigour.

I forced her to sit down and hurried to her father. He was sleeping like a babe. I thought of the asphyxiating sensation I had experienced and stepped gently to my sleeping corner. Kneeling down, I struck a match. The flame burned steadily. Not carbonic acid gas then at all events; but I tried the whole room to make sure, also the interior of the sarcophagus, but without result. So far baffled, I stood up and thought. What agency had been at work to disturb us? I made a tour of the walls and examined the stones of their construction one by one. It seemed just possible that there might be a secret entrance to the chamber; and some robber Arab acquainted with it might be employing it for evil ends. But I was forced to abandon that idea like the other. And no one had entered through the pylon, for the dust about the doorway was absolutely impressionless. What then? I turned to Miss Ottley. She was watching me with evidently painful expectation, her hands tightly clasped.

"What made you think the shadow wished to kill me?" I inquired.

"I saw its face."

"Oh! it has a face now, eh?"

"The face of a devil; and long thin hands. It fastened them about your throat."

"My dear girl."

"Don't be a fool," she retorted stormily; "what aroused you? Did you hear me call?"

I was confounded. "Very good," I said, "I admit the hands at least, for the nonce, for truly I was half strangled. But what do you infer?"

"Can human creatures make themselves invisible at will?"

"My good Miss Ottley, no. But they can run away."

"Do you want to see the shadow's face?"

"Yes."

"Then look on the lid of the sarcophagus and see its portrait in a gentle mood."

"Ptahmes!" I cried.

"Ay, Ptahmes," she said slowly. "We are haunted by his spirit."

I sat down on the edge of the sarcophagus and lit a cigarette.

"I am quite at a present loss to explain my throttling," I observed, "but that is the only mystery. I reject your shadow with the contempt that it deserves. What you saw was some wandering Arab who hopped in here without troubling to tread through the dust in the doorway and who departed in the same fashion. Pish! There, too, is the mystery of my throttling solved."

"Perhaps," said she, "indeed I hope so." She was still trembling in spasms.

"Are you minded for the experiment?" I asked.

"What is it?"

"I wish to drive this foolish fancy from your mind." I took out my revolver and showed it to her. "Spirits are said to love the dark best. Let us put out the lamp. It's their element. How, then, can we better tempt old Ptahmes from his tomb?" I wound up with a laugh. "I can promise him a warm reception."

Miss Ottley shivered and grew if possible paler than before. But her pride was equal to the challenge. "Very well," she said.

I drew up a stool near hers, put out the lamp and sat down. When my cigarette had burned out the darkness was blacker than the blackest ebony.

"An idea runs in my head that spirits respond most surely to silent wooers," I murmured. "But I have no experience. Have you?"

"N-no," said Miss Ottley.

The poor girl was shivering with fear and too proud to admit it. I sought about for a pretext to comfort her and found one presently.

"Don't they join hands at a séance?" I inquired.

"I—I—t-think so," said Miss Ottley.

"Well, then."

Our hands encountered. Hers was pitifully cold. I enclosed it firmly in my left and held it on my knee. She sighed but ever so softly, trying to prevent my hearing it. Thereafter we were silent for very long, listening to the sick man's quiet breathing. No other sound was to be heard. But soon Miss Ottley's hand grew warm, and the fingers twined around mine. It felt a nice good little hand. It was very small, yet firm and silken-smooth, and it possessed a strange electric quality. It made mine tingle—a distinctly pleasurable sensation. I fell into a dreamy mood and I think I must have indulged in forty winks, when all of a sudden Miss Ottley's hand aroused me. Her fingers were gripping mine with the force of a vice. She was breathing hard.

"What is it?" I whispered.

"There is some—presence in the room," she gasped. "Don't you feel it?"

And as I live, I did. I struck a match and sprang afoot. Three paces off a man's face glowered at us in the fitful glimmer of the lucifer. Its characteristics were so unusual that it is not possible ever to forget them. The eyes were large, dark and singularly dull. They were set at an extraordinary distance apart in the skull, six inches, I should say, at least. But the head, though abnormally broad thereabouts, tapered to a point in the chin and was cone-shaped above the wide receding temples. The cheek bones were high and prominent. They shone in the match light almost white in contrast with the dark skin of the more shaded portions of the countenance. The nose was long and aquiline, but the nostrils were broad and compressed at the base, pointing at negroid ancestry. The mouth, wide and thin-lipped, was tightly shut. The chin was long, sharp and hairless. The ears were bat-shaped.

Recovering from my first shock of amazement, I addressed the intruder in Arabic.

"What are you doing here? What do you want?" I cried.

He did not answer. Enraged, I started forward and hit out from the shoulder. Striking air. The match went out. I lit another. The man had vanished. I relighted the lamp and carefully examined the chamber. But our visitor had not left the slightest sign of his intrusion.

I shook my head and went over to Miss Ottley. She was leaning against the wall with her eyes shut, her bosom heaving painfully.

I touched her and she started—suppressing a shriek. Her lips were trickling blood where she had bitten them. Her face was ghastly and she seemed about to swoon.

"Pish!" I cried, "there is nothing to be frightened of. A rascally Arab—knows some secret way of entering this cavern, that is all."

She swayed towards me. I caught her as she fell and bore her to a stool. But though quite overcome she was not unconscious. Yet her fortitude was broken down at last and she was helpless. She could not even sit up unassisted. Placing her on the floor a while, I made her drink some spirit and then, lifting her upon my knee, I rocked her in my arms like a child and did my best to soothe her fears. Heavens, how she cried! My handkerchief was soon as wet as if I had soused it in a basin of water, and yet she still cried on. I spoke to her all the time. I told her that I would answer for her safety with my life, and all sorts of things. And thinking of her as a poor little child, I called her "dear" continually and "darling"— and I let her weep herself into an exhausted sleep upon my breast. And when that happened I did not need anyone to tell me that science was no longer the mistress of my fate or that I, a comparative pauper, had committed the unutterable folly of falling in love with the daughter of a millionaire— whose religion was Pride with a capital P. I held her so till dawn, staring dumbly at her face, and thus when her eyes opened they looked straight into mine. She did not move, and half-unwillingly my arms tightened round her. "The bad dream is over, little girl, "I whispered. "See—the golden sunlight."

"May—May," said Sir Robert's voice.

She started up, her face aflame. I followed her to the bedside. The patient was awake, and strong and hungry. Also querulous. He complained of the pain of the wound and ordered me to dress it. He had seen nothing. But I knew Miss Ottley would not forgive me on that account. I read it in her eyes. After I had dressed the patient's wound and we had fed him, she followed me to the door.

"You had no right to let me sleep—like that," she said imperiously.

There was nothing for it but to insult her or to prove myself an adventurer. I had no mind for the latter course. "Quite right," I returned, "when you behaved like an idiot I should have treated you as such and left you to recover from your own silly terror instead of acting the soft fool and losing my own rest in serving you. I'll do it, too—next time. What will you have for breakfast?"

She swung on her heel and left me.

CHAPTER SIX

ENTER DR. BELLEVILLE

WHILE WAITING FOR the kettle to boil I happened to glance in the direction of the Nile. A column of moving smoke at once attracted my attention. A launch, of course, and what more likely than that it should contain soldiers, Arabs, servants, and a surgeon. "I shall soon be free to return to my work, it seems!" I said aloud, and it is wonderful what a lot of dissatisfaction the reflection gave me. I came within an ace, indeed, of consigning the Nile Monuments to literary perdition. But only temporarily. For I felt that I should need as engrossing mental occupation soon. Work is a fine consoler. The party arrived a few minutes before noon. It consisted of Sir Robert Ottley's dragoman, half a company of Egyptian camel corps under command of a fussy little English-French lieutenant named Thomas Dubois, some twenty swart-faced fellaheen labourers, and two English friends of Sir Robert and his daughter. The latter were rather singular personages. One was middle-aged, short and thick and "bearded like the pard" up to his very eyes. He rejoiced in the name of William Belleville and was a Fellow of the Royal College of Surgeons. The other one was tall and thin and marvellously good-looking. He called himself Captain Frankfort Weldon, and I soon discovered was an Honourable. Preparatory to discharging myself in toto of my responsibilities, I took charge of the entire crowd. I have been assured by my best friends that I am a natural autocrat. Those who are not my friends have sometimes described me as an arrogant and self-assertive egotist. I contend, however, that I was eminently well qualified to judge what was best to be done, in that instance, at all events, and it is not my fault that Weldon and Belleville chose to consider themselves slighted because I did not ask their advice. Within ten minutes I had sent the camel soldiers packing across the desert in the direction taken by the Arab robbers. They did not want to go in the least, but I put my foot down hard, and they went. Without losing a moment thereafter I made the fellaheen erect a large double tent in a shaded cleft in the mountain at some distance from the temple. It did not take them long, for I directed their operations personally. I then marched them to the temple. Miss Ottley was talking to the Englishmen in the pylon. I bowed and passed her, followed by the fellaheen. I gave to each man a task, the carriage of some piece of furniture. The two strongest I appointed as bearers of Sir Robert Ottley's cot. The baronet was awake. He questioned me.

"What are you doing, Pinsent?"

"I'm going to move you to a tent for better air, to hasten your recovery," I said.

He only sighed and wearily closed his eyes.

Then the procession started. When Miss Ottley saw her father being carried out, she was so surprised that she stood dumb. Turning round a little later I saw that she and her friends were conversing amiably. Arrived at the tents, I fixed the patient comfortably, then arranged the furniture in both apartments; the outer, of course, was to be Miss Ottley's room.

When all was done, I dismissed the fellaheen to other tasks and walked up to Ottley's cot. "Sir Robert," said I.

His eyes opened and he looked at me.

"You know that your friend, Dr. Belleville, has come?"

"Yes—we have had a chat."

"So. Well, I now propose to turn the case over to him. Your recovery should be rapid. You are already practically convalescent."

"You are leaving me?"

"You no longer need my services."

"How can I ever repay you, Pinsent, for your extreme kindness to me?"

"Easily; let me be present when you open the coffin of Ptahmes."

"What?"

"Ah!" said I, "I forgot." I then told him of my experiment with the sarcophagus, and the perfume. He listened with the most passionate attention. Finally he said:

"You are not certain the sarcophagus does contain the body, though?"

"Not certain, Sir Robert."

"Yet you told me, if I remember aright, that, that—"

"You were dying," I interrupted. "I had to arouse you. But, after all, I feel sure your desire will be gratified. I have no sort of doubt but that a body lies in the coffin."

"Nor I," said he. "The papyrus speaks of an essential oil the mere scent of which arrests decay. Ptahmes alone knew the secret of its preparation. But the sarcophagus must be guarded, Pinsent."

"I'll fix a watch," I said, and held out my hand. "Good-bye, sir."

"You are returning to your camp?"

"Yes."

"Then au revoir, Pinsent. I shall send for you as soon as I am well enough to investigate the coffin."

"Thank you."

But he continued to hold my hand and looked me in the eyes earnestly. "Be careful of yourself," he murmured.

"Careful," I repeated, puzzled.

"Ay," he murmured still lower, "you have incurred the curse unwittingly—but still you have incurred it."

"What curse?"

"The curse which Ptahmes directed against all desecrators of his tomb."

I thought he raved, and felt his pulse. But it was steady as a rock. "Come, come," I said with a smile. "I shall be thinking you a superstitious man, Sir Robert, presently."

"Do you believe in God?" he asked.

"Yes," I cried, astounded.

"Then are you not superstitious, too? But there, I have warned you. I'll say no more. Good-bye. Kindly send my daughter to me."

I found Miss Ottley and the two Englishmen at the door of the outer tent. "Sir Robert wants you, Miss Ottley," I observed, and passed on. I had hardly gone a dozen yards, however, when I found I had a companion on either side of me.

Dr. Belleville immediately opened fire. "You have been taking time by the forelock, Dr. Pinsent," he said softly. "I should hardly have moved the patient for a day or two. He is very weak."

"My name is Frankfort Weldon—Captain Weldon," said the handsome soldier—introducing himself. "I think you have annoyed Miss Ottley, Dr. Pinsent. Seems to me you should have consulted her before acting, at least."

I glanced from one to the other and shrugged my shoulders. "The thing is done," said I. "Gentlemen, good-day." My long legs left them quickly in the rear. There seemed no good reason to waste time in explaining myself to them. They would soon enough find out the reasonableness of my actions for themselves, if possessed of ordinary human curiosity. But a second later I stopped and turned.

"Dr. Belleville," I shouted, "I shall fix a watch at the temple. Ottley wishes it maintained. Miss Ottley will tell you why."

I found the fellaheen collected in a group near the old store house. They eyed me approaching with open sullenness. I chose two among their number and directed them to stand guard before the pylon for four hours. The two I had picked moved off obediently enough, but they were stopped almost on instant by their leader, a big ruffian with a scarred, black face and wild, fiercely scowling eyes. Sir Robert Ottley's dragoman hurried to my side. "Softly, Excellency, or there will be trouble," he muttered. "Let me speak to them. Yazouk is a chief—he will not be commanded. His term of service does not start till to-morrow. He is angry."

"Silence, you," I responded in the same tone. "There is but one way to crush a nigger mutiny."

I stepped smilingly forward, looking into Yazouk's eyes. The black giant—he stood six feet four in his bare feet and was a splendid physical specimen—put his hand on the knife in his belt. But before he could guess at my intention he was sprawling on the sand. He uttered the yell of an angry wild beast and, springing up, rushed at me with bare blade. I stepped aside and kicked him in the stomach. He collapsed, howling dismally. I marched up to the rest, who were all handling their knives, and showed them my revolver. Two minutes later they were all disarmed and I was a walking arsenal. I turned to the dragoman. "I am going away, Mehemet—to my own camp. But so that you will have no trouble with this scum, I shall take their chief with me. I need a servant."

Mehemet bowed to the very ground. "Your Excellency knows best," he muttered reverently.

"Yazouk," said I, "yonder is my ass. Go saddle him for me."

Yazouk went. He returned with the ass saddled and bridled before I was half through a cigarette. I mounted forthwith and started towards my long-deserted camp. "Come, Yazouk!" I called out carelessly, and I took good care not to look back. There is no means surer of making an African obey you than to act as if you are certain he has no alternative. Perhaps Yazouk hesitated for a moment, torn with fear and hate, but he followed me. Soon I heard the patter of his footsteps on the sand. Then I said to myself, "Now, if this man is to remain with me and be my servant I must make him fear me as he would the plague. But how?" I solved the riddle at the end of five miles. I must show him that I despised him utterly. So I stopped. He stopped. Twenty paces separated us. "Yazouk," I said, "come here!"

He approached, eyeing me like a wolf. "From this day for a month, Yazouk, you shall be my slave," I observed calmly. "If you prove a good slave I shall pay you when the term ends at the rate of fifty piasters a day. If you offend me by so much as winking an eyelash I shall not only pay you nothing, but I shall ask Poseidon to transform you into a hyena. Will you like that?"

Yazouk did not remark on my dreadful threat, but there was murder in his eyes. I smiled at him, and, always looking him full in the face, I took one by one the knives I had taken from his fellows, from my belt and cast them on the sand at his feet. "It is not fit for a lord to carry such trash when he has a slave," I said. "Pick up those knives."

Yazouk obeyed me. When he stood upright again there was a great doubt in his eyes. I thought to myself, it would be quite easy for this ruffian to murder me at any time in my sleep, and already I am a wreck for want of sleep. I -threw my revolver on the sand. "Carry that, too!" I commanded loftily—and spurred my ass on. Probably a volume might be written on the state of Yazouk's mind as he trudged along behind me to my camp—a whole compendium of psychology. But I cannot write it, because I never once glanced at him, and, therefore, I can only guess at the turmoil of his thoughts. But the event justified my expectations. I was so mortally wearied when I reached my camp that I had no heart left even to discover whether my precious manuscripts had been disturbed by some chance wayfarer of the wilderness. It sufficed me that my tent was standing and that it contained a cot. I cast myself down, without even troubling to remove my boots, and I slept like the dead for sixteen solid hours. When I awoke it was high noon. A steaming bowl of coffee stood upon my table and a mess of baked rice and fish. Beside the plate lay my revolver, and every one of the knives I had given Yazouk to carry. Yazouk himself stood at the flap of the tent, a monstrous, stolid sentinel. When I arose he bent almost double. I swept the armoury into a drawer and attacked my break-fast with the relish of a famished man. Then I set to work with the energy of a giant refreshed; and with short intervals for meals, sleep and exercise, I toiled at my book thereafter till it was roughly fin-ished. So twenty days sped by. Throughout Yazouk waited upon me like the slave of Aladdin's lamp. I had not a fault to find with him. Indeed, he was a perfect jewel of a servant, and he stood in such abject terror of my every movement, nod or smile or frown, that I could have wished to retain his services for ever. But that was not to be. On the twenty-first morning he accidentally dropped a cup and broke it. I heard the smash and looked up. It was to see Yazouk flying like a panic-stricken deer into the desert. I shouted to recall him, but he only sped the faster.

CHAPTER SEVEN

THE ONE GODDESS

I SPENT THE rest of the day covering up the stele I had unearthed with sand. There was no use thinking of attempting to transport it to Cairo under existing circumstances. But I had no mind to be deprived of the credit attached to its discovery. So I hid it well. Afterwards I gathered up my portable possessions, including my tent, and packed them in a load for my ass's back ready for the morrow. For I had resolved to set out on the morrow for the Hill of Rakh. Surely, I thought, Ottley will be quite recovered by this. I wondered why he had not sent for me before—in accordance with his pledge. Had he forgotten it? The desert was exceptionally still that evening. There was a new moon, and although it gave but little light, it seemed to have chained the denizens of the wilderness to cover. I lay upon the sand gazing up at the stars and listening in vain for sounds, for hours, then, at length, I fell into a quiet doze. The howling of a jackal awakened me. It was very far off, therefore I must have slept lightly. A long sleep, for the moon had disappeared. The darkness that lay upon the land was like the impenetrable gloom of a rayless cave. But the heavens were spangled with twinkling eyes, that beamed upon me very friendly wise. I had lost all desire to repose, but I had found a craving for a pipe. I took out my old briar-wood, therefore, charged it to the brim and struck a match. "My God!" I gasped and scrambled afoot. The tall Arab who had terrified Miss Ottley in the cave temple at Rakh stood about three paces off intently regarding me. I struck a second match before the first had burned out, then felt for my revolver.

"Tell me what it is you want," I cried in Arabic, "and quickly, or I fire."

He did not speak, but very slowly he moved towards me. I raised the pistol. "Stop," I said. He did not stop. "Then have it!" I cried, and pulled the trigger.

He did not flinch from the blistering flash of the discharge. It seemed to me that it should have seared his face and that the bullet should have split his skull. I had a momentary glimpse of a ghastly, brownish-yellow visage and of two dull widely separated eyes peering into mine. Then all was dark again and I was struggling as never I had struggled in my life before. Long, stiff fingers clutched my throat. A rigid wood-like form was pressed against my own and my nostrils were filled with a sickly penetrating odour which I all too sharply recognised. It was the perfume that had issued from the sarcophagus of Ptahmes when I drove my chisel through the lead. At first I grasped nothing but air. But clutching wildly at the things that gripped my throat, I caught hands at last composed of bone. There was no flesh on them, or so it seemed to me. Yet it was good to grip something. It gave me heart. I had a horrible feeling for some awful seconds of contending with the supernatural. But those hands were hard and firm. They compressed my windpipe. Back and fro we writhed. I heard nothing but my own hard breathing. I was being slowly strangled. It was very hard to drag those hands apart. But I am strong, stronger than many men who earn their living by exhibiting to the vulgar feats of strength. Impelled by fear of death, I exerted my reserve of force, and driving will and muscle into one supreme united effort I tore the death grip from my neck and flung the Arab off. Uttering a sobbing howl of relief and rage, I followed him and caught him by the middle. Then stooping low, I heaved him high and dashed him to the ground. There came a sound of snapping wood or bones, but neither sigh nor cry of any sort. "We'll see," I growled, and struck a match. The sand before me was dinted, but deserted. The Arab had vanished. My senses rocked in horrified astonishment. My flesh crept. A cold chill of vague unreasoning terror caught me. I listened, all my nerves taut strained, peering wildly round into the dark. But the silence was unbroken. Nothing was to be heard, nothing was to be seen. Were it not for the dinted sand and the marks of feet other than my own where we had stepped and struggled, I could have come to the conclusion I had dreamed. After a while spent in soothing panic fears, I sneaked off to my baggage and extracted from the pile a candle lamp. This I lighted and, returning, searched the sands on hands and knees. The stranger's footprints were longer than my own and they were toe-marked. Plainly, then, he had stolen on me naked-footed. Looking wide around the dint made by his falling body I came presently upon some more of them. They were each a yard apart, and led towards the Hill of Rakh. Yet only for a little while. Soon they grew fainter and fainter. Finally they disappeared. Tortured by the mystery of it all, I halted where the footprints vanished and, putting out the lamp, squatted on the ground to wait for dawn. It came an hour later, but it told me nothing fresh. Indeed, it only rendered the riddle more intolerably maddening. Where had my Arab gone? And how had he come? For there was not a single footprint leading to the camp. Of course he might have thrown a cloak before him on which to walk; and thus he might have progressed and left no trace. But wherefore such extraordinary caution? And why should he be so anxious to conceal himself? It was hard to give up the riddle, but easier to abandon than to solve it. Calling philosophy to my aid and imagination, I determined that my Arab was some mad hermit upon whose solitude Ottley had intruded in the first instance, and I in the second. And that he had conceived a particular animosity for some unknown reason against my humble self and wished to kill me. Without a doubt, he had some secret hiding-place and feared lest I should seek to discover it. Perhaps he had found some treasure of which he had constituted himself the jealous guardian. I felt sure, at any rate, that he was mad. His actions had always been so peculiar and his speechlessness so baffling and astonishing and crassly unreasonable. But he or someone had killed my donkey. I found the poor beast lying in a hollow, dead as Cæsar. A knife had been employed, a long, sharp-pointed knife—perhaps a sword. It had searched out the creature's heart and pierced it. I made a hasty autopsy in order to be sure. The circumstance was most exasperating. It condemned me to the task of being my own beast of burthen. And the load was not a light one. I made, however, the best of a bad job, and having fortified myself with a good breakfast, I started off laden like a pack-horse for the Hill of Rakh. Having covered four miles, I stopped. Miss Ottley and Captain Frankfort Weldon had suddenly come into view. They were mounted. I sat down on my baggage, lighted a cigarette and waited. Common elementary Christian charity would compel them to offer me a lift. It was a good thought. It is not right that a man should work like a beast. And, besides, it was cheering to see Miss Ottley again. She came up looking rather care-worn and a good deal surprised. I arose and doffed my hat like a courtier. Captain Weldon touched his helmet with his whip by way of salute. He might have just stepped out of a bandbox. I felt he did not like me. The girl looked at me with level brows.

"Sir Robert well and strong again?" I asked.

"Quite," said Miss Ottley.

"We were on our way to pay you a visit," observed the Captain.

"Sir Robert wants me," I hazarded.

Miss Ottley shrugged her shoulders. "Does he?" she asked, then added with a tinge of irony, "You seem content to be one of those who are always neglected until a need arises for their services. Does it appear impossible that we might have contemplated a friendly call?"

"I have no parlour tricks," I explained.

Her lip curled. "You need not tell me. You left without troubling to bid me as much as a good-day. How long ago? Three weeks. Why?" Her tone was really imperious.

"But I left a benediction on the doorstep," I responded. "You looked cross and I was in a hurry."

Her eyes blazed; they were beautiful to see. "Where are you going?" she demanded.

"To call on your father."

"You have a load," observed the Captain.

"A mere nothing,"

"Is not that a tent?"

"I am shifting camp."

"That nigger chap—Yazouk—came along last evening. But he vanished during the night. We fancied something might have happened."

"Oh, Yazouk. He broke a cup and feared I would turn him into a hyena, so he ran away."

"What!" shouted the Captain.

"A superstitious creature," I shrugged.

The Captain shook with laughter. "We wondered how you had tamed him," he chuckled presently—"after the bout. 'Pon honour, you served him very prettily. Straight from the shoulder and savate, too. The dragoman declares you have the evil eye."

"Have you lost your donkey, Dr. Pinsent?" demanded Miss Ottley.

"He expired suddenly last evening."

Captain Weldon frowned and sat up very straight in his saddle.

"Eh?" he said and looked a question.

"I had an Arab visitor. My visitor or another killed my donkey with a knife. I should like to have caught him in the act."

"My dream," said Miss Ottley, and caught her breath.

"By Jove," said the Captain, "it is really wonderful—but wait—you had a visitor, Doctor?"

"I believe it."

"Did he offer to attack you?"

"The spirit of the cavern!" cried the girl.

"A lunatic of an Arab," I retorted, "and so little of a spirit that I had hard work to prevent him throttling me."

"But the face. Did you see the face?"

"Our friend of the cavern," I admitted.

Miss Ottley glanced at the Captain, then back at me. She was as white as a lily.

"I knew it," she said. "I saw him kill the donkey and steal upon you—in a dream. His hands were bloody—and, look, there is blood still on your throat."

"My cask was empty, so perforce I could not wash," I murmured. The Captain looked thunderstruck. "It's the most wonderful thing," he kept repeating, "the most wonderful thing in the world."

"And I never thought of looking in the mirror. It was packed up," I went on. I took out a rather grimy kerchief and began to rub at my neck.

"Has that wretched Arab—worried you at all—since I left, Miss Ottley?"

"I have seen him twice—and once more" (she shuddered) "in my dream."

"And where did you see him out of dreams?"

"Once in the cavern and once in my father's tent. Each time at night. Each time he vanished like a shadow."

"Did anyone else see him?"

"My father and Captain Weldon."

"The most hideous brute I ever saw," commented the Captain; "you could put a good-sized head between his eyes. And such eyes. Dull as mud, but horribly intelligent."

"Well, well," said I. "We'll know more about him some day soon, perhaps, that is, if we stay long enough at the Hill of Rakh. He has a hiding thereabouts—without a doubt. Your father is pining to open the tomb of Ptahmes, I suppose, Miss Ottley?"

"He has opened it," she answered.

"Oh!" I exclaimed—and stopped dead in the act of naming Sir Robert a thankless perjurer.

The girl was looking at me hard. "You are surprised?"

"Curious," I growled. It was hard to say, for I was furious.

"I cannot enlighten your curiosity," she said.

"No?"

"He permitted no one to be present to assist him. It took place the day before yesterday in the cave temple. And the tomb is now closed again."

"You are then unaware what is discovered?"

"Perfectly."

"And Sir Robert?"

"You will find my father greatly changed, Dr. Pinsent."

"Indeed."

"He seems to be quite strong, but he has aged notably, and he will hardly condescend to converse with anyone, even me. Moreover, the subject of Ptahmes is tabooed. The very name enrages him. Dr. Belleville has forbidden it to be mentioned in his hearing."

"Humph!" said I. "If my donkey were alive I should go to Kwansu straight. But as it is I shall have to trespass for a stretch on your preserves at Rakh. I hate it, too, for your father has broken faith with me."

"Ah!" cried the girl. "He promised that you should help him open the tomb."

"Exactly."

"You must not be hard on him. I believe that he is not quite himself."

"Oh! I am accustomed to that sort of treatment from the Ottleys," I replied.

It was brutal beyond question, but I was past reckoning on niceties with rage. Captain Weldon turned scarlet and raised his whip. "Dr. Pinsent," he cried, "you forget yourself. For two pins—" then he stopped—having met my eyes. I laughed in his face. "Why not?" I queried jibingly. "It would be not only chivalrous—a lady looking on—but safe. Have you ever seen a St. Bernard hurt a spaniel?"

He went deathly and slashed me with his whip. Poor boy. I never blamed him. I'd have done the same myself. As for me, the blow descended and cooled my beastly temper, which was an unmitigated blessing. I took his whip away and gave it back to him. Then I laughed out, tickled at the humour of the situation, though it only told against myself. "I had intended accepting your offer of your mule for my belongings," I chuckled. "You haven't offered him, but that's a detail. And now I can't." I shook with laughter.

Weldon leaped on instant to the ground. "Do, do!" he almost groaned.

He was a generous youngster. "And forgive me!" he said. "If you can—it was a coward blow."

"Gladly I'll forgive you," I replied, and we clasped hands.

"I'll help you load the beast," said he.

But I put my foot on my baggage. "That mule," I said, "belongs to Sir Robert Ottley. I'll not risk the breaking of his back."

We looked at one another and I saw the Captain understood me. He turned rather sheepishly away, but did not mount immediately.

Miss Ottley was gazing over the desert. "You must know you are behaving like a child," she cuttingly remarked.

I shook my head at the Captain. "That means you are keeping a lady waiting," I observed.

He smiled wrily in spite of himself. "Scottish, are you not?" he asked.

"From Aberdeen."

He climbed on the mule's back. "I'm thinking Dr. Pinsent would like to be alone," he said.

Miss Ottley nodded and they rode off together. I picked up my swag and trudged after them. It was dry work. About twenty minutes later Miss Ottley rode back alone. She did not beat about the bush at all.

"I want you to put your things on my donkey," she said; and slipping afoot, she stood in my path.

"Not to-day," said I.

"But I'm in trouble, I need your help," she muttered.

"With such a cavalier as Frankfort Weldon?" I inquired.

She coloured.

"And Dr. Belleville. Old friends both, I am led to fancy."

She bit her lips.

"And both of them in love with you," I went on bluntly.

"Dr. Pinsent," said Miss Ottley, "it is my opinion that my father is not quite right in his mind."

"Dr. Belleville is a F. R. C. S.," said I.

"I am afraid of him—my own father," she said, in a tragic tone. "I have a feeling that he hates me, that he wants to—to destroy me."

"Captain Weldon would lay down his life for you, I think," said I.

She put a hand on my breast and looked me straight in the eye. "I could not tell this to Dr. Belleville, nor to the other," she half whispered.

I thrilled all over. "All right," I said, cheerily. "Just stand aside till I load your little beastie, will you?"

Her whole face lighted up. "Ah! I knew you would not desert me," she said.

But we did not speak again all the way to the Hill of Rakh. We were too busy thinking; the two of us. When we arrived she flitted off, still silent. Captain Weldon came to me. "I want you to share my tent," said he. "I have a tub for you in waiting, and some fresh linen laid out, if you'll honour me by wearing it."

"You are a brick," I replied, and took his arm. But at the door of the biggest tent in the whole camp to which he brought me I paused in wonder. It was a sort of lady's bower within. The floor was laid with rugs, and the sloped canvas walls were hung with silken frills; and women's photographs littered the fold-up dressing-table. They were all of the same face, though, those latter; the face of Miss Ottley.

"Sybarite!" I cried.

He winced, then squared his shoulders. "Well—perhaps so," he said with a smile.

"But your gallery has only one goddess," I commented, pointing to a picture.

He gave a shame-faced little laugh. "You see, Doctor, I have the happiness to be engaged to marry Miss Ottley," he explained. Then he left me to my tub.

CHAPTER EIGHT

OTTLEY SHOWS HIS HAND

THE CAPTAIN'S LINEN he had laid out for my use on his damask-covered cot was composed of the very finest silk. Even the socks were silk. I was positively ashamed to draw my stained and work-worn outer garments over them; and I thought, with a sigh, of my two decent suits of tweed lying, like the Dutchman's anchor, far away—in a Cairo lodging-house, to be precise. I shaved with the Captain's razor and wondered why I did not in the least mind resting indebted to his courtesy. The removal of my beard laid bare the weal the Captain's whip had raised. Perhaps that was the reason. He came in just as I had finished and he saw the weal on instant. "I wish to the Lord you'd just blacken one of my eyes," he said remorsefully. "The sight of that makes me feel an out-and-out cad. Not ten minutes before it happened Miss Ottley had been telling me the angel of goodness you had been to her."

I sat down on the edge of the cot and grinned. "It gives me quite a distinguished appearance," I replied, "and, say, didn't it give me back my temper nicely, too."

"Little wonder you were wild," said he. "But why didn't you break me up while you were about it? You could have, easily enough. Lord! how big and strong you are."

"And ugly," I supplemented.

He flushed all over his face. "You make me feel a silly girl-man by comparison," he cried. "A man ought to be ugly and strong-looking like you. I'd give half my fortune to possess that jaw."

"What a boy it is!" I said delightedly, for I was proud of my jaw, and I love flattery.

"I'm having a cot made now; it will be put over there for you. You'll share my diggings, won't you? I want us to be friends," beamed the Captain.

There was something so ingenuous and charming in his frankness that I assented at once.

"It's funny," he said afterwards. "But I detested you at first. Have a cigar. This box of Cabanas is for you. They're prime. I've more in my kit when they are finished. Lie down and rest while you smoke one, won't you? Lunch won't be ready for an hour yet, and you must be fagged."

I wasn't a bit, but I lay back and puffed a mouthful of delicious smoke with a long-drawn sigh of luxury.

"You needn't talk. Miss Ottley says you don't like talking," said the Captain. He lit a cigar and sat down on his kit box. "I'm a real gabbler, though," he confessed. "Do you mind?"

"No, fire away, sonny!"

He fired. It was all about himself and Miss Ottley: how they had been brought up together, predestined sweethearts: how they had quarrelled and made up and quarrelled again: how really and truly in their hearts they adored each other: and how—if it had not been for the girl's intense devotion for her father, they would have been married long ago. He characterised Sir Robert as an extremely selfish man, who, ever since his wife's death, had used his daughter as a servant and secretary because he could get no other to serve him as well and intelligently. "But he doesn't really care for her a straw," concluded the Captain. "And he would sacrifice her without remorse to his beastly mummy hobby for ever if I'd let him. But I won't. I'm going to put my foot down presently. I've waited long enough. He has done nothing but drag her all over Europe translating papyri for him for the last six years. And she has worked for him like a slave. It's high time she had a little peace and happiness."

"Translating papyri," I repeated. "A scholar, then?"

"Between ourselves," replied the Captain, "Sir Robert's fame as a scholar and an Egyptologist rests entirely upon his daughter's labours. Without her he would be unknown. She did all the real work. He reaped the credit. She is three times the scholar he is, and I know a Frenchman who regards her knowledge of cuneiform as simply marvellous. He is a professor of ancient languages, too, at the Sorbonne, so he ought to know."

"Queer she never mentioned a word of it to me," said I.

"Oh!" cried the Captain, "she is the modestest, sweetest creature in the universe. I sometimes think she is positively ashamed of her extraordinary ability. Whenever I speak of it she apologises—and says she only learned the things she knows to be a help to her dear old father. Dear old father, indeed! The selfish old swine ought to be suppressed. He loathes me because he fears I'll persuade her to leave him. If she wasn't so useful she could go to the deuce for all he'd care. But it's got to end soon or I'll know the reason why. Don't you think I'm right? We've been engaged now seven years."

"I consider you a model of patience," I replied.

"Besides," said the Captain, starting off on a new tack, "the old man is positively uncanny. It's my belief he has an underhanded motive in his love for mummies, especially for his latest find, this Ptahmes. He's a spook-hunter, you know—and he told me one day in an unguarded moment that he expected to live a thousand years."

"What's a spook-hunter, Captain?"

"Oh! I mean a spiritualist. He has a medium chap, he keeps in London—a rascally beggar who bleeds thousands a year out of him. They have séances. The medium scamp pretends to go into a trance and tells him all sorts of rubbish about the Nile kings and prophets and wizards and magicians and the elixir of life. It is dashed unpleasant for me, I can tell you. There's always some wild yarn going round the clubs. And as I'm known to be Ottley's prospective son-in-law, I have the life chaffed out of me in consequence. The latest was that the medium chap—Oscar Neitenstein is his name—put Ottley in the way of finding an old Theban prophet's tomb—this very Ptahmes, don't you know. And though he has been underground 4000 years, Neitenstein has fooled Ottley into expecting to find the prophet still alive. It's too idiotic to speak seriously about, of course; but on my honour the yarn drove me out of England. It got into the comic papers. Ugh! you know what that means. But I'm not sorry in one way. So I've come here to have it out with Ottley. And I'm going to—by Gad."

"You haven't spoken to him yet?"

"I have, but he treated me like a kid. Told me to run away and play and allow serious people to work. I stormed a bit, but it was no use. It made him so angry that he nearly took a fit—and I had to leave. Since then he has been shut up with his infernal mummy, in that cave temple over there—and he won't even let his daughter go within yards of the door. That's curious, isn't it?"

"Very."

"And there's that business about the mysterious Arab," went on the Captain. "The ugly horror that tried to throttle you and has been frightening Miss Ottley. She thinks it's a ghost. But I reckon not."

"Ah!"

"I reckon Sir Robert knows all about that Arab, though he pretends he does not know. In my opinion it's another of those spook mediums of his, and he is keeping the ugly beast hidden away somewhere. Probably the fellow is some awful criminal who has got to hide. Sir Robert would shelter Hill or even that Australian wife-murderer Deeming [1] if he said he was a medium."

"You extend my mental horizon," I remarked. "The Arab mystery is clearing up."

The Captain simply beamed. "So glad you catch on," he said. "Do you know, I am depending heaps upon you in this business."

"How?"

The monosyllable disconcerted the Captain. He stuttered and hawed for a while. But, finally, he blurted out, "Well, you see, she won't leave her father under existing circumstances on any account, that's the trouble. But I'm hoping if we can convince the old man he is being fooled by a pack of scoundrels he will return to his sober senses and live sensibly, and then—" he paused.

"And then—wedding bells," I suggested.

"Exactly," replied the Captain. "And see here, I have a plan."

"Ah!"

"It's to lay for that Arab, as a first step—and catch the brute."

"And what then?"

The Captain looked rather foolish. "Well," he said, "well— oh!—we'd be guided by circumstances then, of course. We might induce him to confess—don't you think?"

I could not help laughing. "If you want to know what I think," I said, "it is, that you are in the position of a man who knows what he wants but does not in the least understand how to get it. Still count on my help. If we can lay the Arab by the heels we shall not harm anyone deserving of consideration, and we will put Miss Ottley's mind at rest, at all events; I hate to think that she is worried by the rascal. What do you propose?"

"I thought of hiding by the temple to-night. I passed it late last evening, and though Sir Robert was ostensibly alone, I could swear I heard voices. What do you say?"

"Certainly."

---

1. Frederick Bailey Deeming (1853–1892) was born in England but immigrated to Australia in 1882 with his first wife Marie. Deeming initially incurred the wrath of the law through theft and swindling (for which he served prison sentences), but his main claim to infamy was as the murderer of his wife Marie and their four children in Rainhill, England, and Emily Mather, a woman he bigamously married, in Melbourne—both murders having taken place in 1891. Deeming was arrested in Southern Cross, Western Australia in 1892, extradited to Melbourne for trial, then convicted and hanged in the same year. There was contemporary speculation that Deeming might have been Jack the Ripper.

"Shake," said the Captain. We shook. "Now let's go to lunch," said he. We went.

"That's Belleville's shanty," observed the Captain, pointing to a neighbouring tent. "I don't like the fellow, do you?"

"I don't know him."

"He's a spook-hunter like Sir Robert."

"Ah!"

"The beggar is in love with Miss Ottley."

"Oh!"

"He had the impudence to tell her to her face one day that she would never marry me. He declared that it was written—by spooks, I suppose. One of these days I'll have to break his head for him. But he is not a man you can easily quarrel with. You simply can't insult him. He comes up smiling every time."

"An unpleasant person."

"A bounder," said the Captain with intense conviction. "Lord, how hot it is!"

We entered the eating tent as he spoke. The table was already laid. Dr. Belleville stood near the head of it talking to Miss Ottley. A couple of Soudanese flitted about affecting to be busy, but effecting very little. At sight of me both shuddered back against the canvas and stood transfixed. One held a spoon, the other a plate. They looked extremely absurd. I told them in Arabic that only the dishonest had occasion to fear the evil eye, and took a seat. Instantly both rushed to serve me. My companions, not possessing the evil eye, were forced to wait. Miss Ottley became satirical, but I was hungry and her shafts glanced off the armour of my appetite. When I had finished my first helping of currie she sat down. "There's no use waiting for father," she sighed. "I shall take his lunch to him by-and-by."

Dr. Belleville echoed the sigh. "My dear young lady," said he, "permit me now," and he vanished a minute later carrying a tray.

"You see," said the Captain, sotto voce, to me.

"More currie," I said, addressing, not the Captain, but the tent. Immediately one of the Soudanese slipped and sprawled on the floor in his eagerness to serve. The other leaped over his fellow's prostrate body and whisked away my plate. He returned it loaded in about five seconds. Miss Ottley broke into a half-hysterical laugh. It kept up so long that at last I looked at her in surprise. She had a knife and fork before her, but nothing else; also the Captain. "What is the matter?" I demanded.

"Look," she gurgled. Following her finger I turned and saw both Soudanese standing like statues behind me. "Wretches," I cried, "have you nothing else to do?"

They uttered a joint howl of terror and fled from the tent. But the joke had staled. I took after them hot foot, caught them and drove them back to work, to find that my companions in the meanwhile had helped themselves. Dr. Belleville, however, entered a moment later, and at a nod from me the trembling Soudanese became his abject slaves.

Dr. Belleville had something to say. "The negroes are frightened of you," he began.

"They fancy I have the evil eye."

"Humph!" cried the Doctor. "Talk German—they understand English. It's not that."

"What then?"

"Sir Robert Ottley sent one of them to you—with a message—last night. He returned this morning with three ribs broken. He is lying in the hospital tent now—in a high fever."

"A tall, thin man—the eyes set far apart in the skull?" I asked.

Dr. Belleville shook his head. "No. Short, thick-set, snub-featured, but a giant in strength."

"How did he explain his accident?"

"That unwittingly he angered you."

"The man is a liar," I declared indignantly. "I had a set-to with a skulking rogue last night. That is true enough. But the fellow I encountered and threw was taller than myself."

The Doctor shrugged his shoulders. "It was a dark night, I believe." Then a minute later— "Ottley is much annoyed. This Meeraschi was an excellent subject. Ottley was experimenting with him."

"How?"

"Hypnotically."

I glanced at the others, but they were talking apart.

"Ottley sent me a message?" I asked, returning to the Doctor.

"Yes," replied Belleville between mouthfuls. He was gulping down his lunch like a wolf in a hurry. "He wants you," he went on.

"Needless to say I received no message."

"Needless?" repeated Belleville. "And you here?"

The tone was so insulting that I arose and walked quietly out of the tent. The sun was blazing hot. I thought of the cool cave temple and wandered towards it. Why not see Sir Robert at once? Why not, indeed. Two black sentinels guarded the middle pylon, skulking in the shadow of a column. When I approached they stood bolt upright. They were armed with rifles. They barred the way.

"Ottley!" I shouted. "Ottley!" and once again "Ottley!"

At the third the little baronet's face appeared in the stone doorway.

"Oh! Pinsent," he said, and stared at me. I read doubt in his glance, some fear and anger and uneasiness. But there was much else I could not read. His skin was as yellow as old parchment, and he did not look a well man by any means.

"It is roasting—here," I observed.

He swallowed audibly, as a woman does recovering from tears. "Ah, well," he said. "Come in—here."

The blacks vastly relieved, it appeared, lowered their arms and gave me passage. Sir Robert, however, still blocked the door. I traversed the pylon and stood before him. "We can talk here," said he.

But I had no mind to be treated like that. I looked him in the face and talked to him like this: "I am not welcome. I can see it. But it matters nothing to me. I have rights. I gave you back your life. You made me a promise. You broke your promise. That relieves me of any need to be conventional. I am curious. I intend to satisfy my curiosity. Invite me into the cavern and show me what you have there to be seen. Or I shall put you aside and help myself. I can do so. Your blacks do not frighten me, armed or unarmed. As for you, pouf! Now choose!"

"Dr. Pinsent," said Sir Robert. (He was shaking like an aspen.) "In about ten minutes my dragoman is setting out for Cairo. If you will be good enough to bear him company he will hand you at the end of the journey my cheque for a thousand pounds."

"I ought to have told you," I murmured, "that it is a point of honour with me to keep my word."

"Two thousand," said Sir Robert.

"At all costs," said I.

"Five thousand!" he cried.

"You rich little cad!" I growled, and looked into the muzzle of a revolver.

Sir Robert's eyes, seen across the sights, glittered like a maniac's. "Go away!" he whispered. "Go—or——"

I thought of an old, old policeman trick and assumed an expression of sudden horror. "Take care," I cried. "Look out—he will get you."

The baronet swung around, gasping and ghastly. In a second I had him by the wrist.

"What was it?" he almost shrieked.

"A policeman's trick," I answered coldly, and disarmed him.

"Curse you! Curse you!" he howled, and doubling his fists, he rushed at me, calling on his blacks the while. The latter gave me momentary trouble. But it was soon over. I propped them up like lay figures against the columns, facing each other, afterwards, and extracted the charges from their guns. Looking over the sand, I saw Miss Ottley and Dr. Belleville and the Captain walking under umbrellas towards the tanks. I felt glad not to have disturbed them. Sir Robert had disappeared within the cavern. I followed him. He had put on a large masque which entirely covered his face, and he was fumbling with the screw stopper of a huge glass jar at the farthest corner of the cavern. The sarcophagus had been overturned. It now rested in the centre of the cavern, bottom upwards. And on the flat, leaden surface of the bottom was stretched out, stiff and stark, the naked body of a tall, brown-skinned man. The body glistened as if it had been rubbed with oil. It was almost fleshless, but sinews and tendons stood out everywhere like tightened cords. One might almost have taken it for a mummy. It had, however, an appearance of life— or rather, of suspended animation, for it did not move. I wondered and stepped closer to examine it. I looked at the face, and recognised the Arab who had attacked me on the previous night, the Arab who had frightened Miss Ottley and myself more than once. His mouth was tight shut; his eyes were, however, open slightly. He did not seem to breathe. I put my finger on his cheek, and pressed. The flesh did not yield. I ran my eyes down his frame and uttered a cry. Three of his ribs were broken. Then I felt his pulse; it was still. The wrist was as rigid as steel—the arm, too—nay, the whole man. "He is dead," I exclaimed at last, and looked at Sir Robert. The little baronet was re-stoppering the glass jar, but he held a glass in one hand half filled with some sort of liquid. Presently he approached me—but most marvellously slowly.

"This man is dead," I said to him. "He attacked me last night. I threw him and perhaps broke his ribs. But I did not kill him, for he fled. How comes it he is dead?"

Sir Robert, for answer, threw at my feet the contents of the jar. Then I understood why he wore the masque. The cavern was filled with the fumes of the deadly perfume of the sarcophagus on instant. One sniff and my senses were rocking. I held my breath, but in spite of that the cavern swung round me with vertiginous rapidity.

It seemed best to retire. I did so, but how I hardly know. Somehow or another I reached the pylon, passed the blacks and stepped upon the sand. About fifty paces off I saw a beautiful grove of palm trees suddenly spring up out of the desert. Such magic was most astonishing. I said to myself, "They cannot be real, of course. I am merely imagining them." But their shade was so deliciously inviting that I simply had to accept its challenge. I entered the grove and sat down beside a little purling stream of crystal water. It was very pleasant to dip my hands in it. Presently a lovely Naiad rose up out of the pool, seized my hands and pressed them to her lips. That was pleasant, too. Then she came and sat quite near me on the banks of the rill and drew my head upon her lap and stroked cool fingers through my hair, crooning a tender love song all the while. That was pleasantest of all. But her crooning made me drowsy. Like the Lorelei's song, it charmed away my senses, and I slept.

CHAPTER NINE

A COOL DEFIANCE

OF COURSE, I had swooned, and equally, of course, not on the bank of a rivulet and under the cool shade of palm trees, but in the full blaze of the mid-day sun and on the smooth, unprotected burning surface of the desert. It was the accursed sarcophagus perfume that had worked the mischief. Fortunately Miss Ottley saw me fall; otherwise I might have had a sunstroke. Belleville and the Captain carried me between them to the shade of one of the pylons, and Belleville opened a vein in my left arm—a proceeding I am prevented from commenting on by considerations of professional etiquette. Happily, I recovered consciousness in time to save a little of my precious blood. I told Belleville my opinion of him in one comprehensive scowl, which he interpreted correctly, I am glad to say, and then got up. I bandaged my arm myself and made off for the Captain's tent. That gentleman followed me. There arrived, I cast myself upon the cot and swore at ease. Weldon listened in spellbound admiration. He afterwards assured me that he had never before encountered such proficient fluency in objurgation and invective. I was madder than a hatter, and the more because I was as weak as a cat, and I wanted to be strong, with all my soul. Yet, five days passed before I felt well enough to be able to attack the task in front of me. Meanwhile, I told the Captain very little and Miss Ottley nothing. How could I let her know I knew her father to be a confounded old rascal? She was very good. She visited me every day and spent hours reading aloud by my bedside, while the Captain and I watched her face and thought much the same thoughts; though I took care, for my own part, not to let my features reflect the fatuous devotion of the Captain's. On the sixth morning I found I could lift that young man shoulder-high with one hand without wanting to sit down and pant afterwards, so I got up. It was just after daylight. The Captain wanted to accompany me, but I thought differently. He was annoyed, but I let him watch me from the tent flap. I found Sir Robert talking to Dr. Belleville at the door of the cave temple. His greeting was quite affectionate. "So glad you are better again, my dear young friend," he said, and he warmly invited me into the chamber. It was almost empty. The jar of perfume had gone; the sarcophagus had disappeared. It contained only a table and a cot. "Sit down," said Sir Robert.

"Where is the sarcophagus?" I demanded.

The old rascal grinned. "I had it quietly transferred last night on a truck to a punt," he replied, "while you were enjoying your beauty sleep. Dr. Belleville and I have not been to bed at all. It is now on the road to Cairo—and England."

I sat down on the cot. "And the dead Arab?" I questioned.

Dr. Belleville choked back a laugh. Sir Robert smiled.

"The dead Arab you saw was the mortal casket of Ptahmes," said he. "I am not surprised at your mistake. The body is in a perfect state of preservation. It is not a mummy in any sense of the expression. I regret very much that your sudden indisposition prevented you from examining it closely and me from explaining the circumstances of its preservation and discovery on the spot. However, I can tell you this much now. We found it steeped in an essential oil which an hermetic process had defended from evaporation. The oil began to evaporate immediately it was exposed to the air: but I contrived to save a certain quantity with which, later, I purpose to experiment in London. The Egyptian authorities have been very good to me. They have given me all necessary powers to deal with my discovery as I please. I tell you this lest professional jealousy should lead you to attempt any interference with my actions."

"In plain words, Sir Robert, you wish me to understand that your discovery is for you and not for the world."

"Hardly that, my dear Pinsent. Merely that I propose to choose my own time for taking the world into my confidence—and that of Dr. Belleville," he added, bowing to his friend.

"An unusual course for a professed scientist to adopt."

"I have very little sympathy with conventionality," cooed Sir Robert.

"And I," said Belleville.

"The point of view of two burglars," I observed. I scowled at Belleville.

"You shall be as rude as you please. You saved my life," said Sir Robert.

Dr. Belleville cleared his throat. "Ahem—Ahem," said he, "the discourtesy of the disappointed is—ahem—is a tribute to the merits of the more successful."

In my rage I descended to abuse. "You are a nasty old swindler," I said to Sir Robert, "but your grey hair protects you for the present. But, as for you, sir," I turned to Belleville, "you black bull-dog—if you dare so much as to open your lips to me again, I'll wring your flabby nose off."

The baronet turned scarlet; the Doctor went livid; but neither of them said a word.

I strode to the door intending to quit, but there rage mastered me again. I swung on heel and once more faced them. "One word more," I grated out; "you're not done with me yet, either of you. I'm a peaceful man by nature, but no man treads on my toes with impunity. Spiritualists or spirit-summoners you are, I hear. Weldon calls you spook-hunters—a very proper term. You'll need all the money you possess between you and all the spirits' help you'll buy from your rascal spirit-rappers to keep me from your trail. Looking for the elixir of life, I'm told. It will go hard if I don't help you find it. The elixir of public ridicule, that I'll turn upon you, will hand your names down to posterity. I'll help you to that much immortality, at least, and gratis, too. Good-day to you!"

"Dr. Pinsent!" shouted Ottley.

I paused and glanced at him across my shoulder. He gazed at me with eyes that simply blazed.

"Be warned," he hissed, "if you value your life, let me and mine alone. I'll send a cheque to your tent to-day; keep it, call quits, and I'm done with you. I owe you that consideration, but no more."

"And suppose, on the other hand—"

"Cross me and you shall see. You sleep sometimes, I suppose. My emissary will not always find you wakeful. He never sleeps."

"Your rascal Arab!" I shouted.

"Pah!" he cried.

"Murderer, it was to you I owe that rough and tumble a week ago at my own camp in the desert."

"To me," he mumbled. "To me. Whom else? My agents are spirits and invisible. They do not love you for despising them. They have tortures in reserve for you when you are dead and you, too, are a spirit. But I would be merciful—I shall send you a cheque. Return it at your peril. Now go, go, go."

On a sudden I was cold as ice. The man was evidently insane. He seemed on the brink of a fit. He was frothing at the mouth.

"Softly, softly, Sir Robert," I said soothingly. "No need for excitement. Calm yourself; after all this is a business transaction."

"Oh!" he gasped, then broke into a wild laugh. "A mere matter of price. I should have known it; a Scotchman!"

"Exactly," said I. "And my price is a million. Good-morning."

The whole camp was astir. The negroes' tents were all down and rolled. The mules and asses were being loaded heavily. Evidently Sir Robert was about to flit after the corpse of Ptahmes. I found Miss Ottley and the Captain talking over the apparent move. The girl was agitated. She had not been consulted. It was not a time to mince matters. I told her frankly everything that had passed between her father and myself, and hardly had I finished, when she rushed off hot foot to visit him. The Captain went with her. I made a passably good breakfast.

CHAPTER TEN

THE CAPTURE OF THE COFFIN

ABOUT NOON—I saw no one but blacks in the meanwhile—the Captain came with a letter. "From Sir Robert—catch!" said he. I tore it open. A single sheet of note enclosed a cheque signed in blank.

> "Dear Dr. Pinsent," ran the letter. "You will find that my signature will be honoured for any sum it may please you to put upon my life in your esteem. Permit me to express a hope that you will not hurt my vanity in your selection of numerals.
>
> "Sincerely yours, ROBERT OTTLEY."

I handed the note to Weldon. He read it and whistled loud and long.

"You might beggar him!" he cried. "The man is stark mad."

"Either that or he has made a truly wonderful discovery," I rejoined. "And there is Belleville to consider. That man, I fancy, is a rascal—but also a sane one."

"It has me beat," said the handsome Captain. "The whole thing from start to finish. Ottley is up there now spooning his daughter like a lover. He was as sweet as pie to me, too. I feel like a stranded jelly-fish. What will you do?"

I enclosed the cheque in a blank cover, sealed it and gave it to the Captain.

"Will you be my courier?"

"Of course," said he, and swung off.

He returned at the end of my third cigar, with a second letter. It ran,

> "My dear young friend,
>
> Your refusal has deeply pained me. The more, because it deprives me of the pleasure of your company on the road to Cairo. I beg you, nevertheless, to choose from my stores all

62

that you may require that may serve you during your continued sojourn at Rakh. We start at sunset for the Nile and north.

> "Ever yours attachedly,
> "R. OTTLEY."

When the Captain had mastered this precious effusion, he collapsed upon a stool. "He intends to leave you here alone in the desert. It's—it's marooning, nothing less!" he gasped.

I lighted a fourth cigar and lay back thinking hard. In ten minutes I had made up my mind. I sat up. The Captain was anxiously watching me. "See here, my lad," I said, "in that bundle yonder is the manuscript of a book I have been working hard upon for three years and more. It is the very heart of me. Take good care of it. One of these days—if I live—I'll call for it at your diggings in London. I have your address in my notebook."

"Oh! Oh! Oh!" said the Captain. "But what's the game?"

"Diamond cut diamond. I'm going a journey. But I'll say no more. Mad or sane, you are eating Ottley's salt, and are beholden to him for his paternity of the exceptionally gifted young woman you propose to marry. Good-bye to you."

I held out my hand. He sprang up and wrung it hard. "You are sure you are doing right?" he asked.

I filled my pockets with his cigars. "I am sure of nothing," I replied, as I did so, "except this—I have been abominably ill-used by a man who under Heaven owes his life to me—and this—I resent it."

I put on my helmet, nodded and left the tent.

The Captain cried out, "Good luck!" Five minutes later I turned and waved my hand to him. He was still standing by the tent flap gazing after me. I thought to myself, "He is as honest as he is good to look upon. He will make May Ottley a gallant husband." I am a reasonably bad Christian, and quite as selfish as many worse, but somehow or another the reflection brought no aftermath of bitterness. The handsome, happy-hearted boy—he was little else for all his three and thirty years—had crept into my heart, and I felt somehow the chamber he occupied was next door to that wherein May Ottley's visage was enshrined. But I had work to do; so I turned the key on both. The sun was so hideously hot that I was forced to hasten slowly. But I reached the Nile under two hours, and found, as I expected, Sir Robert Ottley's steam launch moored to the bank. Her smoking funnel had been the beacon of my march. She was in charge of an old French pilot, a Turkish engineer, and

four Levantines, piratical-looking stokers, mongrels all. I stalked
aboard with an air of paramount authority. The Frenchman came
forward, bowing. He wore a sort of uniform. "Steam up, Captain?" I
asked.

"Since morning, monsieur!" he replied.

"Then kindly push off at once. I must overtake the punt that
started last night without delay."

His mouth opened. "But monsieur," he protested, "I—"

"You waste time," I interrupted.

He rubbed his hands nervously together. "But monsieur is unknown to me. I have my written orders from Sare Roberrrrt.
Doubtless monsieur has authority. But monsieur vill perceive—"

"That you are a punctilious old fool," I retorted. "Here is my
authority!" What I showed him was a revolver. He jumped, I vow,
two feet in the air, and hastily retreated. But I followed more
quickly still, and forced him to the bridge. There he became very
voluble, however; so much so, indeed, that I was constrained to
cock my pistol. That settled him. He thundered out his orders and
we were soon racing at ten knots an hour down stream. When
rounding the nearest bend to the Hill of Rakh the temptation was
very strong in me to sound the steamer's whistle. But I am proud to
say that I refrained. It would have been a little-minded thing to do.
About midnight, feeling weary, I ran the steamer's nose gently into
a mud bank, drove the captain down to the deck and locked him
with the rest of the crew in the engine-house. Then I foraged round
for eatables, made a hearty supper and snatched about five hours'
sleep. When morning came I awoke as fresh and strong as a young
colt. After bath and breakfast, I released my prisoners, made them
eat and then push off the bank. We lost an hour at that job, but, at
length, it was accomplished, and our race for the punt recommenced. We overhauled it about four o'clock the same afternoon. It
was just an ordinary flat-bottomed Nile abomination, towed by a
tiny, panting, puffing-billy, with twenty yards of good Manilla.
Twelve Arabs squatted round the sarcophagus. Seated on the sarcophagus, under a double awning, was a burly-looking Englishman.
He was smoking a pipe, and one look at his face told me exactly
why he had been entrusted with Sir Robert Ottley's priceless
treasure. He was, as plain as daylight, a gentleman if one ever lived,
a brave man, too, shrewd and self-reliant and as incorruptibly devoted to his duty as a bull-dog with a thief's hand between his jaws.
I wondered if I would get the better of him. As a first step towards
that desideratum, I assured the French captain that I entertained too

much regard for him to put him to a lingering death should he disobey me. I had previously locked the rest of the crew in the engine-house. Then we bore down on the punt and I shouted for the tug to be stopped. This was done. As it lost way, we nosed up, going easy until we were alongside the punt. Then I ordered half speed astern until we, too, were stationary. Some power of suction or attraction began immediately to draw the two crafts together. The tug, however, continued to remain, say thirty feet off. The Englishman ordered out rope fenders and asked me what the blazes I was doing. I answered that I had come after him from Sir Robert Ottley—which was in a sense perfectly true—and that he could hardly expect me to shout out urgent private business before listeners, which was also a reasonably veracious statement of the facts. The Englishman—I never learned his name—observed, with some heat, that he would not leave his charge for a second for any man living except Sir Robert Ottley; and that if I had something to tell him I must go aboard the punt.

I said "Very well," and as the crafts touched I helped myself to the punt with a rope.

"Well, what is it?" he demanded, and he eyed me most suspiciously, one hand in his breast. Doubtless he had there a revolver. Had he been warned? And of me? It is a thing I have still my doubts about. But I looked him frankly in the eyes and told him the truth to the very best of my ability.

"It has lately come to Sir Robert Ottley's knowledge," I began, "that one of his guests—a man named Pinsent" (he started at the name) "has conceived a bold design of relieving you of this very charge of yours, which you are guarding with such praiseworthy solicitude."

"Oh!" said the Englishman, "and how would he go about it?" The idea appeared to tickle him. He laughed.

"He would follow you and attack you," said I.

The Englishman put his hands on his thighs and simply roared. "He would have to swim after me," he chuckled. "There is not another launch save these two between here and Ham!"

"I am honestly glad to hear it," I replied, and, indeed, I was.

"It's a mare's nest," declared the Englishman.

"Oh!" said I. "This Pinsent is a desperate fellow and resourceful. Do you know, he actually; tried single-handed to seize that launch."

"The *Swallow!*" cried the Englishman. "Impossible."

"On the contrary!" I retorted. "He succeeded. He stands before you. My name is Pinsent. Permit me!"

He was a trifle slow-witted, I fancy. He still looked puzzled, when his face emerged above the Nile water, after his dive. But I would not let him return to the punt. Immediately I discovered that the Arabs were only armed with knives. I had taken the trouble to throw overboard all the firearms that I could find on the *Swallow*; so I just drove them aboard the launch and ordered the Frenchman to sheer off and return to Rakh. He was charmed at the permission.

The Englishman fired at me twice from the water, but he had to keep himself afloat, so he naturally missed. When he was well-nigh drowned I hauled him up with a boat hook. It was easy to disarm him in that condition. I had intended to put him on the tug, but I waited too long. The tug cut the tow rope before my eyes and without so much as by your leave puffed after the *Swallow*. The Englishman and I were thus left lonely on the punt; in middle stream. The current was fairly strong at that point and making towards a long, low-lying sweep of reedy flats. I had no mind to land there, however, so after tying up the Englishman neck and crop, I contrived to hoist a sail and steered for the opposite bank.

The Englishman and I had nothing to say to each other. No doubt he recognised the futility of conversation in the circumstances; as for me, I never felt less inclined to talk. About five o'clock we grounded under the lee of a pretty little promontory. It was populated with crocodiles. Nice companions—at a distance— crocodiles—musky-smelling brutes.

CHAPTER ELEVEN

GOOD-BYE TO THE NILE

THE ENGLISHMAN WAS evidently something of a gourmet. I found foie gras, camembert cheese, pressed sheep's tongues and bottled British ale in his private locker. But he was as sullen as a sore-headed grizzly. He sourly declined to eat even though I offered to free his hands, and he strove to make my dinner unpleasant by volunteering pungent information on the punishment provided by law for the crimes of piracy, robbery under arms, burglary, assault and battery, and false imprisonment. Those, it seems, were the titular heads of some of my delinquencies. He felt sure that I would get ten years' hard labour, at least. I did not argue the point with him. After dinner I examined the sarcophagus. The lid was fastened on with crosswise-running bands of hinged steel, padlocked in the centre. But it was, strange to say, wedged at one end with iron bolts about an inch ajar, as if on purpose to allow air to pass into the coffin. After a little search I discovered a toolbox in the shallow hold of the punt; and I attacked the bands with cold chisels and a mallet. Ten minutes' work sufficed. I tossed the broken bands aside and levered off the lid. My heart beat like a trip-hammer as I looked into the coffin. I was prepared for a surprise. I received one. My Arab gazed up at me. The mysterious Arab with the three broken ribs, who had frightened Miss Ottley and tried to throttle me and whom I had last seen lying—a corpse—in the cave temple at Rakh. Of course, Sir Robert Ottley had declared the corpse in the temple to be identical with that of Ptahmes, the four thousand years dead High Priest of Amen-Ra. But that was ridiculous. I had only had time to make a cursory examination of the dead Arab in the cave temple, it is true, but I am a surgeon, and I had convinced myself that the fellow, so far from being a mummy, had not been long dead. I had yet to discover an essential error in my cave temple investigation. My very first impression had been not death, but suspended animation. And I must have been right. The later speedy diagnosis had, in sober truth, misled me. The man was not dead. It had been a case of suspended animation. The Arab lying in the sarcophagus before me was alive. His broken ribs were neatly set and bandaged. Otherwise he was swathed from head to foot in oiled rags. He was lying in an easy position on his back—upon a doubled feather tick. He was breathing softly but unmistakably. And he was awake. His extraordinary eyes—they were set fully five inches apart in his abnormally broad skull—were wide open and staring at me in a way to make the flesh creep. They were horrible eyes. The whites were sepia-coloured, the pupils were yellowish, and the iris of each a different shade of black flecked with scarlet spots. His cone-shaped forehead was moist and glistening with oil or perspiration. His mouth was held open by two small rubber-tipped metal bars joined together, against which his teeth—great brown fangs—pressed with manifest spasmodic energy.

Now what was Ottley's purpose in taking such extraordinary pains to transport a living Arab in a dead man's coffin from Rakh to Cairo, and, perhaps, London?

Perhaps the Arab could tell me. Burning with curiosity, I stooped down and took from his mouth the mechanical contrivances which held the jaws apart. The Arab uttered on the instant a deep, raucous sigh. His eyeballs rolled upwards and became fixed. He appeared to have fainted. I rushed away to procure some water. That water was in the hold. Seizing a dipper, I sprang down the steps, hurried to the cask and filled it. The whole business occupied only a few seconds. I certainly could not have been away from the deck half a minute, but when I returned the sarcophagus was empty. The Arab had disappeared. Utterly astounded, I gazed about me. Had the whole thing been a dream? It appeared so, but no—I caught sight of a tall, dark figure making off hot foot across the promontory. He had leaped ashore, a distance of twelve feet or more, and was running towards the desert. In a second I was after him. I thought of the crocodiles while in mid-air; but it was too late to turn back at that juncture. My feet landed in a patch of oozy sand. I scrambled out of it and up the slope among the reeds. A loud rustle and a stink of musk warned me of a saurian neighbour. I gave a mighty leap and cleared the reeds. Then I ran as I had never run before, for my Arab was in front, and a hungry monster came hard upon my heels. A log lay in my path. It was another crocodile. I cleared it with a bound and gained the desert. I was hunted for some seconds, I believe, but I never looked back, so I do not know at what point the saurian gave up the chase. The Arab was a marvel. He had a lead of one hundred yards and he maintained it. He had three broken ribs and I was as sound as a bell. Yet, at the end of twenty minutes not his breath but mine gave out. I was forced to pause for a spell. He ran on. His lead doubled. Setting my teeth, I resumed the chase. But I might have spared myself the trouble. He gradually grew farther and farther away from me. I did my best, but at last I was compelled to admit myself beaten. The Arab's tall form grew less and less distinguishable against the stars. Finally it melted into the mists of the horizon. I was alone on the desert. I sat down to rest and took counsel with myself. I had turned pirate and committed, technically, a number of other atrocious crimes for absolutely nothing. Plainly I could not return to the punt.

First of all, in order to reach it I should have to face the crocodiles. And even should I escape their jaws again, what could I do on the river? Sooner or later I should be caught. And I had a very strong suspicion that Sir Robert Ottley would not hesitate, once I was in his power, to plunge me into an Egyptian prison. He had evidence enough to get me a long term of hard labour, and I felt little doubt but that he would go to a lot of trouble for that, and *con amore* after the way that I had served him. It did not, therefore, take me long to resolve to risk the desert rather than rot in an Egyptian gaol. I had spilt a lot of milk. I was foodless, waterless, and Gods knows where. Also, I was as thirsty as a lime kiln. But no use crying. What to do? That was the question. For a start, I lay down and pressed my cheek against the ground. The horizon thus examined showed a faintly circled unbroken level line in all directions except the northwest. There it was interrupted for a space by a mound that was either a cloud-bank or a grove of trees. It proved to be the latter. I found there water to drink and dates to eat. Next morning I took my bearings from the sun, and giving the river a wide berth I pressed on north for two days and nights on an empty stomach. Then I shot an ibis with my revolver in a reedy marsh and ate it raw. Next day I climbed into the mountains and looked back on Assuan and Philæ. But it is not my purpose to describe my wanderings minutely. It would take too long. Suffice it to say that I changed clothes with an Arab near Redesieh and entered Eonah dyed as a Nubian a week later, after crossing the river at El-Kab in a fisherman's canoe. The Nile was still ringing with my doings, so I judged it best to proceed on foot to Luqsor. But there I got a job in a dahabeah that was conveying a party of French savants back from Elephantine to Abydos. I stayed with them three weeks, hearing much talk, meanwhile, of a certain rascally Scotch doctor named Pinsent. It was supposed he had perished in the desert. One day, however, hearing that Sir Robert Ottley, who had been lying at Thebes, had been seen at Lykopolis, I deserted from my employ, and walked back to Farschat. There I bought a passage on a store-boat and came by easy stages to Beni Hassan. Thence I tramped to Abu Girgeh, where I lay for a fortnight, ill of a wasting fever, in the house of a man I had formerly befriended. A large reward had been offered for my arrest, but he was an Arab of the better sort. So far from betraying me to outraged justice, he cashed my cheque for a respectable amount and procured me a passage to Cairo on a river steamer. I entered the ancient city of Memphis one day at dusk, a wreck of my old self and as black as the ace of spades. Not daring to reclaim my goods at my lodging-house, I proceeded forthwith to Alexandria with no wardrobe save the clothes upon my back, and so anxious was I to escape from Egypt that I shipped as stoker on a French steamer bound for Marseilles. I could find none that would take a negro as passenger. The dye pretty well wore off my face and hands during the voyage, but the circumstance only excited remark among the motley scum of the stokehole, and I was permitted to land without dispute. Heavens! how beautiful it was to dress once more as a European, to eat European food, to sleep on a European bed, and not to be afraid to look a European in the face. In Europe I did not care a pin for Sir Robert Ottley and all that he could do to hurt me. In Egypt his money and influence would have left me helpless to resist him; but I felt myself something more than his match in the centre of modern civilisation. He had the law of me, of course, but I had a weapon to bring him to book. I could hold him up to public scorn and ridicule. Were he to prosecute me I could put him in the pillory as a wretch ungrateful for his life saved by my care and skill, a promise-breaker and something of a lunatic. On the whole, I decided he would not venture to put me in the dock. And so sure did I feel on that head that I proceeded to London as fast as steam could carry me.

CHAPTER TWELVE

THE MEETING

WHENEVER IN LONDON my practice for years had been to put up at my friend Dixon Hubbard's rooms in Bruton Street. We had been schoolfellows. He was one of the most fortunate and unfortunate creatures in the world. Born with a silver spoon in his mouth, he had inherited from some cross-grained ancestor a biting tongue and a gloomy disposition. He was an incurable misanthrope and unpopular beyond words. At college he had been detested. Being a sickly lad, his tongue had earned him many a thrashing which he had had to endure without other reprisal than sarcasm. Yet he had never spared that. His spirit was unconquerable. I believe that he would have taunted his executioners while they burned him at the stake. I used to hate him myself once. But one day after giving him a fairly good hammering I fell so in love with the manly way in which he immediately thereafter gave me a sound excuse for wringing his neck that I begged his pardon for being a hulking bully in having lifted hand against a weaker body but a keener brain and more untamable spirit than my own. That conquered him. From that moment we were inseparable chums, and on an average the privilege cost me at least two hard fights a week, for my code was—hit my chum and you hit me. His gratitude lay in jibing at me if I lost the fight, and if I won informing me that I was a fool for my pains. But we understood each other, and our friendship bravely withstood the test of time and circumstance. I found him nursing an attack of splenitic rheumatism before a fire in his study, and we were still only in the middle of July. His man, Miller, had just broken a Sévres vase, and Hubbard was telling Miller in a gentle, measured way his views of clumsiness in serving-men. Miller—a meek, dog-like creature usually—stood before his master glowing but inarticulate with rage. His fists were clenched and his lips were drawn back from his teeth. Hubbard was evidently enjoying himself. He watched the effect of his placid exhortation with a sweet smile—and he applied his mordant softly uttered gibes with the pride of a sculptor at work upon an image. Each one produced some trifling but significant change in Miller's expression. Probably Hubbard was experimenting—seeking to discover either how far he could go with safety or exactly what it would be necessary to say in order to make Miller spring at his throat They were both so engrossed that I entered without disturbing them. I listened for a moment and then created a diversion. Miller's tension was positively dangerous. I walked over, took him by the collar and propelled him from the room. "You'll find my bag downstairs," I said. "I've come to stay."

Miller gave me the look of a dog that wants but does not dare to lick your hand. His gratitude was pathetic. I shut the door in his face.

Hubbard did not rise. He did not even offer to shake hands. He half closed his eyes and murmured in a tired voice: "The bad penny is back again, and uglier than ever."

I crossed the room and threw open a window. Then I marched into his bedroom, seized a water jug, returned and put out the fire.

"You've been coddling yourself too long," I remarked. "Get up and put on your hat. It's almost one. You are going to lunch with me at Verrey's"

"I have a stiff leg," he remonstrated.

"Fancy! Mere fancy," I returned.

The room was full of steam and smoke. Hubbard said a wicked thing and got afoot, coughing. I found his hat, crammed it on his skull and crooked my arm in his. He declined to budge and wagged a blistering tongue, but I laughed and, picking him up, I carried him bodily downstairs to a cab. He called me forty sorts of cowardly bully in his gentle sweetly courteous tones, but before two blocks were passed his ill-humour had evaporated. He remembered he had news to give me. We had not met for eighteen months. Of a sudden he stopped beshrewing me and leaned back in the cushions. I knew his ways and talked about the weather. He endured it until we were seated within the grill-room. Then he begged me very civilly to let God manage His own affairs.

"I am very willing," I said.

He impaled an oyster on a fork and sniffed at it with brutal indifference to the waiter's feelings. Satisfied it was a good oyster, he swallowed it.

"I am no longer a bachelor," said he. "I have taken unto myself a wife."

"The deuce!" I cried.

"Exactly," he said. "But the prettiest imp imaginable."

"My dear Hubbard, I assure you—"

"My dear Pinsent, you have blundered on the truth."

"But—"

He held up a warning finger. "It occurred a year ago. We lived together for six weeks. Then we compromised. I gave her my house in Park Lane and returned myself to Bruton Street. Pish! man, don't look so shocked. Helen and I are friends—I see her once a week now at least, sometimes more often. I assure you I enjoy her conversation. She has a natural genius for gossip and uses all her opportunities. She has already become a fixed star in the firmament of society's smartest set and aspires to found a new solar system. I allow her fifteen thousand pounds a year. She spends twenty. My compensation is that I am never at a loss for a subject of reflection. We shall call on her this afternoon. A devil, but diverting. You will be amused."

"Do I know her, Hubbard?"

"No; you are merely acquainted. Her maiden name was Arbuthnot."

"Lady Helen Arbuthnot!" I cried.

He smiled and shrugged his shoulders. "You will find her changed. Marriage has developed her. I remember before you went away—was it to Egypt?—she tried her blandishments on you. But then she was a mere apprentice. Heaven help you now—if she marks you for her victim."

"Poor wretch!" I commented. "I suppose you can't help it. But you ought to make an effort, Hubbard, really."

"An effort. What for?"

"To conceal how crudely in love with your wife you are."

He bit his lips and frowned. "Children and fools speak the truth," he murmured. Then he set to work on the champagne and drank much more than was good for him. The wine, however, only affected his appearance. It brought a flush to his pallid cheeks and made his dull eyes sparkle. He deluged me with politics till three o'clock. Then we drove to Park Lane. Lady Helen kept us waiting for twenty minutes. In the meantime, two other callers joined us. Men. In order to show himself at home Hubbard smoked a cigarette. The men looked pensively appalled. They were poets. They wore long hair and exotic gardens in their buttonholes. And they rolled their eyes. They must have been poets. Also they carried bouquets. Certainly they were poets. When Lady Helen entered they surged up to her, uttering little artistic foreign cries. And they kissed her hand. She gave their bouquets to the footman with an air of fascinating disdain. Their dejection was delightful. But she consoled them with a smile and advanced to us. Certainly she had changed. I had known her as a somewhat unconventional and piquant débutante. She was now a brilliant siren, an accomplished coquette and a woman of the world. Her tiny stature made her attractive, for she was perfectly proportioned and her costume ravishingly emphasised the petite and dainty grace of her figure. Her face was reminiscent of one of those wild flowers of torrid regions which resemble nothing grown in an English garden, but which, nevertheless, arrest attention and charm by their bizarrerie. It was full of eerie wisdom, subtle wilfulness and quaint, half-humorous diablerie. In one word, she was a sprite. She greeted her husband with an unctuous affectation of interest which would have made me, in his place, wish to box her ears. Hubbard, however, was as good an actor as herself. He protested he was grateful for the audience and claimed credit for introducing me. Lady Helen looked me up and down and remembered that I had owed her a letter for nearly thirty-seven months. She gave me the tips of her fingers and then rushed away to kiss on both cheeks a lady who had just entered. "Oh, you darling!" she twittered. "This is just too lovely of you. I have longed for you to come."

It was May Ottley. She did not see me at once. Lady Helen utterly engrossed her. I had, therefore, time to recover from the unexpected shock of her appearance. I was ridiculously agitated. I slipped into an alcove and picked up a book of plates. At first my hands shook so that I could hardly turn the pages. Hubbard glided to my side. I felt his smile without seeing it. "I smell a brother idiot," he whispered.

I met his eyes and nodded.

"In Egypt, of course?"

"Yes."

"She marries a guardsman next month, I hear."

"Indeed."

"The poor man," murmured Hubbard. "Come out and let us drink his health."

"No, thank you."

"You'd rather stay and singe your wings, poor moth."

"And you?"

"Mine," said he, "were amputated in St. James Church. She is a lovely creature, Pinsent."

"Which?"

He chuckled without replying. A footman pompously announced: "Mrs. Carr—Lord Edward Dutton."

"Bring the tea, please," said Lady Helen's voice.

"She is staring this way at you," murmured Hubbard. "She recognises your back. No, not quite, she is puzzled."

"She has never seen me in civilised apparel," I explained.

"Are you afraid of her, my boy?"

"Yes."

"Well, you are honest."

I began to listen for her voice. The air was filled with scraps of conversation.

"Three thousand, I tell you. He cannot go on like that. Shouldn't wonder if he went abroad. Like father, like son. Old Ranger had the same passion for bridge."

"You can say what you like, names tell one nothing. In my opinion the man is a Jew. What if he does call himself Fortescue? Consider his nose. I am tired of these rich colonials. I have no time for them. Heaven knows what they are after."

"She will spoil her lower register completely if she keeps on. Her voice is a mezzo and nothing else. You should have seen the way old Delman sneered when he listened to her last night."

"My test of a really fine soprano is the creepy feeling the high C gives one in the small of the back. Delicious. She never thrills me at all."

"Oh! Lord Edward, how malicious. What has the poor man done to you?"

"He plays billiards too well to have been anything but a marker in his youth. I believe he kept a saloon somewhere in the States."

"They say it will end in the divorce court. That is what comes of marrying a milkmaid. And, after all, she did not present him with a son. Ah, well, it's an ill wind that blows nobody any good. Young Carnarvon is his heir still, and his chances of succeeding grow rosier every day."

"My dear Mrs. Belvigne, if it was not for her red hair, she would be as commonplace as—as my dear friend Mrs. Sorenson. What you men see in red hair—"

"Conscience, Lady Helen, is a composition of indulgences. It is a marriage de convenance between the conventional instinct and the appetite."

"Dr. Pinsent," said Miss Ottley, "is it really you?"

I turned and looked into her eyes. They were all aglow and her cheeks were suffused with colour. She gave me both her hands. The room was already crowded. People entered every minute. Hubbard pointed significantly at the tea-cups. Miss Ottley and I drifted to the divan. We watched the crowd through the parted curtains, sipping our tea. We might as well have been in a box at the theatre watching the play.

"I knew you would escape," she murmured, presently. "The others believe you to have perished in the desert."

"They consoled themselves, no doubt?"

"My father especially."

"Did he recover his Arab?"

"What Arab?"

"The creature he had imprisoned in the sarcophagus."

"The mummy, you mean. The body of Ptahmes? Oh, yes, that was safe enough, but he was in a fearful state until we found the punt. He feared that you would either steal or destroy the mummy, I believe."

"Miss Ottley!" I cried.

"You must not blame him too much," she murmured; "you know how he had set heart—"

"Look here!" I interrupted. "Do you mean to tell me that you found the mummy in the sarcophagus?"

"Certainly. Why?"

"Did you see it?"

"Yes."

"The mummy?"

"Why, of course."

"A dead body, a mummy?"

"Dr. Pinsent, how strangely you insist."

"I'll tell you the reason. When I opened the sarcophagus—"

"Yes."

"It contained not a mummy, but a living man."

"Impossible."

"You think so? The Arab was the very man who frightened you so often in the temple at the Hill of Rakh."

"Dr. Pinsent!"

"When I removed the lid he leaped out of the sarcophagus, sprang ashore and fled to the desert. I followed him for several miles. But I could not catch him. I was compelled to give up the chase. And now you tell me that you afterwards found a mummy in the coffin which I had left empty."

"One of us is dreaming," said the girl.

"What was this mummy like?"

"A tall man—with a curious conical-shaped head —and eyes set hideously far apart in its skull—but you have seen the Arab who frightened me—and indeed he attacked you at your camp. His mummified counterpart."

"And some of his ribs were broken?"

"I do not know."

"But his body was bandaged. Otherwise he was almost nude."

"Good heavens!" she exclaimed. She put down her cup. "You make me very unhappy. You force me to recall my horror—in the cave temple. The wretched uncanny sense of the supernatural that oppressed me there. You make me remember that I was tortured into a fancy that the mummy was a ghost—that we were haunted— that—oh! oh! And father has been so kind to me lately, kinder than ever before."

"He is in London?"

"Yes"

"And the mummy?"

"Yes."

"And Dr. Belleville?"

"He is staying with us."

"Captain Weldon?"

She turned aside her head. "He is in London, too."

"You are shortly to be married, I am informed."

She stood up. "I must really be going," she observed constrainedly; then she held out her hand. I watched her pick her way through the crowd to our hostess. It was a well-bred crowd, but it stared at her. She was worth looking at. She walked just as a woman should and she bore herself with the proper touch of pride that is at the same time a personal protection and a provocative of curiosity. Some people call it dignity. Hubbard materialised from the shadow of a neighbouring curtain. "My wife has invited me to dinner," he announced. "You, too. I have made her your excuses because I have a money matter to discuss that should not be postponed."

"You have my deepest sympathy," I answered, and left him as puzzled to know what I meant as I was. Something was whispering over and over in my ear—"Work! work! work!" and whispering in the imperative mood. I determined to call upon Captain Weldon and procure from him my manuscript, at once. I remembered he lived in Jermyn Street. I walked thither as fast as I was able.

CHAPTER THIRTEEN

HUBBARD IS JEALOUS

I ENCOUNTERED THE Captain on his doorstep. He was just going out, hatted and gloved, but on seeing me he abandoned his intention. His delight was that of a child, and so manifestly genuine, so transparently sincere, that it warmed my heart. He dragged me into his sitting-room and wrung my hands again and again, expressing his pleasure in tones that made the windows rattle. One cannot help liking a man so simple and at the same time so kind. There are too many complex people in the world. He had grieved for my supposed loss more than at his own brother's death, he said, and I believed him. Very few men care much for their brothers. Then he told me all about his approaching marriage. It was to take place in five weeks and he was dreading the ordeal already. He had just finished furnishing his Wexford country house from top to bottom. They were to settle there after a honeymoon in Italy and adopt the life and manners of country magnates, only coming to town for the season. It was Miss Ottley's desire; she did not care for London smart society, it seemed, and although he did, he was quite willing to give it up or anything else indeed to please her. It was pleasant to hear him rhapsodise concerning her and to watch his happy face. Its spirit made him ten times handsomer, and although his speech was boyish it did not detract him from his exuberant virility. He was a man from the crown of his head to the soles of his feet,—a splendid animal, with just enough brains to be a force to command respect, and a heart big enough to fill the whole world with his affection. There was not a single bitter drop in the cup of his happiness. He was about to marry the woman he adored. He was enormously wealthy, and his wife-to-be was the only daughter of a millionaire. His plans for the future were Utopian. He dreamed of enlarging his estates and providing for at least the welfare of a hundred families. Wealth was given one in trust for others, he declared, and he was resolved to make every one around him happy and contented. As a wedding present to his tenants he had already ordered the rebuilding of their homes and cottages on a scale of almost lavish grandeur. Each farmhouse would be a model of luxury; each labourer's cottage would be a miniature castle with tiled walls, and hot and cold water attachments. Other landlords were annoyed with him and had not hesitated to express their resentment. He was spoiling his own tenants and making them dissatisfied, they said. But the Captain asked me with eyes aglow how could one want to keep all the good things of life to benefit a single class? It was monstrous, impossible, absurd. He only wished he could at one stroke make all the poor in the world comfortable. "You ought to hear May on the subject," he cried out in a burst of confidence. "You'd think she was a socialist. But she is only an angel." Thence he wandered to her father. Sir Robert had given up all his old stupid ways. He had reformed and was as sane as any man in England. He had repudiated his ancient attachment to "spooks" and spirit-rapping, and Mahatmas, and had sent his famous medium, Navarro, to the right about, much to that gentleman's disgust and indignation. Sir Robert was now engaged with Dr. Belleville in compiling a history of the dynasty from papyri they had found in the tomb of Ptahmes. The Captain still thought that Ottley had treated me very badly, but he begged me to forgive the old man as he had evidently not been quite in his mind at the time. "You excited his professional jealousy, don't you know, old chap," said Weldon. "Sir Robert has one fault—he is dreadfully vain and he wanted to get all the credit out of his discovery. He told me so himself. He quite opened up to me on the voyage home."

A vision of Sir Robert Ottley "opening up" to the Captain occurred to me. The little, old, inscrutable, shut-in face of the baronet peering slyly into the frank and unsuspicious countenance of the handsome, simple-minded guardsman and making a confession of his faults the while! For why? I could not guess, but I had a feeling that it was for no straightforward purpose. We dined together, and while we ate I questioned him about Dr. Belleville. For the first time I saw a shade on his face. He did not like the doctor. I pursued the investigation. For a while he fenced with my questions but finally it all came out. "I have an idea," said he, "that Belleville annoys May. He is in love with her. Of course one can't blame him for that, but as a guest in her father's house and her father's closest friend, he has opportunities to force his attentions, and I believe the brute abuses them. She does not complain and will tell me nothing—but all the same I have my opinion. You see, she worships her father so much that she will run no risk of hurting his feelings. She would put up with almost anything rather than distress him, and

Belleville knows it. He has Sir Robert under his thumb far more than I like. I hate to think I may be wronging the fellow—but upon my soul I cannot help distrusting him."

"But you have nothing definite to go upon?"

"Nothing—except this: One day about two weeks ago I went in unannounced and found her—in tears. I had passed Belleville in the hall a second earlier. He looked as black as night. And she—well, she told me, weeping, that she would marry me when I pleased. Up till then she had always put off naming the day. What would you make of it, Pinsent?"

"What did you?"

"I concluded that he had been persecuting her and that—well, that she felt safer with me than with her father. Don't rag me for being vain, old chap. If you'd seen her cry. She is not that sort of a girl either. It was the first time I ever knew her to break down, and I've known her all my life."

"Did you speak to Belleville about it?"

"She forbade me to—but all the same I did. I behaved like an idiot, of course. Lost my temper and all that sort of thing. He was as cool as a cucumber. He denied nothing and admitted nothing. He pretended to think I had been drinking, and that enraged me the more. I was fool enough to strike him. He got all the best of it. He picked himself up smiling sweetly and said that nothing could induce him to resent anything addressed by a person in whom Miss Ottley was interested. The inference was that he loved her in an infinitely superior way to me. I felt like choking him for a bit. And would you believe it—he actually offered to shake hands."

"A dangerous man, my lad. Beware of him."

"He gives me the creeps," said the Captain. "But let's talk of something else pleasanter."

We talked of Miss Ottley, or rather he did, while I listened, till midnight. Then he strolled with me to Bruton Street and we parted at Dixon Hubbard's doorstep as the clocks were striking one.

I found Hubbard seated before the fire, smoking, and staring dreamily up at a portrait of his wife that rested on the mantel.

"I've found out why I married her, Pinsent," he said slowly. "It was to benefit a Jew named Maurice Levi—the most awful bounder in London. She had been borrowing from him at twenty-five per cent, to pay some of her brother's gambling debts. Levi wanted to marry her, and would have, too, if I had not stepped in to save him. She is the dearest little woman in the world. She shed some tears. They cost me about a thousand pounds apiece."

"Good-night, Dixon," I said gently.

"Tears, idle tears," he murmured. "The poet, mark you, did not speak of woman's tears." Then he closed his eyes and heaved a deep sigh. "You find me changed, Pinsent?"

"A little."

"For better or worse? Be frank with me."

"For the better. This afternoon for the first time in our acquaintance I beheld you in a lady's drawing-room. You are growing tolerant of your kind."

"I am no longer a misanthrope, but I am rapidly becoming a misogynist. Yes, I am altered, old friend, greatly altered. At the bottom of my former misanthropy was a diseased conviction born of vanity that I was the only person in the world really worth thinking badly about. But marriage has compelled me to think more badly still of somebody else. The less selfish outlook thus induced has broadened my mind. I begin to look forward to a time when my perversion will be complete and I shall be able without blushing to look any woman in the face and acknowledge her superiority in innate viciousness."

"I begin to pity your wife, Dixon."

"A waste of sentiment. She has married five and twenty thousand pounds per annum, and she would be the last to tell you that the institution is a failure. Few women contrive to dispose as advantageously of the sort of goods they have to sell. Lady Helen would have made a fortune as a bagman. But there, I do not want to prejudice you against her. She likes you, I believe. Perhaps—who knows—but there—good-night."

I was glad to get away.

CHAPTER FOURTEEN

THE PUSHFUL MAN

A DAY OR two afterwards, while spending an hour in the rooms of the Egyptology Society I was introduced to a new Fellow, who had been appointed during my absence from England. His name was Louis Coen. He was in private life a broker, but his heart and soul were wrapped in the Cause. He evidently spelt it with a capital, in sympathy, perhaps, with the vast sums in cash he had already put at the disposal of the Society for exploration work. He was intensely entertaining. He took me aside and confided that it was his ambition to transform the Society into a sort of club. We needed a liquor license and more commodious premises, it seemed. Then we would *boom*. He offered to provide all the money requisite and he begged me to use my influence with other members to get his views adopted. He was one of those men whose mission in life is to "run" every concern into which they can manage to insinuate themselves. I was afraid I disappointed him, although I did my best to be polite. But he was nothing daunted. He declared he would galvanise the "old fogies" into fresh activity and make us see things from his point of view or die in the attempt. We might be as serious as we pleased, but he would force us to be sociable. He had a nose like a parrot, and was already on the committee of management. He even proposed to change our name. The Royal Egyptian Club seemed to him a "real smart monniker." He saved me from an impending mental and physical collapse by mentioning the name of Sir Robert Ottley. Ottley, it appeared, was his latest convert. Ottley agreed with him that we wanted new blood, that our methods were too conservative. Ottley thought it was ridiculous that everything a member did or discovered should have to be reported to, and judged about, by a lot of old fossils. What right had those old "stick-at-homes" to appropriate the credit of the exertions of the energetic? "Would you believe it," cried Mr. Coen, "they have had the impudence to demand from him an account of his recent find—the tomb of an old johnny named Ptahmes—which he unearthed at his own expense entirely! They have had the 'hide' to insist that he shall immediately hand over the mummy to the British Museum and place the papyri before them—them—them—for the purpose of translation, et-cetera! I never heard a more cheeky proposition in my life. My friend Ottley would act rightly if he told them to go to the deuce!"

"What has he told them?" I inquired.

"Oh, he is temporising. He has written to say that he will place his discoveries at their disposal when he has satisfied himself of their authenticity, et-cetera. Of course that's all '*gyver*.' The mummy is genuine enough, so are the papyri. But he naturally wants to have first 'go' at them, and he is fighting for time. Meanwhile, I am organising the progressives. We can never hope to get this show properly on the move till we shake things up and reform on sound commercial lines. I tell you, sir, before I've done with it, I'll make this Society a power in the land. I'm going to take it up in both hands and chuck it right in the eyes of the B. P., that means the British Public. And you take it from me, it's going to stay there. Good-day to you. I'm glad to have met you. You are a bit antiquated in your notions; but you're a young man yet, and you'll find you'll have to join my crowd. S'long!"

He shook my hand very energetically and bustled off. I sank into a chair and began to fan myself. A moment later the president, Lord Ballantine, entered the room. The poor old gentleman was purple in the face, spluttering: "Has-has-has that man Coen been can-can-canvassing you?" he thundered.

I nodded.

"I-I-I'll resign—by God!" cried Lord Ballantine. "It-it-it's too much. I-I-I," he stopped—gasping for a word, the picture of impotent rage and misery.

But I felt no sympathy for him. "Why did you let him in?" I asked.

"We-we-we were short of funds."

"And now?"

"He's bought us, or thinks he has, body and soul."

"Who nominated him?"

"Ottley."

I was not surprised to hear it. "He—he's Ottley's broker. Ottley and he are running the market-change—together. Have you heard? They have cornered South Africans. They made half a million between them yesterday. All London is talking about it. And they want to turn us into a beer garden."

"You'll have to turn them out."

"How can we? We owe them, Lord knows how much."

"Then if you cannot," I said calmly, rising as I spoke, "you'll have to grin and bear the infliction you have brought upon yourselves. After all, it's a question of voting."

"You'll stand by us, Pinsent?" he implored.

"My resignation is at any time at your disposal, Ballantine. All the same, I don't pity you a scrap. You are getting little more than you deserve. I have been working for three years for the Society without remuneration, and I am a poor man. Many of your older members are as rich as Crœsus, and yet you must needs import a vulgar Semitic broker to help you out of a hole. Good-afternoon."

I left the poor old fellow helpless and speechless, staring after me with anguished eyes and mouth agape. That evening I received a letter from Louis Coen offering to finance my book on the Nile Monuments. He said he felt sure it would prove a work of rare educational value, and on that account he was willing to furnish every library in the English-speaking world with a free copy. Aware, however, that I was not a business man, he would conduct all the business arrangements himself. On receipt of the manuscript, therefore, he would forward me a cheque for £1000 as an instalment in advance of my share of the profits—fifteen per cent, he proposed to allow me—and he wound up as follows: "Your acceptance of my offer will commit you to nothing as regards our chat of this morning. My good friend, Sir Robert Ottley, put me up to this venture. He has the brightest opinion of your ability and he is sure your book will prove a success. I am going blind on his say so. Let me have an answer right away."

I thought a good deal over this precious epistle, but in the end I did not see why I should not make a little money. I knew very well that under ordinary circumstances it would be impossible for me to make £100, let alone a thousand, out of the Nile Monuments. But I felt little doubt that Mr. Coen had a plan to make even more— somehow or other. But I had done the man injustice—it was not money he was after. Reading the *Times* two mornings later I came upon the following announcement:

"A PATRON OF LEARNING"

"We are informed that Mr. Louis Coen, F. R. E. S., has induced the well-known Egyptologist, Dr. Hugh Pinsent, to commit the results of his recent archæological researches on the Nile to the enduring care of the printer's ink. Mr. Coen has purchased the rights in advance for a large sum of the projected volume, which it is said will take the form of an exhaustive treatise on the Nile Monuments. It is not, however, Mr. Coen's object to direct his enterprise to his own financial benefit. It is his intention to produce a splendidly illustrated edition of the book for presentation to educational establishments all over the United Kingdom in the hope of thus fixing public attention upon the enormous historical importance of the work now being carried on by the Royal Egyptologist Society, of which Society Mr. Coen is a member, and a generous supporter. Mr. Coen is to be congratulated upon his latest effort in the interest of popular education. It will be remembered that last year he endowed a chair in the University of Newcome for study of the ancient Egyptian tongue; but it may be confidently expected that his exploitation of Dr. Pinsent's history will go much further in popularising a subject which is now practically confined to the ranks of leisured scholars."

It was not pleasant to think that I had been idiot enough to allow Mr. Coen to use me as a stepping-stone to notoriety. But it was too late to object. The thing was done. My consolation was a bigger banking account than I had had for years. Not even the fact that during the day I received a score of sarcastic congratulatory telegrams from members of the Society, could rob me of that satisfaction. But I sent in my resignation all the same. I felt that I had no right to belong to any institution run by Mr. Coen. I might meet him there—and if I did, a police court case of assault and battery would infallibly result.

CHAPTER FIFTEEN

A Quaint Love Pact

ONE EVENING, AFTER a hard morning's work on my book, and a particularly fatiguing afternoon spent in vainly trying to lift Hubbard out of a funereal mood, I thought I should make myself a present of a few minutes' conversation with Miss Ottley. I argued that she would be sure to spend the evening out somewhere, so I knocked at her father's door a few minutes before eight o'clock. A gloomy-looking footman opened the door. Yes, Miss Ottley was at home. He would give her my card. Would I wait? I would, though I wondered. I heard Dr. Belleville's voice. It issued from a room that opened on the hall. He was talking shrilly as though he were angered, and in French, perhaps to spare the feelings of the servants. He kept repeating that he had made up his mind and that he would not wait another day for God Almighty. All of a sudden the door opened and he stalked out looking like the baffled villain in a melodrama. We came face to face. He stopped dead and glared at me. "You!" he gasped. "What are you doing here; what do you want?"

I glanced beyond him and saw Miss Ottley. He had been speaking to her, then, and like that. My blood began to boil. I advanced upon him trying to smile. I had seen Miss Ottley's face. "I want you to go right back into that room and pretend you are a gentleman," I said. The girl had put a kerchief to her eyes. "Quickly!" I added.

Dr. Belleville returned into the room. I followed and closed the door.

"Dr. Pinsent—" he began as I turned. But I cut him short.

"On your knees," I commanded. He went livid.

"Dr. Pinsent," said Miss Ottley, "I beg you not to interfere. You will only make it the harder for me."

She might as well have spoken to a fence. I never took my eyes from Belleville. "You know what you ought to do," I murmured. "If you compel me to teach you, you'll repent the object lesson in a hospital."

He fell on his knees before the girl. "I apologise," he groaned out in a choking voice.

I bowed him out of the room as deferentially as if he were a woman. He vanished silently. Miss Ottley was dressed for the opera.

"You are going out?" I asked.

"Y-yes," she said. She was powdering her face before a mirror.

"To the opera?"

"Yes. To meet there Mrs. Austin."

"Dare you walk there—with me for a companion?"

"Oh, yes," she said.

A moment later we found ourselves in Curzon Street. She took my arm. We walked for two blocks in absolute silence, save that every now and then she choked back a sob. She was her own mistress again at length, however. "Why did you come—of all times to-night?" she asked.

"I do not know."

"Did you wish to see my father?"

"No. You."

"Why?"

"I had a subconscious conviction that you might be needing me."

"Truly?" she cried—and pressed my arm.

"That or something else. At any rate, I felt obliged to call. It may have been from a desire to reassure myself about the colour of your eyes."

"Ah! I suppose you are wondering—because—Dr. Belleville—because—I—," she paused.

"I am human," I observed.

"I want you to forget it. Will you, Dr. Pinsent?"

"On the spot."

"That is good of you." Her tone was crisp with disappointment. "You are indeed a friend."

"But not in need a friend, eh? Come, come, Miss Ottley, you are in trouble. I am strong and trustworthy and capable. There are times when a man may tell the truth about himself, and this, I think, is one of them. Can I help you?"

"No one can help me," she said sadly, "you least of all."

"And why least of all?"

"Because you hate my father."

"Is he in trouble, too?"

"He is the willing but unwitting victim of a wicked, wicked man—but, oh, what am I saying? Dr. Pinsent, please, please let us talk of something else."

"You are trembling—May."

"Oh!" she said—and looked at me.

"It slipped out—unconsciously," I stammered. "I did not mean to be impertinent. I think of you—by that name. Is it impertinent to think—"

"No, no."

"Then you'll forgive me?"

"What is there to forgive?"

"All that the circumstance implies. Come, after all, I am not sorry for the slip. Why should I twist its meaning either, like a coward. It is only the weak who need the shelter of hypocrisy. Look straight before you—May—and do not turn your eyes. May again, you see."

"You have something to tell me," she said gravely.

"The old, old story, May," I answered with a short but reckless laugh.

"Should you—Dr. Pinsent—do you think?"

"Yes, because the husband you have chosen is a gallant fellow and my friend. I am too fond of him to wish to do him an ill turn, even in my own adventure. Why, look you, May, were you to turn to me and say, 'I love you, Hugo Pinsent,' I would answer, 'Yes—and we both love Frankfort Weldon.' "

"Yes," said Miss Ottley. She stopped and we looked deep into each other's eyes.

"Yes," she said again. "And we both love Frankfort Weldon."

"God help us," I exclaimed.

"It is a good prayer. God will hear it," she said softly.

"What made you?" I asked a little later; we were walking on again—but now apart.

"You," she said.

"It is very wonderful."

"And sad," said she.

"But grand and beautiful."

"I shall not go to the opera to-night," she said. "Will you put me in a cab?"

"You will go home?"

"Yes."

"And Belleville?"

"He will be at work. I shall not see him."

"He threatened you?"

"Not me, but Captain Weldon. He demands that I shall marry him. My father also wishes it. You see I tell you everything—now. You will help me, will you not?"

"Of course. But you must teach me how. In what fashion does Belleville threaten Weldon?"

"He vows—that unless I do as he demands within this week—Captain Weldon will be found dead in his bed."

"Murder!" I cried.

"He does not scruple to conceal the fact. He declares he has nothing to fear. He pretends to possess a secret which gives him as great a power over life and death as Providence. An esoteric power, of course. It is connected with the discovery of Ptahmes. He claims to have already tested it. My father has used it in other ways. He has been experimenting on the Stock Exchange. In ten days he has already doubled his fortune. Surely of that you must have heard."

"I have heard that he has been speculating with extravagant success. But that his luck was due to supernatural agency I decline to believe. In my opinion Belleville is simply putting up a scoundrelly game of bluff."

"I wish I could think so, too. But I cannot."

"But, my dear girl, consider the probabilities. Belleville's story belongs to the Middle Ages."

"Yes—but he believes it. I am as sure of that as that I live."

"And is that a reason why you should believe it, too? The man is perhaps a lunatic."

"Ah!" she said. "I knew that you would take this view. That was partly why I felt you could not help me."

But her distress cut me to the quick. "It does not matter what view I take," I muttered hastily. "I'll do anything you wish."

"Anything?"

"Did you doubt it?"

"No."

"Then—"

"Then go and stay with Captain Weldon. He will welcome you, for he likes you out of mention. Spend the week with him. Do not let him from your sight at night. Especially guard him while he sleeps. Is it too much to ask?"

"No."

"There is a cab—stop it, please! Thanks. Now say good-bye to me."

"Good-bye—May." I helped her into the vehicle. "Would it be permissible to kiss your hand?"

"No!" she said, "but give me yours."

I felt her lips upon my fingers, and with a sort of groan I snatched them away from her grasp. That was our good-bye.

CHAPTER SIXTEEN

LADY HELEN PRESCRIBES FOR HER HUSBAND

NEXT MORNING EARLY I picked a quarrel with Hubbard, and left him biting his finger nails. I went straight to Jermyn Street with my valise. Weldon was in bed. I told him I had had a fight with Hubbard and asked to be put up for a few days. He agreed with acclamation, though I am sure he was perfectly astounded at my strange request. I proceeded to astound him further. I mendaciously informed him that my nerves were in rags and that I was obsessed with a horrible hallucination of a mysteriously threatened life at night. Would, then, he give me a shake-down in his own bedroom, just for a week? It is wonderful how easy lying comes to one after the first plunge. I did the thing thoroughly. Mind you, I felt all along the utmost scorn for Dr. Belleville's threats against young Weldon's life. But Miss Ottley had asked me to look after him, and I was determined to fulfil the trust to the very foot of the letter. He was a splendid fellow to live with. It gives me a heartache to remember the anxiety to make me comfortable, the almost absurd cordiality of his welcome, the unselfish sincerity of his desire to please. One would have thought me a superior creation, a sort of divinity in disguise, the way he treated me. I had never awakened such affection in any living thing before, except in a mongrel retriever which once upon a time followed me home and which I had to turn away after it had licked my hand. And the amazing thing was, I had done nothing in the world to deserve it. I had never put myself out of my way in the smallest particular to serve the Captain. When we first met I had treated him with the scantest courtesy and afterwards with a sort of good-natured contempt. Even now I cannot understand it properly. It may have arisen from a secret disposition to hero-worship. Some men are like that. They are fond of investing a sentient figure-head with exaggerated attributes of majesty and bowing down before it. It is the survival of an aboriginal instinct to glorify the insubordinate. Weldon admired two things above all others: strength of body and strength of mind. In both these gifts he felt himself inferior to me, therefore he must needs put me on a pedestal. His gratitude in finding me willing to stoop to ask a favour of him was unbounded. It resembled that of an Eton fag to a monitor kind enough to take an interest in his doings. I have said before that he was essentially a boy at heart. But what an honest, clean-minded, fresh, wholehearted boy! I found myself liking and admiring him more and more each day. He taught me one of the greatest truths a man may learn. It is this—there is a more admirable thing in the world than intellect. Weldon's intellect was not of the first order. That is why I began by very nearly despising him. But he was the straightest, truest, manliest and simplest-minded man I have ever met. And I ended by half-humorously but none the less sincerely, reverencing him. If it were only for his sake I shall while I live regard the highest type of brain as incomplete without a paramount ideal of morality. And the best thing about Weldon was that he was utterly unconscious of his goodness. He was perfectly incapable of posing, but he had a fine, robust vanity of sorts, and he liked to regard himself as a bit of a "sad dog!" Romance was at the bottom of this. He envied the more than questionable experience of some of his acquaintances. It was because of the glamour of their perfumed wickedness. But their callous self-extrication from entanglements after growing weary of their chains made him long to wring their necks. For his own part, a certain shop girl had once fallen in love with him. He twirled his moustache and cast furtive glances at the mirror near him. It appears he had dallied with the temptation for a while—the "sad dog"—but Miss Ottley's portrait had saved him. He had kissed the shop girl once—horror of horrors!—in the Park after dark. He apologised to her father with a thousand pounds and fled to South America. When he came back she was married. He had confessed the whole of his truly dreadful criminality to Miss Ottley in a letter—and she had kept him waiting three miserable days for a reply. He believed he would have gone to the dogs headlong if she had refused to pardon him. But she did not. Vanity told him the reason. But it was beautiful to see the colour flush his cheeks and his eyes sparkle as he protested that he couldn't understand why she ever brought herself to speak to him again. I believe that was as far as Weldon ever got to telling a downright falsehood; the dear, great gander.

On the third afternoon of my stay at Jermyn Street I was busily at work writing, when a knock sounded. Weldon was out; he had gone to take Miss Ottley for a drive in his newest dog-cart. His man, too, had a day off, so I was quite alone. I said "Come in," and there entered Lady Helen—Hubbard's wife. She was a vision of lace fripperies and arch, mincing daintiness.

"So! run to earth!" she cried.

I sprang up and offered her a chair.

She settled into it with a swish and a sigh. "Been searching for you everywhere! I had thought of applying to the police."

I suppose I looked astonished, for she laughed.

I stammered, "Why have you been searching for me?"

She gave me a glance of scorn. "Should a dutiful wife regard with indifference the sudden desertion of her husband by the only friend he possesses? Just tell me that."

"You take my breath away."

"No," she flashed, "the 'dutiful wife' did that. Confess!"

"Well, since you insist—I admit that Helen becomes you better than Joan," I said audaciously.

Her eyes glittered. "May be, my fine gentleman—but would you say 'Dixon' was synonymous with 'Darby'?"

"Not quite. Still, they both commence with a 'D.' That is something, eh?"

"So does another word which rhymes with lamb," she retorted cuttingly. "Oh! I might have known that you would take his part. You men always stick together."

"I beg your pardon, Lady Helen. I consider that you deserve well of your country. You have improved Hubbard past belief. He is worth improving."

She smiled. "I have humanised him, just a little, don't you think?"

I nodded.

She leaned forward suddenly and looked me in the eye. "It's only the commencement, the thin edge of the wedge."

"Oh!"

She began speaking through her teeth. "I'll make a man of him yet if I have to beggar him in the process."

"I beg you to excuse me."

She fell back and began to laugh. "Oh, how solemn you are. You disapprove of me. Ha! ha! ha! You don't even begin to hide it."

"You see I do not understand you."

"Yet you disapprove?"

"No. I wonder."

"You are a man, Doctor, that one can't help trusting!" She stood up and began to move about the room. "I am going to confide in you," she announced, stopping suddenly.

"A dangerous experiment," I observed.

"One risks death every time one crosses a car-crowded thoroughfare. I'll take the risk."

I shrugged my shoulders.

She frowned. "You used to like me once. What stopped you?"

"I haven't stopped."

She smiled bewitchingly and, gliding forward, placed her hand upon my arm. "He wanted to take me away to South America—he owns a ranch there—and to bury us two for ever from the world. That was his idea of marriage. It all came of a rooted disbelief in his own ability to keep me interested in himself while I possessed an opportunity to contrast him with his social equals. He saw a rival in every man I looked at or who looked at me. He should have been born a Turk. I should then have been the queen of his zenana. But no, I must do him justice—he is not polygamously inclined. Still, he would have shut me up."

"The poor devil," I muttered. "It is his disposition. He cannot help himself."

"But he may be cured of it," said Lady Helen. "He thinks every woman is a rake at heart. But he is mad. I for one am not. Mind you, I love society. I like men. I live for admiration. But as to—pshaw!"—she spread out her hands.

"You quarrelled?" I inquired.

"No, we argued the matter out and came to an arrangement. We are good friends. But he does not conceal his opinion that some day or another I will go to the devil. He thinks it inevitable. Pride, however, forbids him from looking on except at a distance. That is why he separated from me. He imagines that no woman can keep true to one man unless she is immured. The fool, the utter fool! As if walls and locks and keys were ever an encumbrance. Love is the only solid guarantee of a woman's faith."

"But my dear Lady Helen, your husband has not the faintest idea that you love him!"

She drew back gasping. "You—you—you!" she cried. She was scarlet. Then she said, "How dare you!" She looked so lovely that I no longer wondered at Hubbard's infatuation.

"You should not have kept it from him," I said severely. "But there, it's wonderful. How did you ever manage it? He is not an attractive man. And you—a butterfly. It is a miracle. There must be depths in you. Are marriages made in Heaven? I thought—he thinks—you married him for his money. And you love him! I shall never get over this. Lady Helen, you are a most amazing woman!"

She rushed at me panting with rage and, seizing my arm, shook it with both hands. "If ever you tell him—I'll—I'll kill you!" she hissed.

"But why?"

"He must find out himself. He must suffer. He deserves it. He has bitterly insulted me. He has shamed my sex. He must gnaw out his heart. In no other way can he be made like other men. I'll teach him. I'll teach him. Oh, if you dare to interfere! But you shan't— you would not dare."

"No," I said, "I would not dare."

Next second she was in another mood. Her anger melted to pathos and the little siren began to plead to me. "You know what I really want you to do is to help me," she murmured, oh! so prettily. "And it is all for Dixon's sake, or really and truly I would not ask. You see, Doctor, I am working on a system. Goodness, how I am trusting you! And you can help, oh! ever so much."

"Only tell me how."

"Do not lose a chance to revile me."

I was staggered. "I beg your pardon, Lady Helen!" I cried.

"Ah! I thought you would understand. Don't you see you are his only friend? More than that, you are the only man he ever speaks to. He is a hermit. Well, then, who else is there to reproach me to his ears? To put his own thoughts of me into words?"

"But what on earth do you want that done for?"

"It will compel him to defend me, first by lip, then by heart."

I confess I whistled.

"I felt it to be necessary to have this talk with you," went on Lady Helen. "Hitherto he has done all the reviling and you the defending of me. Is it not so?"

"You little witch."

"And that is not right, since it is he, and not you, who is my husband."

"Lady Helen, you are surely the cleverest woman in the world."

"I have thought the matter out," she answered, with a sad little smile. "Is it wonderful that a woman should wish to be happy and that she should fight for that with every weapon she can find?" She rose and held out her hand. "You will go and make friends soon, will you not? He is fretting because you have deserted him."

"In a very few days, Lady Helen. I wish I could this moment, but I cannot."

"You are very busy, eh?"

"I have a task to carry out. It will be finished at the end of the week."

"So!" she said and shrugged her shoulders. "And are you quite engaged? Could you not come to me to-night? Your friend Captain Weldon comes, and some others. We are to have our fortunes told. Signor Navarro has promised us a séance. Miss Ottley has arranged it. She tells me he is a truly marvellous clairvoyant, medium, etcetera. Have you a curiosity to know your future? Do come! Dixon will be there."

"Thank you very much; yes, I shall be glad to go."

I opened the door for her and she blew me a kiss from the stairs. I returned to my work, but it was very little I was able to do the rest of that afternoon. What could have induced Miss Ottley to arrange this séance? Were her nerves giving way under the strain of Dr. Belleville's threats? Did she really believe this rascal Navarro capable of predicting events? Was she becoming superstitious? These reflections profoundly disturbed me.

CHAPTER SEVENTEEN

THE SÉANCE

NAVARRO EVIDENTLY BELONGED to the highest and most ingenious order of charlatanry. He had no assistant, no machinery, no accomplice. It was almost impossible to suspect any of the audience. There were only Lady Helen, Miss Ottley, Mrs. Greaves (wife of a Parliamentary Undersecretary), the Countess von Oeltzen (the Austrian Ambassador's wife), Weldon, Hubbard, the Count von Oeltzen and myself present. And the medium scouted the idea of turning down the lights. He left such devices to impostors, he remarked. He was a tall, thin fellow, with big, black eyes and a thick-lipped mouth. He had the most beautiful hands and feet. His fingers were covered with valuable diamond rings. He had a big bulbous nose and he wore a *tire-boucheau* moustache and beard consisting of about sixteen coarse stiff black hairs; four on each side of his upper lip and eight on his chin. He plucked at the latter continually in order to display his hands and his rings. It would have been a difficult matter to find his match in vulgarity, in ugliness, and impudence. But he was certainly impressive. He talked of himself in a booming baritone, like a Barnum praising an elephant. He adored himself and expected to be adored. He spoke with a strong Irish-Spanish accent. Probably he was an Irishman who had lived in Spain. But he posed as a full-blooded Castilian who had learned English from a Cork philomath.

After he had exhausted his vocabulary in describing some of his clairvoyant achievements he needlessly directed us to be silent. He had permitted none of us a chance to speak thitherto. We were to wait, he said, till he began to breathe in a peculiar heavy manner, and then who so wished to experiment, must take his hands and hold them firmly for a little while, thinking of the matter next the experimenter's heart; and then we should see what we should see. With a smile of lordly self-confidence he reposed his limbs upon a couch and sank back on the cushions. I glanced around the throng and saw they were all staring at Navarro—Miss Ottley with parted

lips and rapt intentness. Her expression irritated me. Soon afterwards I met Hubbard's eyes. He gave me a scowl. I looked at
Weldon. He turned and frowned at me. I directed my attention to
Lady Helen. She grew restless and, presently moving in her chair,
glanced rapidly about. She started when our eyes encountered and
impulsively placed a finger on her lips. I hadn't thought of speaking. I was disgusted. Mrs. Greaves, the Countess and the Ambassador all in turn gave me scowling glances. It was as if everybody
recognised and resented my secret scepticism. It appeared I was the
only sane person in the room. Oh! no, there was Navarro. He was
sane enough undoubtedly; the rogue. He was making his living. It
was his business to make fools of people. I returned to contem-
plating him with a sense of positive relief. At least I could hope to
be amused. He had closed his eyes and was therefore uglier than
ever. His whole body was tense with silent effort. I wondered if
some of his audience were unconsciously imitating him. They all
were, except myself. I felt inclined to get up and shake them for a
pack of self-delivered dupes, lambs self-abandoned to the sacrifi-
cial rites of this High Priest of Thomas-rot. Soon, friend Navarro
began to breathe stertorously. So did his audience, for a minute or
two. Then they turned and looked at one another and at me; and I
rejoice to say my calm smile disconcerted them. But I refrained
from glancing at Miss Ottley. I could not bear to see her look
foolish. Perhaps she did not. They pointed at one another. They
feared, it seemed, to speak. Who would be the first? And who
would dare the oracle? The Count von Oeltzen arose. Brave, noble
man! He approached the couch and took Navarro's hand in his own.
The medium was now in a trance. His body was quite limp. A
breathless silence fell upon the gathering. It lasted about four
minutes. Then Navarro began to speak, not in his ordinary booming
baritone, but in a high falsetto—his spirit organ, no doubt. The
language employed was German.

"I see," said he, "a short fat man in the uniform of an Austrian
courier. He is seated in a railway train. He is smoking a cheroot. He
has on his knees a small, flat iron box. It is a despatch box. It contains letters and despatches. He is coming to England—"

"Ah!" sighed the Count.

"Ah! Ah!" sighed the Countess.

"He is on his way to you," went on Navarro. "The despatches are
for you. One of them is in a cipher. It relates to your recall. It—"

But the Count on that instant dropped Navarro's hands as if they
had burnt him and abruptly rose up, the picture of agitation. He

turned and looked at the Countess. She stood up, most agitated, too. "My friends," he began. But the Countess said "Hush!" He bowed to her, bowed to Lady Helen and offered his wife a shaking arm. They forthwith left the room. It was most dramatic. For a little while everybody sat under a sort of spell. I was glad, because I felt disinclined to break up the party by expressing my views on Navarro's revelation, and if any one had said a word I should have been compelled to speak, I was so angry that sensible people could allow themselves to be imposed upon so easily. Moreover, I wished to learn what Miss Ottley's object was. When, therefore, Mrs. Greaves quietly arose and moved to the couch, I said a little prayer of thankfulness.

Presently the high falsetto squeaked forth in Irish-Spanish-English. "I see—a large building, square, very tall. It is made of steel and stone. It is in America—in New York. It is a hotel. I see in it a room. There are tables and chairs. Then one—two—three—four—five six are there. They play cards. The game is poker. One loses. He is young. He is English. He has a little cast in his left eye. His name is Julian Greaves. The floor is littered with cards. Julian Greaves is annoyed because he loses. He—"

The voice ceased.

Mrs. Greaves was returning to us. She was smiling. She said to Lady Helen in her calm, slow way, "I believe, my dear, that my naughty son is at present occupied exactly as you have heard described. Signor Navarro has a great gift. Goodnight, my dear—No, I cannot stay—I promised the Bexleys. Do not trouble—"

She had gone.

Dixon Hubbard walked over to the couch. I glanced at Lady Helen. She was biting her lower lip—and holding her breath. I stole across the room on tip-toe and sat down beside her.

"I see," said Navarro, after the proper interval, "a woman. She is young and very beautiful. (Oh! artful Navarro.) Her mind is deeply troubled. The person she cares most for despises her. On that account she is wretchedly unhappy, although she permits no one to suspect it. She is not far away. She—"

But Hubbard had dropped the medium's hand like hot potatoes.

"It is your turn, Captain Weldon," he said, with a poor attempt at jocularity. "Step forward and have the secret of your life laid bare."

He gave his wife a scorching glance and sauntered out of the room.

"How much did you pay Navarro for that last?" I whispered in Lady Helen's ear.

She gave me a radiant smile. "Nothing to call me beautiful," she whispered back.

Weldon had taken the medium's hands. Immediately he did so, Navarro heaved a portentous sigh. I watched his face very narrowly, and somewhat to my surprise I observed it to turn to a horrid, fishy, whitish-yellow colour. Presently his eyelids slightly opened, disclosing the whites. The eyes were fixed upwards rigidly. He looked simply monstrous. For the first time I doubted his mala fides. There were many signs of cataleptic trance about him. I stole over to the foot of the couch and inserted a pin into the calf of his leg. Not a muscle twitched. Evidently he had hypnotised himself. I tried the other leg, with an equal result. I became furious. It seemed just possible that the fellow had some esoteric faculty after all. Science, of course, scouts the phenomena of clairvoyancy, but in my younger days I had witnessed so many experiments with hypnotised subjects in Paris that I had ever since kept an open mind on the question. This time we waited for quite a while for the medium to begin his manifestations. Perhaps ten minutes passed and he was still silent. But by that time I felt convinced of his unconsciousness. "Ask him some question, Weldon," I said quietly. "He is not shamming, I believe. In my opinion he is in hypnotic sleep and cannot act as his own Barnum."

Weldon laughed, but before he could adopt my hint Miss Ottley glided to the couch and standing at the head of it put her fingers lightly on the medium's eyes.

"I know what to do," she said, looking at me. "I have seen him in this state before. He is not a charlatan, Dr. Pinsent, at least when he is like this. Presently you will see. He will astonish you, I think."

"I wish you'd ask him where the lost key of my Saratoga is, May," whispered Weldon.

Navarro answered the question instantly, and in his natural reverberating baritone.

"It is lying on the top of the canopy of your bed in your bedroom in Jermyn Street."

"By Gad!" cried Weldon. "That's where it is as sure as I stand here. I tossed it up there a month ago and more—and forgot all about it."

"Hush!" said Miss Ottley. "Think of Dr. Belleville, Frankfort, please."

Weldon frowned. "You might have chosen a pleasanter topic," he muttered.

"Hush!" said the girl again.

A moment later she bent over the medium. "Speak!" she commanded. "Tell us what you see!"

Navarro sighed. "I see a large room," he began. "It is half library, half laboratory. One part of it is filled with racks of books and parchments. At the other end is a dispensary made up of shelves containing jars of different oils and phials filled with drugs. In the middle of the room is a table spread with maps and papyri. The papyri are inscribed with hieroglyphics. Beside the table, standing on two steel trestles, is a large sarcophagus of lead and iron lined with silver. The lid is propped against the wall near by. It is ornamented with the leaden cast of a man. An inscription states that this man is Ptahmes, a high priest of Amen-Ra. His body was once enclosed within the sarcophagus. It is now, however, reclining on a couch at a little distance from the table—"

"Describe it!" said Miss Ottley.

"It is apparently the body of a man of latter middle age. It is of great proportions. It is almost seven feet in length. But the body is very lank and shrunken and ill nourished. The head is of extraordinary shape and dimensions. It is very large and long, and broad. It is surmounted by a crown of jet-black hair that has recently been cut. It tapers like a cone above the temples and again like an inverted cone from the cheek bones to the chin. The nose is long and hooked like the beak of an eagle. The eyes are closed; I cannot see them. But they are almond shaped and set far apart in the skull. The mouth is shrivelled and almost shapeless. The chin is long and pointed. The skin is dark brown, almost black. It looks unhealthy. The body is clothed in ordinary European garments. One arm is fastened in a sling. The chest is, underneath the clothes, swathed in bandages. On the feet are fastened rubber shoes, on the soles of which are particles of fresh-dried mud. That is all."

"Proceed!" said Miss Ottley. "There are living people in the room, are there not?"

"Two," replied the medium after a short pause. "One is seated before the table poring over a torn piece of papyrus. Beside him on the table is a dictionary of hieroglyphics to which he constantly refers. He is a big, thick-set man with black eyes, strongly marked features, and a black bushy beard. In his hand is a pen. He writes with this pen upon the paper before him. He is engaged in translating the papyrus. Ha! he stops. He is looking up at his companion. He is speaking."

"What does he say?"

"He says, 'I cannot altogether reconcile our subject's statements with the records, Ottley. Either in his long sleep his memory has somewhat failed him, or in his sleep he has learnt more than he knew before. It is most annoying; we shall have to question him again.' The other—a little old man, with white hair and very bright small grey eyes—replies, 'You are too damned pernicketty, Doctor. Haven't we the formula, and hasn't it nobly stood the test of practical experience? What more do you want? Your infernal curiosity would ruin everything if I let you have your way. Once for all I tell you that Ptahmes belongs to me, not to you. Damn your science! You've had enough out of him. I'll not allow him to be used again except for my purposes. He has disappointed me with the elixir. Well, he'll have to atone by making me the richest man in the universe. I'll not be satisfied till every shilling in the world belongs to me—every shilling—every shilling.' The little man is now laughing like a lunatic. The big man watches him with a frown, bending his big black brows together. 'But you fool!' he says very angrily, 'do you forget that these things here—' he points to the body of Ptahmes—'will soon wear out? Every time that you drive it to work the friction sheds into dust a portion of its matter. Is it not better to use its brain than its body? Remember that we cannot repair his tissues. Unless we make absolutely certain of the composition of the invisible oil while we have the chance, we may be left stranded in the end. His body is of secondary importance after all. It serves you now, but you can just as well serve yourself by using the oil and doing your own dirty business. But the thing is to make sure of learning how to replenish the oil when our stock gives out. That is the all-important matter. And that is why his brain is of paramount interest to me, and should be to you.'

"The little man says,—'I won't have it, I tell you, we know enough!' The big man replies,—'Be sensible, Ottley! Remember he lost five pounds in weight yesterday! He is melting away before our eyes. Come! I'll make you a proposal. Let me do what I like with Ptahmes and I'll take his place for your money-making purposes. I'll be the ghost of the Stock Exchange and find out all you want to know. Now, what can be fairer than that?'

"The little man is biting his lip. He seems to be thinking," (there was a pause in the narration). Presently Navarro went on. "The little man speaks again; he says:—'That is all very well, Doctor, but you know as well as I do—that you intend to use Ptahmes to destroy your rival. You haven't the courage to do it yourself.' The big man answers very quickly, 'And are you brave enough to tackle Pinsent?

Yet his existence threatens all our plans. I firmly believe he has a notion of our ideas already. He is no fool and an adept at putting two and two together. Do you suppose he hasn't guessed at the reason of the success of your enormous transactions on 'Change?' The little man grinds his teeth. 'Curse him!' he shouts. 'Curse him to Hell!' The big man smiles. 'With all my heart,' he says, 'may he rot there for ever and ever! But all this proves to us how careful we should be of the waning strength of our magician. Remember the last time he tried odds with Pinsent on the Nile he got all the worst of the encounter. Three broken ribs! It's true we are more advanced in knowledge since then, and now we can make him quite invisible. But all the same we cannot afford to trifle with the strength of our subject, considering the two great tasks before him.'— Ah!—"

The last expression was a groan. The medium moved restlessly, then groaned again.

"Proceed! I command you!" said Miss Ottley in a trembling voice.

But Navarro for a third time groaned, and he began to struggle on the couch.

"Oh, God! he is waking up!" cried the girl. "Hold his hands tightly, Frankfort. He must tell us more! He must, he must!"

But Navarro with a sudden spasmodic writhe and twist, broke away and sat erect. He was shaking like a man in an ague, and he began to pant and groan like a wounded animal.

Miss Ottley gasped "Too late!" and wrung her hands.

I handed the medium a glass of water, but he was trembling too violently to take it of himself. He spilt half the contents on his knee. I forced the rest into his mouth. It revived him. A little later he stood up. He was bathed in perspiration, and looked sick. But he rejected all offers of assistance. He seemed to be very angry. He declared that we had treated him most cruelly, and that we might have killed him. He would not be appeased, and he went off in the care of a footman filled with petulant resentment and mouthing stupid threats. It may have been a pose, part of his "business" intended for effect to impress his clients;—probably it was. But I am not sure. He certainly seemed to be in a highly over-wrought, nervous condition; he could not easily have affected that.

After he had gone we all sat back in our chairs and stared at one another. Nobody was in the least haste to speak; we had so much to think about; and it was plain that "Fancy"—"Well, I never!" and ejaculations of that ilk did not even begin to meet the conversational demands of the occasion. Lady Helen was the first to speak.

She said, "Well, I am trying hard to be an ideal hostess and not ask any questions that might seem impertinent. But will someone tell me, is it Sir Robert Ottley and Dr. Belleville who are making preparations for Dr. Pinsent's funeral. I wish to know real badly, because I want him to do quite a lot of things for me before he crosses over the divide, and if necessary I shall go to Sir Robert and ask him for my sake to give Dr. Pinsent a little time to say his prayers."

It was just the flippant tone needed to bring us back to earth again. Everybody laughed. Everybody was so relieved that the laugh was unconventionally loud, and it had a tendency to overdo itself.

Then we trotted out the "well-I-nevers!"

"Did you ever hear such a lot of rubbish talk?" demanded Lady Helen.

"It quite took my breath away," said Miss Ottley with a gallant effort to attain the correct, approved, sociably foolish affectation of brainlessness.

"The fellow deserves three months without the option for his villainous slanders," said the Captain heartily. He was honest, anyhow. "Lord knows I can't stand Belleville at any price," he continued. "But Navarro went a bit too far, by Gad! I never heard anything more malicious in my life than his vile insinuations."

"A discharged servant," I observed. "Malice was to be expected from one of Navarro's type."

"And a foreigner to boot," said the Captain, in the manner of one absolutely clinching an argument. "Ah, well!" he suppressed a yawn, "he entertained us—and that's something. Seen the 'Japanese Marriage' yet, Lady Helen? Miss Ottley and I did an act or two last night. It's ripping. So—ah! so jolly unusual, don't you know. You get left every time you think something is going to happen; and when you least expect it one of the funny little beggars ups and wants to make his friend a present of his liver on a plate, or cut off his rival's head, or something."

"Miss Ottley's carriage," announced a footman.

"I asked for it," said the girl to Lady Helen. "My father has been very poorly all day."

Weldon went away with her. She did not even spare me a glance.

Lady Helen consoled me with the best cigar I have ever received at the hands of a woman.

She lit a cigarette for herself and curled up on a pile of cushions.

"That man Navarro is a rapacious rascal," she observed presently. "He wouldn't take a penny less than a hundred to say what he did say to Dixon. But I did not tell him to call me beautiful," she added.

"I am glad to be certain that the fellow is a rascal," I muttered half underbreath. But she heard me.

"Surely you knew. His ravings did not take you in," she cried scornfully. "Everyone knows he simply loathes Sir Robert Ottley. He used to be the little old millionaire's tin god. Sir Robert hardly dared to breathe without consulting his oracle. And they say the man bled him of thousands. No wonder he went mad to find that Sir Robert had escaped his influence. Ever since then he has been saying the most awful things. Lots of people believe them, I know, but I never thought you would."

"I don't." I smiled. I could smile now, for I felt wonderfully relieved. "But tell me, Lady Helen, just why you employed him to say that to your husband?"

She puffed out a cloud of smoke. "Dixon is superstitious at heart," she replied. "He will not want to, but he will end by believing what Navarro told him."

"What! that you care for him despising you?"

"Silly!" she cried. "No—not that I care for him—but for another man despising me—the man for whom *I care*. Have you forgotten Navarro's words?"

"But why on earth deceive your husband?"

"To make him jealous."

"Of a chimera?"

"No, my friend," said Lady Helen, smiling very strangely. "Of you! Remember, you have promised to revile me to him. That alone would fix a suspicious mind like his on you. But to make assurance doubly sure, I told him this afternoon that it hurt me very much to find that he had given you a poor opinion of me."

I sprang to my feet, aghast. "But look here—my girl," I cried. "This is a dangerous game you are playing."

"Are you afraid—are you then a coward?" she flashed.

"Hubbard is my oldest friend. You will make him hate me!" I protested.

"And you will refuse to risk that for his happiness and mine?" she asked. "Remember, he is my husband, and soured, twisted creature that he is, I love him!"

"Ah!" said I.

"I could have made you serve me in ignorance," she cried, "but I am incapable of playing you or any other—save him—a trick like that. However, say the word and the play ends—this instant. I have no claim upon you. I'll save you the trouble of telling me that. I am only a woman fellow-creature, and knight-errants are out of fashion now-a-days. Well—what is it to be?"

Her words stung like nettles. Such a little spitfire I had never seen before. But that was the proper way to treat me, and I believe she knew it. She was as sharp as any needle, that young woman.

"I am not in the habit of breaking my word once given," I growled out. "Good-night!" Then I stalked off most indignant. But she caught me at the door, flung her arms round my neck and kissed me on both cheeks.

"You are a darling," she whispered. "And—well—Dixon will have to hurry and reform—or else—but there—go!"

That is the way clever women bind foolish men to the further-ance of their caprices. A cuff, a kiss, a piece of subtle, thrilling flattery, and the trick is done. I was heart and soul in love with another woman, and yet from that moment Lady Helen Hubbard possessed the right to walk over me, if she wished to do it. And, mind you, I am not an out-of-the-way brand of idiot as fools go. It's just a matter of armour and the weak spot. No suit of armour ever existed that hadn't one. Some women are born with the faculty of being able to put their soft little fingers on those places right away.

CHAPTER EIGHTEEN

THE UNSEEN

"FOR MY SAKE, watch! It is but for two days longer,—the fatal week will then be over. Oh! I implore you not to let your scepticism make you careless. I trust you and depend upon you." Weldon gave me the note himself. It was not signed. He watched me curiously as I read it. I tore it up and threw the pieces in the grate.

"Miss Ottley is afraid that your friend Belleville meditates doing you an injury," I said carelessly, "and knowing that I am your guest, she has appointed me your guardian angel. Evidently she imagines that you are a more sensible person than I am. She said nothing about it to you?"

"No," replied the Captain. "But she made me promise not to leave your side for the next two days." He gave a sheepish laugh. "I'm afraid she has let you in for a lot of boredom, old man. But don't you bother to be polite! If you feel like kicking me at any time to relieve your feelings I'll take it lying down. You see, I couldn't help myself. She has such a way with her—and although I argued and protested and begged her to consider you—it was no use. I had to give in."

"You needn't apologise, Weldon. I believe I am strong enough to survive the infliction, and I promise not to kick you. How is Miss Ottley?"

"She is well, although she seems nervous and depressed. That is probably because her father is ill and she has been nursing him. You have heard, I suppose, of his latest doings?"

"No. As you are aware, I have not been out of doors for two days, and I have carefully refrained from newspapers."

"He has cornered the copper market. They say his fortune is increasing at the rate of half a million a day. But he is not strong enough to bear the excitement. In my opinion it is killing him. I saw him this afternoon. He looks ghastly. He was a little delirious, I fancy. They left me alone with him for a moment or two and he took the opportunity to warn me not to sleep to-night if I valued my life.

He said a terrible danger is hanging over my head. But Dr. Belleville came in just then, and it was surprising how sensible he got again, immediately. Naturally I said nothing of this to May. It would only have made her miserable. It is wonderful how she dotes on the poor old fellow. I don't know what she would do if he were to die."

"How did Belleville treat you?"

"For a wonder with the greatest courtesy. He took me aside and begged me to forget any occasion of offence. He appealed to me as the successful one—and he gave me his word, unasked, that he would never again do anything to hurt May's feelings or mine. After all, he's not such a bad fellow, Pinsent. One must make allowances. It's not his fault that he is in love with May. He can't help that. My wonder is that every man who knows her is not."

"I suppose you forgave him?"

"We shook hands, certainly. You wouldn't have me bear malice, would you? Remember! I'm in a position to be generous—and he made the advance."

"My dear lad," I answered slowly, "I wouldn't have an atom of you changed for worlds. You are an absolute ass and all that sort of thing, but somehow or other you make me want to be the same sort of idiot, and I feel positively ashamed at times that I cannot."

You should have seen his face flush, and the hangdog way he tried to pass over the compliment by cursing an untied shoestring and me at the same time for trying to "pull a fellow's leg."

We went for a ride in the park that afternoon, and just to be pleasant the Captain forced on me the gift of his finest Arab and a permanent stall in his stable in which to keep the animal. He knew, the dear fool, that I could not afford to keep it myself. I believe he would have suffered tortures had I refused him. But indeed I had no thought. The gift completely captivated me; I felt like a child with a new toy, and as proud as any peacock. The horse was a noble creature. I named him forthwith "Abd-el-Kadir," and the pair of us spent the evening petting him, until it was time to dine. We had the gayest possible meal and afterwards went to the Empire, reaching home a little before midnight like reputable bachelors. The Captain, as usual with him, fell asleep almost as soon as his head touched the pillow. But I had a trust to fulfil and, ridiculous as it may seem, as soon as I heard young Weldon's quiet breathing it began to weigh upon me. All sorts of mad questions began to ask themselves over in my mind. What if Sir Robert Ottley and Dr. Belleville had really discovered some wonderful secret of Nature? What if Belleville had

really determined to assassinate his rival? What if—in that act—he
purposed to make me appear to be the criminal? What if—as the
medium had hinted—they had found a way to make themselves
invisible? It was no use calling myself names, and saying mentally:
"Pinsent, for Heaven's sake be reasonable." Something had come
over me. For the first time in my life I was nervous. Mysterious
fears obsessed me. For an hour I lay on my side and watched the
Captain. Then I could stand it no longer. I got up and stole over to
the door. It was locked securely. I looked under both beds and
peered into wardrobes and cupboards. When I had perfectly convinced myself that Weldon and I were the only occupants of the
room I felt a little better. But only a very little. I resolved to spend
the night watching. I lighted a cigar and then threw myself into an
armchair, fixing my eyes on the Captain. He slept like a babe. I do
not know when it was exactly that I became actually aware of a
third presence in the room. Probably the idea had been gradually
growing upon me, for I experienced no sudden shock of surprise
when conviction displaced doubt. I said to myself, "This person,
whoever he may be, has come here intending to strangle or smother
Weldon in his sleep. But my watchfulness has baffled him. What
will he do?" I was soon to be informed. A slight, a very slight, noise
drew my attention to the farthest corner of the room. Over a little
cupboard hung the Captain's sword in his scabbard. The sword, but
not the scabbard, was moving. The blade was gradually appearing;
and my flesh crept to see that it was, apparently of its own volition,
moving, not downwards, but upwards along the wall.

I distinctly saw its shadow appear and lengthen on the wall. But
no other shadow was cast to explain the cause. For a moment I was
petrified—paralysed by an abhorrence of the supernatural. Then the
sword entirely left the scabbard. It advanced slowly, point downwards, borne on air into the room. As it moved it swished slightly to
and fro. The invisible hand that held it must have been trembling.
The thought recovered me. I stood up. The sword stopped. I flashed
a glance around the room. The poker in the fireplace attracted my
attention. I gave a sudden bound and reached it. The sword flashed
across the room towards Captain Weldon's bed. God knows how I
got there in time to save him, but I did. The point was quivering at
his throat when I dashed it aside and with the return blow crashed
the poker upon a hard thickness of transparent matter. The clang of
steel awoke Weldon, but I had no time for him. The sword was in
retreat. I followed it. It was making for the door. I raised the poker
for another blow, but on the instant the blade fell crashing to the

boards and I heard the key turning in the lock. I hurled myself against the panels and was brought up against a body. Thank God, though I could not see it I could feel it. It was a man. "Weldon!" I shouted, and was locked in a deadly struggle. Over and over we rolled; the invisible man and I. Weldon stood over us, looking on like one in a dream. He could only see me, and he thought I had gone mad and was behaving as maniacs sometimes do. The invisible man was strong—strong. He twined his hands around my throat and I could not prevent him. But slowly, steadily, surely, I forced his chin back. I wished to break his neck. I have an impression he was nude, but cannot be sure. I twined my right hand in his hair, with my left around his neck. I drew him to me. I was undermost. To save himself he began to beat my skull against the boards. It was then that Weldon intervened. He seized my wrists and tried to lift me up, to save me, as he thought, from doing myself an injury. But all he did was to save the life of the invisible man. Weldon's grasp on my wrists forced mine in some measure to relax. I put forth all my strength, but in vain. The invisible man used his chance and writhed away from me. I struggled afoot, casting Weldon off, but too late. The door opened before our eyes and our enemy, unseen, fled, banging the door behind him. I heard the patter of feet as he departed. The Captain uttered an oath. "Oh! you fool, you fool!" I cried at him.

"By George!" gasped Weldon. "Did you see that door?" He rushed forward and opened it again, peering out into the passage.

I fell into a chair spent and panting.

Presently Weldon came back. He picked up his sword and examined it. There was a great gap in the edge near the point where I had struck it with the poker. "What is the meaning of all this?" he cried. I told him as soon as I was able. But from the first he did not believe me, and he was honest enough to say so. How could I blame him? The story sounded incredible, even to me, while I was telling it. Weldon adopted the most charitable possible view. I had dreamed everything and acted the somnambulist. He admitted that it was a queer circumstance, the door opening and shutting so unexpectedly. But no doubt one of the other lodgers in the house had tried it in passing—some late bird a bit under the weather, Weldon thought—and finding it yield had banged it shut again. It was no use retorting that the door had been locked—Weldon merely laughed and asked what more likely than that I had turned the latch before smashing his best blade? He was quite upset about his sword. It had been carried by his grandfather at Waterloo. He plainly considered the damage I had done to it was the only serious occurrence of the night. But he strove, like a hero, to keep me from realising just how bad he did feel about it. I ceased protesting at last, and abandoned the vain task of trying to convince him of the deadly peril that had menaced him. He returned the sword to its scabbard and with a subdued sigh got back into bed again. Within ten minutes he was fast asleep. As for me, I paced the floor till morning, thinking, thinking, thinking. I have no shame in confessing that I was horribly afraid; not of the immediate present, but the future. I did not expect our mysterious assailant to return that night. But what of the morrow? I am not a believer in the supernatural or I must have set down the unseen marauder as a spirit. But I had felt and wrestled with the thing, and knew it for a man. I had heard the patter of its feet. Moreover, the memory of the séance and Navarro's dramatic recitation supplied me with a sort of clue. What if Navarro had not been acting, but had really been clairvoyant? Who shall dare to define the limits of the possible? Was it more marvellous that he should have heard and seen things really happening in a trance, than that I—in full possession of all my faculties—had wrestled with a man invisible in the bright glare of an incandescent lamp? I said to myself: "It is necessary to assume that Navarro is a true medium, if only for the sake of argument. Well, in that case it is clear that Dr. Belleville and Sir Robert Ottley had found in the tomb of Ptahmes a papyrus containing a tremendous scientific secret. This secret is one which teaches its possessors how to control forces of Nature, in a manner which my imagination can only guess at, for the production of a physical result which I have actually experienced. They have learned how to override the laws of light. They have discovered a means of not only rendering opaque objects transparent, but positively invisible. And they are using their secret knowledge to further their nefarious designs. Sir Robert Ottley is using it to increase his fortune by spying out the financial secrets of his business rivals. Dr. Belleville is using it to accomplish the destruction of Captain Weldon, his rival in love. And, in all probability, they both intend it to remove me from their path because they fear that I suspect them."

It must not be supposed that I adopted these conclusions with any sort of confidence. They entered my mind and remained there. But I received them churlishly and treated them as unwelcome guests. And the only reason that I did not expel them was because I could not discover, try as I would, any more substantial or sensible explanation of an event which they pretended to explain.

When the dawn broke and the light of day began to steal into the room between the shutters I looked around and shook my head. After all, had I fallen asleep against my will and dreamed the whole thing, as Weldon believed? It might be so. The intellect is a strange, elusive, shadowy affair. It slips from one's control at times. The memory easily clogs. The imagination is easily overheated. And one is not the best judge of one's own experiences. Science had taught me so much, at least, that one cannot always accept the evidence of sense. I began to doubt, to cast about me, and to vote myself absurd. With the rising of the sun, I flung back the shutters and looked forth on a vista of chimneys and leaded roofs. They were so manifestly real and solid and prosaic that all my brain expanded to a sense of ridicule except one small part, which began to shrivel up under the douche I poured upon it, of what I called cold common-sense. But it did not entirely shrivel up. It insisted on certain reservations. It said to me, "Pinsent, my man, there are more things in heaven and earth than are dreamt of in your philosophy. You have no right to ill-treat a part of your intelligence which —even though it may have erred—served you to the best of its ability. And can you be sure it erred? If it hap that it did not, you would never forgive yourself for flouting it. Be wise in time! Don't prejudge the case! Wait and watch! Take precautions! Guard yourself—and, above all, guard your charge!"

I determined to suspend judgment. Above all, I determined to guard my charge. But I confess it was with a curling lip I made the resolution. There is something in sunlight, some all-subduing power which irresistibly dries up the fountain springs of the imagination. I cannot conceive a novelist writing a fanciful story in the sunlight. Can you? And the sunlight was pouring into the room when I came to my resolve.

CHAPTER NINETEEN

THE FIRST VICTIM

WHEN WELDON WOKE he did one of the three things of which only
gentlemen of the finest sensitiveness are capable. He gave me one
quick, laughing glance, but perceiving in my solemn visage a pre-
disposition to resent badinage, he immediately said, "Good-
morning, old chap. Hope you rested well. As usual, I slept like a
log—all night." Now, who could help liking a man of that stamp?
Not I, most certainly. And not satisfied with pretending to have
forgotten everything, he resolutely refrained from so much as
glancing at his treasured sword, which I had broken. My heart went
out to him in such a flood of feeling that in order to conceal how
fond of him I was and how grateful, I simply had to be insulting.

"You needn't tell me you slept," I growled. "You snored like a
whole sty-full of hogs" (which was a lie). "It's a wonder to me you
did not wake yourself."

"Why didn't you shy a boot at my head?" he asked. "I'm awfully
sorry, Pinsent. I can see I kept you awake. You look quite washed
out."

"Oh! I'm alright, or will be after a hot bath," I replied ungra-
ciously, and left the room.

When I returned he had a bottle of champagne ready for me, as a
pick-me-up; and he was hard at work polishing my boots—all this
by way of apology. I swallowed some wine and allowed myself to
unbend. I suggested a ride to work up an appetite for breakfast. He
joyously agreed, so we dressed and went out. A gallop in the park
made us as jolly as a pair of sand boys. We had dejeuner at Verrey's, and then went to call on Miss Ottley. She was out, however,
so I dragged my charge to an eye specialist in Harley Street. I pretended an eye-ache and had my eyes thoroughly examined. The
specialist could find nothing wrong with them. On the contrary, he
congratulated me on a singularly perfect vision. After that we went
to Weldon's club, dawdled there for a hour and then on the sug-
gestion of Lord William Hurlingham, commonly known as "Bill,"
we ran down to Maidenhead for a row on the river. It was a perfect

day and we enjoyed ourselves amazingly, so much so that we lost count of time and were obliged to dine at a Maidenhead hotel. It thus came about that it was after nine when we strolled to the station to return to town. There was a considerable crowd of holiday-makers on the platform, and one party gave us much amusement. These details are important to explain what followed. The party consisted of half a dozen Jews and as many Jewesses. They were all as gorgeously attired as if they had been attending a regal audience. But their conversation, conducted in tones loud enough to provoke general attention, informed us that they had been spending the day on the houseboat of a certain well-known nobleman of notorious impecuniousness.

Lord Bill, a bit of a wag, made a remark that I did not catch, about the Jews and their nobleman, which sent Weldon into a convulsion of laughter. He then turned to me and began to repeat it for my benefit. Just at that moment the train came rushing into the station. Weldon stood near the edge of the platform with his back to the line, glancing sideways at the Jews and trying to restrain his mirth. I had bent my head the better to hear Lord Bill, who was a short man, but my eyes were on Weldon. Conceive my surprise to observe him stagger backwards of a sudden, as though he had been struck on the forehead. He uttered a startled cry and clawed the air with both hands. For a brief second he tottered at an angle as though he held on to something which supported him. But next instant, as if carried off his feet by a great rush of wind, he went back, back—over the edge of the platform, and before I could move a muscle or utter a word he had fallen and was lying on the rails under the very wheels of the onrushing engine. Men shouted, women shrieked. I sprang forward, and hardly aware of the peril, would have leaped upon the line, but that a dozen hands restrained me. It would have meant infallibly my death as well as Weldon's, for the train was not more than a dozen feet off. But I was incapable of reasoning at the moment. I struggled like a madman with my captors and broke away from them at last—to stand dazedly staring at the engine for some horrid seconds. It had stopped. But had it—? With a great effort I dragged myself forward. The edge of the platform was lined with a crowd of white-faced, silent people. They made room for me. Several railway officials were stooping over a frightful object lying between the pavement and the nearest iron rail. One of them shouted for a doctor, and there was an immediate movement in the crowd. Two or three men set off through the station at a run. I closed my eyes. I had never been so shaken in my

life. I had never lost my self-control so utterly. The wheels of the
engine had completely amputated both poor Weldon's legs midway
between the knee and trunk. There followed a hiatus in my reckoning. When I came properly to my senses I was hard at work tying
up the arteries, assisted by a medical student who had been a passenger in the fatal train, and a nurse who had apparently been hol-
iday-making on the river. I remember how anxious she was to save
her pretty muslin gown from the spouting blood. Presently a surgeon who had been called, appeared armed with proper instruments. With his aid I hastily replaced the imperfect tourniquets I
had improvised out of kerchiefs and neck-cloths with gutta percha
bandages, and we removed poor Weldon from the station to the
villa of a gentleman who had charitably placed his house at our
disposal. From the very first I felt that there was no hope. Not only
had my luckless friend lost his limbs and an immense quantity of
blood, but he had suffered internal injuries and a severe occipital
concussion. Within an hour, in spite of all we could do, symptoms
of lung congestion supervened. When it became manifest that no
human skill could save, I wrote a note to Miss Ottley and sent Lord
Bill to London to escort her to her lover's bedside.

After that there was nothing to do but wait. Weldon was deep in
a state of coma. I sat down beside him and watched his poor, wan
face. Every few minutes I administered a stimulant, yet each time
asked myself what use? And were it not better to let him cross the
bar in painless sleep than try to bring him back for a few moments
to the agony of suffering and hopeless separation? Yet I was
plagued with the most hateful doubts and ideas, and so, beyond
expression miserable that when two hours had gone and I marked
his pulse failing visibly with the fleeting minutes, I did that at length
which, perhaps, I should have postponed till Miss Ottley's arrival.
But then, it might have been too late. Who knows? He opened his
eyes and looked at me. I could hardly see for sudden womanish
tears.

"Give me your hand!" he whispered. I did so, and he pressed
within it a hard, bulbous object. "Put in—in your pocket. Keep it
safe!" he gasped. "It will—ah."

I obeyed him without glancing at what he had given me. Then I
got up and rang the bell. A great change had come over him. The
surgeon responded to my call.

"It is the end!" he said.

Weldon broke into a fit of coughing and beat the bedclothes with
his hands. We bent over him, seeking to help and soothe him. The

paroxysm passed and for a moment he seemed to sleep. Soon, however, he gave a strong shudder and opened his eyes again. "Pinsent—you will avenge me—you have the clue," he said. It was but a breath, but I heard. Yet I cannot say I comprehended. Indeed, I thought he wandered. But I answered softly: "Trust me, lad!" And at that he smiled and lay still, gazing up at me with eyes of deep affection.

"I have sent for her," I whispered.

"Yes," he sighed. "I know; but she will be too late. Tell her—not to fret!" and at the last word the light faded from his eyes and he was dead.

Long afterwards Miss Ottley came into the room. She was pale, but invincibly composed. I gave her his message and left her alone with the dead. The owner of the house, Lord Bill and the surgeon led me out into the garden. They spoke to me in decorous hushed voices for a while, then let me be. I walked up and down the pathway till break of day, and what I thought about I cannot tell. I remember being closely questioned by a policeman. Then Miss Ottley took my arm and we walked to the station. I thought it my place to be kind to her, yet she was kind to me.

"One might think you cared," she said, and smiled into my face. We got into a train and as soon as it started Lord Bill broke out crying. He declared that Weldon was the best fellow in the world and that he would miss him dreadfully. Then he said in the midst of life we are in death, and laughed, and without asking permission, he began to smoke a cigarette. It is strange how differently people are affected by emotion. I was mentally dazed, and I fancy part of my brain was benumbed. Miss Ottley was poignantly awake, but her pride, and her strength of mind served her for a mask. Lord Bill, on the other hand, acted as responsively to his feelings as an infant. And yet each of us behaved naturally. I reflected on these things all the way to town. Lord Bill bade us farewell at the station. Miss Ottley and I drove to her home in a hansom. During the drive she spoke about the funeral quite calmly and mentioned poor Weldon's love for big, red roses. His coffin should be smothered in roses, she declared.

When I helped her to the pavement, she pointed up at a window that was open. "Dr. Belleville's room," she said, and smiled. "He is enjoying his triumph. He kept his word to the letter. It is the seventh day. The seventh day, Hugh Pinsent; that is a terrible man. How shall I possibly withstand him?"

I shook my head. "You are wrong," I answered dully. "He is not responsible for this. It was an accident."

"Are you sure?" she asked.

"I am sure of nothing," I replied. "But it seems to me an accident—and yet. But there. I am incapable of reasoning in my present mood. I shall see you again. In the meanwhile—think of Weldon's last words to you and do not grieve too much!"

"And you?"

I shrugged my shoulders. "I have never felt more miserable. And already I am beginning to fancy I might have saved him."

"How?"

"By going yesterday to your father and Dr. Belleville and forcing them at the muzzle of a revolver to tell me things they know and which I want to know."

"You rave," she muttered coldly, and slowly climbed the steps.

I followed her and rang the bell.

"If you persist in thinking my father a bad man, I never want to speak to you again," she whispered.

There were steps, in the passage. I took off my hat to her. "I must mend my thoughts," I said.

The door opened and Dr. Belleville appeared upon the threshold.

The girl gave him a quick look before which he quailed. But he recovered quickly. "I sincerely trust you bring good news," he said, in tones of deep concern.

"The best," answered Miss Ottley, and drawing in her gown she swept past him with a glance of bitter hate, into the house.

Belleville looked after her, then turned to me, plucking at his jetty beard and frowning heavily.

"Weldon is better?" he inquired.

"He is dead," I said.

"Poor, poor fellow," sighed Dr. Belleville. "I am greatly pained to hear it. You were his friend, were you not, Pinsent? I can see that you are upset. Won't you come in and have a glass of brandy? You look quite done up."

"No, thank you," I answered. "I must get home and change these bloodstained clothes—there is to be an inquest this afternoon. Good-morning."

"Good-morning!" he replied. He was staring at the bloodstains to which I had purposely directed his attention. But he did not give a sign of agitation. His face remained as expressionless as wood.

CHAPTER TWENTY

LADY HELEN'S MEDICINE OPERATES

ON ARRIVAL AT Jermyn Street I changed my clothes and, having collected all my belongings, I repaired at once to Dixon Hubbard's flat. I could not endure the thought of spending one unnecessary moment in my poor dead friend's abode. I saw his honest face and gay, mirth-filled eyes in every corner; and he smiled at me from every dark nook and shadow of the trophy-covered walls. Hubbard received me with his usual frozen politeness. He was still in bed. But I felt an overmastering desire for human sympathy, so I ignored his manner and told him what had passed. He was sorry, I think. He had only met Weldon twice, and had merely exchanged a word or two with him, but he admitted having felt drawn to the bright and manly lad; and though he said little, it could be seen that he was shocked to hear of a death so untimely and on all accounts so utterly regrettable. And he strove to cheer me in his way. After a long silence, he suddenly remarked on the iron-bound remorselessness of fate. "There," he said, "was a young fellow just about to taste his cup of long-anticipated happiness. A man with many friends and no enemies; universally liked and respected. Yet destiny, without warning, dashed the cup for ever from his lips. And one cannot console oneself with the reflection that he has been spared the pain and shame of finding the contents bitter-sweet and mixed with dregs; for the girl loved him, I am told, and she was good to look upon, and honest-hearted. What is the meaning of it all? Omar laughingly declares that the Potter is a Good Fellow and 'twill all be well. But how many pots have encountered that experience? Have I—though still I'm here? And you? I'm all awry. The Potter's hand shook in making me. As for you, you started straight, but you grow more crooked every day and it's not your fault; you are a helpless dough puppet in the hands of destiny."

"You think I grow crooked?" I asked, surprised. "Mentally?"

"Morally," he answered, with a sneer. "You picked a foolish quarrel to leave me, and now you are back again. Why?"

"Can you tell me?"

"I have a theory," he said, with kindly eyes. "Tell me if I am wrong. My wife has become interested in you. She has marked you for a victim. At first you were unwilling. You could not even bear to be near me. But now you are more callous."

"You are wrong," I replied—then suddenly remembered that I had given a solemn promise to Lady Helen.

No doubt Hubbard marked the change in my expression. His sneer grew more pronounced. But I had a task to get through somehow.

"Lady Helen, with all due deference to you, Hubbard," I said slowly, "is not a woman I could ever care about. I feel certain she is even less interested in me than I am in her. But even were the reverse the case with her, as you suspect, what odds? I have the utmost contempt for her; and I think that she deserves—but there, you have the misfortune to be her husband, so I'll say no more."

His face was scarlet. "What reason have you to despise her?" he demanded.

"Is it not enough that she has most unwarrantably caused you a great deal of unhappiness?" I retorted. "Besides, you have told me sufficient of her character to convince me that she is one of those flighty butterfly women whom all honest men regard with only one step short of loathing."

"And you are an honest man?" he sneered.

"I try to be," I answered modestly.

He was furious. In order to hide it, he sprang out of bed, flung on his dressing-gown and rushed to the bath. I thought of Lady Helen's acute prevision of the event, and almost contrived to smile. Hubbard had come within an ace of defending his defamed wife with naked fists on my impertinent face, according to the simple rules of the Supreme Court of Appeals of primeval unlettered aborigines.

We tabooed the subject by tacit consent for the remainder of the forenoon, but Hubbard announced his intention of accompanying me to the inquest, and as soon as we were seated in the train he opened fire again.

"I am afraid I have given you an exaggerated idea of Lady Helen's shortcomings," he commenced, looking anywhere but at me. "I am afraid I have created a false impression in your mind. I don't want you to consider her entirely blameworthy, Pinsent; if she were that I should long ago have ceased to care a pin for her."

I shrugged my shoulders and looked out of the window.

He went on presently. "I'm afraid, Pinsent, I have done a foolish thing, perhaps even a caddish thing, in telling you anything about our private quarrel. It did not occur to me at the time that I might prejudice you against her. To be honest, there were faults on both sides, and if you knew all you might consider me the more deserving of censure, her the more deserving of pity."

"My dear old chap," I answered solemnly, "have I known you all these years for nothing? All you have said only the more assures me of your chivalry and generosity and tenderness of heart, and makes me feel the angrier at her insensate incapacity to appreciate your qualities. I grant you that you hide yourself at times behind a mask of surliness, but do you mean to tell me that any true woman, any woman, indeed, even such a frivolous creature as she has proved herself to be, could have failed to penetrate so transparent a disguise? I can't believe it, my boy. In my opinion, Lady Helen knows you perfectly for what you are. But instead of responding with an equal or similar nobility of mind, at the instance of her innate selfishness she is using her knowledge to put upon you, to hurt you, to trifle with you, and to drain your purse, all that she may pass the sort of existence she prefers without the wheel-brake of your tutelage."

Hubbard moved uncomfortably in his seat. He frowned and bit his lip. Then he coughed and put up a hand to his brow.

"Damme!" at length he blurted out. "You're as wrong as you can be. It was I who insisted on the separation."

"But she forced you to it. She broke her marriage vow of obedience, by refusing to accept the rules of life that you had planned."

"I prescribed conditions which she characterised as grossly unreasonable and unfair. I am by no means sure now that she was not right."

"Nonsense, Hubbard. It's a woman's first duty to obey and cleave to her husband at all costs and whatever be the consequences or fancied consequences to her comfort or convenience. Marriage imposes that obligation on the woman in its sacramental character. It is a sacred obligation and it cannot be violated without the guilt of crime. I could have no mercy on such a criminal."

Hubbard unbuttoned his coat and threw back the lapels. He seemed hot. He puffed out his cheeks and began to fan himself with a newspaper.

"Lord!" he muttered. "What strait-laced ideas you have of matrimony. Upon my soul I cannot follow you. They are out of date. There was a time, perhaps, when they were necessary. But now! My dear Hugh, you should reconsider the matter. Your views are somewhat narrow. For years past the world has been allowing an ever-in-creasing license to woman. And who shall say that it is wrong! Woman is a reasoning, responsible being. I—"

"Nonsense, Hubbard," I interrupted. "Woman is the weaker vessel, and the more she is restricted the better for her own protection. Look at the Divorce Court! Thousands of marriages are every year dissolved. That is all owing to the greater freedom which men have conceded woman of latter years. Divorce was, comparatively speaking, an unknown quantity when men asserted the right to confine their wives in proper bounds and forced them to observe and practise the domestic virtues both for occupation and amusement. Look around you and consider what has been brought about by the unwise relaxation of the old, sound laws! A race of social moths and drones and gad-flies has been created, whose chief business in life it is to amuse themselves; whose pleasure it is to spend money often earned with difficulty by devoted fools; whose delight it is to ensnare and to deceive their former tyrants; whose estimate of motherhood is an avoidable and loathsome human incident; whose morality is a resolution to preserve their immorality from public criticism; whose faith is a shibboleth composed of superstitious formulæ, and whose religion is occasionally to attend divine service in some fashionable church arrayed in the latest thing in headgear and a chic French gown."

Hubbard straightened his shoulders. His expression had grown quite superior during my tirade, and when it was over, it was plain that he looked down on me from the heights of a philosophic Aconcagua.

"I would not advertise those opinions if I were you," he observed with a slight sneer. "They have a grain of truth in them, but not enough to conceal the brand of special advocate. I suppose you do not wish to be regarded as a social reformer?"

"I shall be content to reform one woman—if ever I marry," I answered, with a straight face, though it was hard to keep it straight.

"She has my unmeasured sympathy," said Hubbard. "Once upon a time I was a woman-hater—but in my most uncharitable moments I was never such a fool as you. You will forgive my plain speaking?"

"Certainly, Hubbard, certainly. You are not responsible. It is plain to me that Lady Helen has bewitched you. One of these days you'll be lauding her as a creature of incomparable excellences—a very paragon of merit and a pattern of the virtues. I can see it coming. I am sorry, for, of course, I know what she is."

Hubbard turned crimson. He snapped his teeth together and rapped out: "See here, Pinsent, we are very old friends, but I'll be damned if I allow you to disparage my wife. Is that plain?"

I took out my cigarette case. "Perfectly," I murmured.

He glared at me for a moment, then scowled still more blackly and growled deep in throat: "I can't think what has come over you. You haven't the least right or cause to hate her. It's positively unmanly. Especially as she thinks of you far more highly than you deserve. She feels it, too. You must have shown her how you regard her. She made me feel a brute."

"Look here, Hubbard," I cried, with a nicely assumed show of indignation, "I want to oblige you and I want to keep the peace between us, but I shan't be able to if you keep on defending her when you know as well as I—"

"What?" he thundered.

"That she is a butterfly!" I thundered back.

"She is not!" he shouted.

"She is!" I said.

"You, you, you imbecile!" spluttered my poor friend. "I tell you once and for all that is only one phase of her. I don't like it, I admit," (he began to cool off), "but still it is only a phase. She is in reality a woman of great depth of character." (He was quite cool by this.) "I had a conversation with her the other night that astonished me. Of course, I have always known that she is an educated woman, but the extent of her knowledge had previously escaped me. She has a much more than superficial acquaintance with the modern forms of speculative philosophy. She has read Kant and Spencer and Nietzsche with understanding: and she is now engaged in the study of Egyptian history. You have interested her deeply in the subject."

I shrugged my shoulders. "And from all this you conclude?"

"That I have been an idiot not to recognise long ago that she is my intellectual equal. And I have treated her as if she were an irresponsible child."

"But she is a woman."

"Quite so," replied this converted woman-hater, "and because she is a woman, and such a woman, she has the power to bless the man fortunate enough to win her—her affection—as few men are blessed. Now you can appreciate my position. I have blindly sacrificed my chance. I—"

"Pish!" I interrupted. "Tell her what you have told me and be blessed! You'll repent it all your life through."

"It is too late," he groaned. "I have been weighed in the balance and found wanting. Pride, if nothing else, would always prevent her from forgiving me. She—liked me once, I think—but now——" He cleared his throat and forced a wry smile. "She looks upon me as her treasurer and friend. It was my own choice. I have no right to grumble." Then he burst out suddenly, "But it's damnable, Pinsent, damnable!"

Lady Helen's medicine was working like a charm. I thought it best to let well enough alone. So I made a rude effort and changed the conversation. We soon reached our journey's end.

The inquest was a nightmare dreamed by day. The courtroom was filled with poor Weldon's relatives. His father, the old baron, ostentatiously turned his back on me. He seemed to think me in some way responsible for his son's fate. Weldon's sisters, too, whom I knew slightly, vouchsafed me no sign of recognition. His younger brother—now the heir—was the only member of the family who extended the slightest token of civility. He was so manifestly delighted at the unlooked-for promotion of his prospects that I read in his warm hand-grip a secret pæan of joy. He had been intended for that limbo of younger sons and blue-blooded incompetents, the bar. Happily, the inquest was soon over. I was only in the box five minutes, and a quarter-hour later the verdict was recorded: "Accidental death."

Hubbard and I returned at once to London. There arrived, I plunged into work upon my book and for a space of two days I managed to forget that the world contained anything but steles and obelisks and mural hieroglyphic inscriptions which, though always half obliterate with time, had somehow or other to be made sense of and translated into English prose.

CHAPTER TWENTY-ONE

HUBBARD'S PHILOSOPHY OF LIFE

WELDON'S FUNERAL WAS held on the afternoon of the third day following his death. His body was interred in the vault of his family at their seat at Sartley, in Norfolk. I was not invited to attend, but I felt I had to go. Miss Ottley was there with her father and Dr. Belleville. She was clad in deep mourning, and her face was thickly veiled. One of Weldon's sisters sobbed throughout the ceremony, yet I do not think she felt her brother's loss half as deeply as I did. I heard her whisper to her neighbour once—between sobs—(I knelt immediately behind her)—"Have you ever seen such callousness—not a tear, not a sigh?" She was referring to Miss Ottley. I spent the rest of the afternoon on the cliffs beside the sea. I did not wish to return by the same train as the Ottleys, but destiny ruled otherwise, although I waited for the last. It seemed that Sir Robert had overtaxed his strength and had been obliged to rest. I had hardly taken my seat when he was helped into the same compartment by Belleville and the porter. They made him comfortable with cushions, without observing me; but Miss Ottley started as she entered, and raised her veil. "You!" she muttered, then paused as if in doubt, eyeing Belleville. A second later she let fall her veil again and sat beside me. Without asking anyone's permission, Belleville turned down the light, leaving the compartment in comparative obscurity. The porter muttered thanks for the tip and, departing, locked the door.

Plainly my presence had passed unnoticed. But an exclamation from Belleville soon showed he had discovered me. "Excuse me, sir," he said, "this carriage has been specially reserved." Then he recognised me. "Oh!" he cried. "You—but—"

But the train had begun to move. I sank back in my corner. Belleville took the corner opposite. In a few minutes Sir Robert complained of the light, in the manner of a sick man. Belleville sprang up and put it out altogether. The darkness now was absolute.

124

"If you will take this side, I can make you comfortable; there is a cushion to spare," said Belleville's voice. He was not addressing me.

"I prefer to remain where I am, thank you," said Miss Ottley, in a frigid tone.

Belleville sat down silently. Now and then I caught the glimmer of his eyes from the reflection of passing lights, or the glow of the engine smoke and steam, wind-blown beside the train. He was staring into the corner which I occupied. I felt his hatred wrap and heat me like a coat composed of nettles. And the man had occasion, for ere long Miss Ottley's hand stole to mine, and she sighed when mine enclosed and pressed it close. Belleville could not have known, yet he must have felt we were in sympathy opposed to him —just as I felt his hostile influence. It was a silent ride, but not uninteresting. Twice Belleville unexpectedly struck a match and flashed it in our faces. But my rug covered the occupation of our hands. Once instinct warned me that he was bending forward, peering and prying. I raised my foot and brushed it in his beard. He fell back, coughing, to prevent himself from cursing. It was in that moment probably that he resolved upon my death, for I was unable to restrain a low, grim laugh. Sir Robert slept always, even when we paused at stations on the road. At those times Belleville and I exchanged pretty courtesies. He would offer me his flask, or I would offer him a cigarette. We both refused these charming civilities, but our manner was so densely sugar-coated that there might have been detected by a skilled psychometrist a scent of honey in the air. And our eyes beamed upon each other with the sweetest friendliness. Needless to say, whenever the engine whistled or the train slowed down Miss Ottley's hand left mine. She only spoke to me once, and that was on the London platform, while Belleville was assisting her father from the car.

"Do not go out ever between three and five!" she muttered behind her veil, without looking at me. "I shall come as soon as I can. Do not call on me! Do not reply! Just say good-bye!"

"Well—if you'll allow me, I'll say good-bye, Miss Ottley," I announced in ordinary tones. "You might be good enough to let me know your opinion of my book at your leisure, for I value your opinion. You will have an advance copy in a week or two."

"Most certainly, Dr. Pinsent. It is kind of you to remember your promise. Good-bye!"

I lifted my hat and left her; nodding to Belleville as I passed. He looked surprised, also distrustful, but he said something polite. Sir Robert saw me, but chose to ignore my existence.

I walked home to Bruton Street and found Hubbard ensconced before the fire. The night was chilly enough to warrant one, despite the season. He was staring gloomily into the heart of the glowing coals.

I helped myself to a glass of whisky and took an armchair beside him.

"I can't stand this. I'll go abroad," he announced at the end of a good half hour.

"What's the matter, Hubbard?"

"Oh! I've been there again. I couldn't keep away. She was alone, for a wonder."

"You refer to your wife, I suppose. Well?"

He allowed me to finish my cigar before replying, then he said: "I have no business to tell you, but I shall. She is in love, and I believe with you."

"Nonsense."

"I wish it were," he answered dreamily, "but it is not. She has practically admitted it."

"That—she cares for me?" I cried.

"No—but for someone. And I am not so great a fool that I cannot read between the lines, although she thinks so. Her thoughts dwell constantly on you."

"Impossible!"

He turned and gazed at me. "It's so, old man, upon my honour."

"You are mistaken, Dixon."

"I know you are as true as steel," he muttered. "That is why I do not even feel a wish to thwart the fates. I am nothing but an interloper, a marplot. I ought to efface myself. When I am strong enough I shall. But I wish you'd be frank with me—Hugh, entirely frank. You think you despise her now, but you are sure you have no other feeling deep at heart? Think well before you answer, Hugh!"

"Why?"

"Because if I were sure that you cared, too, I would find my happiness in helping. You are worthy of her—and she—as God hears me, is worthy of the best man living."

"Dixon! Dixon!"

"Oh! I know this must sound oddly from my lips. But though I've been a fool, I'm wiser now. I hold a purer, finer faith; a human faith. And it is now my deep belief that the greatest crime of all is the prevention of the fullest union of predestined mates—and all that sin entails—the birth of children generated by the fires of lust and hate upon the copperplate of physical and psychical indifference; the production of a race prenatally ordained to be degenerates; the determination of unhappy souls galled into madness by their chains,—their ultimate destruction."

He got suddenly afoot and raised his hands on high. "I tell you, Hugh!" he cried, with eyes afire, "there is no surer way to damnation, no surer path. We are born into this world for one strong purpose which is told us by our hearts if we will hear them. And this concerns ourselves not half so much as our potentialities of helping by their proper use the unborn spirits placed by Providence at our control and mercy. It is then for us to choose if we will be servants of the good, to assist in their perfection, or the servants of the evil to promote their desolation and to advance the stages of their ruin. No human being has the right to bring any but a love child into the world. That which is not a love child is a child of hate. There is no course between. And because the father of a child of hate is a criminal for whom there is no punishment conceivable, to a finite mind, acute enough on earth his expiation of his crime will but begin at death. You laugh at me."

"On the contrary," I answered gravely, "I accord with you."

"Then you admit my duty. I should stand aside?"

"Ay—but first be sure, my friend! You love your wife; she may love you."

"I am sure that she does not. But you? It is time, Hugh, that you answered me."

I stood up and put a hand on his shoulder. "I love with all my strength another woman," I said slowly. "And just as sure I am that I love her am I that she loves me. Are you answered?"

He stared at me, and in the moment that my eyes held his, his face grew dull and grey. "My poor Helen," he muttered, "I had hoped to help her to her happiness."

"At—any cost?" I demanded.

"Yes, yes," he said.

"Death?"

"I would have welcomed it," he groaned, and turning, he went slowly from the room. He walked like an old, old man. I had never admired him so little, nor liked and pitied him so much. Straightway I wrote a note to Lady Helen and, going out, posted it myself. It contained only these three words: "It is time." I could trust a woman of her proven cleverness to understand.

CHAPTER TWENTY-TWO

The Dead Hand

I EXPECTED MISS Ottley next afternoon, and Hubbard, as though aware I wished to be alone, went out soon after three. But she did not come. Hubbard returned an hour after midnight. He kept me awake by tramping about his room until far into the small hours. Next morning I found the library filled with corded boxes and Hubbard's man padlocking the last of them. "Master's gone to France, and I'm to follow," he announced with an air of suppressed exultation. "He left this letter for you."

The letter contained these lines: "I know you at length for the cunning scamp you are. How you must have laughed at me. But I forgive you. We shall be away a year, at least. As always, everything I have is yours. Let us find you here on our return. I cannot write more. My heart is too full. Pinsent, she loves me! D. H." The last three words were deeply underlined. By the end of that week I had completed the revision of my book and forwarded the manuscript to Mr. Coen. Afterwards, I was uncomfortably lonely and unoccupied. I waited in from three to five every afternoon, but no one came. The rest of the days I spent wandering about the streets nursing the long sickness of too much thinking. The end of it was, I disobeyed Miss Ottley and went one afternoon to call on her. I might as well have saved myself the trouble. She was "out," likewise her father and Dr. Belleville. Two days later I called again. Again everyone was out. Then I wrote a guarded note and sent it with an advance copy of my book, asking for an expression of her opinion. After much waiting, I received a long typewritten disquisition challenging on apocryphal authority my attribution of a stele superscribed by Amen-aken to the fourteenth dynasty. It was signed by Miss Ottley, but I failed to recognise it as her composition. One evening, however, having nothing else to do, I applied to its verbiage the simple rules of a well-known cipher. This gave me an astonishing result. "Impossible see you without endangering your life. Constant supervision." But it was worth testing the matter further. I therefore composed a formal reply to the challenge, showing my reasons for concluding that Amen-aken had unwarrantably altered for purposes of his own glorification the historic record of a predecessor. I used the same cipher and embodied the following message by its aid: "Shall pass the house before midnight Friday. Throw letter from window explaining all! I live to serve you." This document I forwarded to Miss Ottley enclosed in a letter in which I took pains to show that I had been disappointed by her criticism, and that I was not anxious for the correspondence to be continued. Then I waited as patiently as possible for Friday to come round. The hours passed with leaden feet, but they passed—and midnight found me in the lane walking slowly by the house. It was wrapped in gloom from roof to basement, but her window was open. As the clocks began to chime, a white thing flashed out and fluttered to my feet. It was a kerchief weighted with a golden bracelet. I felt a paper crinkle in its folds. Hastily concealing it within my coat, I pressed on and returned by a circuitous route to Bruton Street. Soon I was poring over my treasure. It was typewritten like the challenge. It read: "I have been obliged to typewrite this, because I am a close prisoner and am forbidden the use of pen or pencil. But they make me work as their stenographer some hours each day—and I was forced to seize the opportunity so presented. Thank God you understood the cipher. If you love me give out that you proceed immediately to Egypt. Then go to Paris and return to London under another name and well disguised. Take lodgings East; and wait until you see in Personal Column of *Daily Wire* directions addressed to 'D. Menchikoff!' Follow them implicitly! Am in power of fiends. Open opposition perilous. Must allay suspicion. Otherwise forced immediate marriage B." Here the missive ended.

I sat down before the fire and thought hard for some minutes. The paper was crunched up in my hand. Suddenly the door opened. I turned my head at the sound of the creak, but could see no one. What could have opened the door? I heard the sound of caught breath, a foot on the door and a sigh. In a flash I understood. I had been seen by my enemies picking up the letter in the street, and they had sent their invisible messenger to win it from me. Quick as thought I thrust the paper in the flames and sprang afoot. There followed a deep-voiced oath and a rush of air fanned my face. I struck out with all my strength right and left, half beside myself with rage and fear. But my blows encountered nothing tangible, and a second later the door banged shut. I was so unnerved that I simply walked over and locked it. How can a man fight with an enemy he cannot see? or even follow him? When my hands stopped shaking I began to pack up my trunks. I resolved to follow Miss Ottley's bidding to the letter. To-morrow I would announce my departure for Egypt and cross the Channel in order to put Belleville off the track. Meanwhile I ransacked my wardrobe. Presently I received a shock. From an unremembered corner in a chest I brought out the clothes I had worn on the day of poor Weldon's death. They were covered with dyed bloodstains, the blood of my dead friend. I placed them on the table and eyed them, shuddering. My mind, as if spell-compelled, reviewed all the details of Weldon's death. I saw him stagger back, back, and fall beneath the wheels of the onrushing locomotive. I heard his dying shriek. Once more I struggled desperately, but alas! how vainly with the dark angel, for his life. Once more, as the end approached, I saw his glazed eyes open and look into mine. Once more I heard his dying words—"Give me your hand!"

And but—God in Heaven! How could I ever have forgotten it! Had he not given me something—something I had put in my pocket half unconsciously without looking to see what it was—something he had implored me to "keep safe."

I felt my senses rock at the recollection; and then I went hot all over with shame, to think of my neglect, my inattention. Until that moment—despite his dying direction, I had utterly forgotten his sad trust. And the thing he had given me to keep—where was it now? Where, indeed, but in the pocket of that coat where I had placed it. Oh! It was safe enough, no doubt—but that did not absolve me. For weeks I had been a recreant trustee. I had, I saw it now, I had been a coward. I felt his death so much that I had resolutely put all thoughts of him aside, smothered them with work, fearing the misery which they must bring. And I had been his friend!

I took up the coat and felt in the pocket. Yes, it was there. What was it? I drew it out before the light and saw nothing! Yet I held something heavy and hard. Was I going mad? Was my sight diseased or what? I rubbed my eyes and looked again. Nothing! I strode over to the gas jet and held the thing between my visual organs and the flame. Ah! something now! But how describe it? I saw a small light blur; a sort of shapeless haze off which the rays, the jet of light diffused, recoiled obliquely. It was not transparent, but neither was it in the true sense visible. It seemed to defy the light rays, to repulse them rather than absorb them. When held directly before the flame I could not see the gas jet through it, and yet itself I could not truly see. It confused and disarranged my vision as a watery mote does floating on the surface of an eyeball. Slowly and surely experimenting with the thing, I found that the farther I withdrew it from the lamp the less sensibly my sense became aware of its existence. But when I placed it directly against the lamp the flame became mysteriously obscured. I say mysteriously, because the thing cast no discoverable shadow, and although solid to the sense of touch, it was not otherwise apparently opaque. The flame still burned behind it, and I still saw the flame, yet not through, but over and around an intermediate blur. In that connection the thing did not resemble glass. Had the reverse been the case I should have seen the flame through it directly. As it was, as far as I can make out, the impression of the flame was conveyed to my retina by rays of light that did not travel in a straight path. They climbed over and surrounded the interposed object first, and thus gave me a slightly distorted image of the flame; and instead of revealing the obstacle which they had to overcome in transit, all they did was to indicate vaguely its situation. Thus, above and below the indiscernible point where their straight and proper course was interfered with I perceived a misty, indefinable haze. And at the point where the rays seemed to reassemble and readjust themselves to the resumption of their ordinary business there was a blur. Perhaps the best way to depict the effect was to present the hypothesis of a weak flame held up before a stronger one. This does not exactly describe the phenomenon I witnessed and investigated, but it approximates as closely as I can manage. The chief points of difference are, that every flame casts a shadow, and this thing did not, unless a blur of light be a shadow; and furthermore, a flame may be seen even confronted with a stronger flame, and this thing I held was destitute of a perceptible outline. The pity was that I was then working without a single clue to any comprehension of the thing; and the greater pity is that though my knowledge became fuller, I am still ignorant of the action of the properties which made the thing visually impalpable. I can only guess at them. But I think I guess correctly when I conjecturally assert that it was surface coated with some essence which had the power to compel the great majority of the light rays to travel along its sides and surface and to resume their original direction afterwards. I do not pretend to understand how this essence could so interfere with and control the laws of light. But granting that it could, the explanation is a natural one. And though scientists may frown at me for advancing a theory which I am unable to substantiate, I prefer to incur their scorn rather than adopt the alternative—supernatural agency. I simply decline to believe in the supernatural. It is my profound conviction that nothing has ever happened on this planet, however mysterious and inexplicable, which has not been produced by a purely and perfectly natural cause. And the longer I live the more certain do I become that, deep and wonderful as our scientific acquaintance with Nature undoubtedly is, we have not yet even thoroughly explored the porch of her palace of secrets, her vast treasure-house of wonders.

But I stray from my subject. It is my present business to relate events, not to discuss their basic principles.

To resume then, after a great while spent in experimenting with the thing which poor Weldon had given me, before the light, I was obliged to confess myself baffled. I then fell back upon my other four senses. I got out a pair of scales and weighed the thing. It weighed exactly seven ounces. Then I smelt it. The thing was odourless. I bit it, but it was tasteless. Yet it yielded to my teeth like stiff rubber or leather. Next I placed it on a sheet of paper and traced its outlines with a pencil. That was the first really definite result I got. The tracing showed a bulbous object four inches wide by five long. It was shaped something like a pear. Its base contained four indentations with corresponding rounded protuberances like knuckles. The apex was ragged. Next I took a knife and with the blade scratched its surface. A moment later a long streak of dark, dry tissue was revealed. I could see it plainly. I shook all over with excitement. The mystery seemed to be clearing up. But even as I took up the knife again I paused, convulsed with a wild, improbable idea. What if?—but there. I held my breath and took the thing before the fire to think its problem out. I sat down. My nerves were all jangled. The fire needed replenishing. It was low and I was cold. I stooped down and heaped on some coal. Then came a thought. I put the thing on a shovel and held it over the grate. Heat! Yes, heat! The greatest of great resolvents. Fool not to have thought of it before. Fool, indeed! One minute—two—three. There was a shadow on the shovel. I bent forward. Instantly my nostrils were assailed with the unforgettable perfume of the tomb of Ptahmes! Ah! the flood of recollections that came surging at its bidding to my brain! But I fought them back. I bent right over the fire—and I made out presently, lying on the shovel, the dim form of a tight-clenched human hand.

CHAPTER TWENTY-THREE

I SET OUT FOR THE EAST

IT WAS THE hand of a mummy. It had been half snapped, half torn from the forearm, just above the wrist. Thus the edges of the stock were ragged and the tendons were drawn out and torn; the bone, however, had fractured clearly, just as glass breaks, leaving a hard, smooth edge. But the hand was not an ordinary mummy's hand. The bones were covered with mummified flesh truly, but, although dry, it was neither stiff nor brittle. On the contrary, it possessed the tough consistency of leather and was resilient and kneadable like rubber. The phalanges, when pulled straight, returned to their ordinary and original position, like springs, immediately the pressure was removed. The colour of the skin was a very dark chocolate. It was marvellously preserved. The very pores were still discernible, and the veins and arteries beneath the epidermis, which had been converted by age into fine black cords, could be traced with ease. Now, whose hand was it? From what mummy torn? And how had Weldon become possessed of it? I gave up the attempt to solve the first two problems as soon as I had mentally propounded them. The third, however, answered itself. I knew Weldon too thoroughly to admit a doubt that he would ever have carried about with him such a ghastly trophy. Like most healthy young Englishmen, he had a horror of such things. Well, then he must have snatched the hand, then invisible, from the grasp of someone—in the very moment in which he had been falling to his death. But no one had been near him. That is, no one visible to us or him. But since the hand had been practically invisible until I had subjected it to the influence of heat, was, it not just as likely that it might have been—nay, must have been—carried by an invisible person? But that invisible person must have been very near Weldon. He must have been close enough to have saved Weldon had he chosen. Why had he not chosen? Why, indeed, unless he had wished Weldon to die? And if he had wished Weldon to die, would it not have been easy for him —because invisible—to help Weldon to die? Easy! Good heavens,

how easy! How appallingly easy! And then I remembered how
astonished I had been to see Weldon stagger back, step after step, to
the platform's edge—three steps at least. I understood it now—and
his startled outcry. He had been assailed by an invisible adversary.
He had been forced back. He had been hurled over the platform—and as he fell he had clutched out wildly and seized the
mummy's hand. He had been foully murdered; and we had watched
his murder, comprehending nothing. My flesh began to creep as the
light of understanding broke in upon my brain. For I realised in the
same instant that Weldon's murderer was, in all probability, the
man who had had most occasion to desire his death
—Belleville—my enemy and the enemy, although the lover, of the
woman I loved; the wretch in whose power she was at that moment.
He had warned Miss Ottley that unless she broke off her engage-
ment with Weldon her fiancé would die within the week. He had
died—murdered in cold blood—on the evening of the seventh day.
Belleville had been most terribly faithful to his awful promise. To
the very letter he had kept his dreadful vow. And now—Miss Ottley
was his prisoner in her own father's house; and, no doubt, Sir
Robert Ottley, sick, enfeebled in body and intellect, was Belleville's puppet instrument to the furtherance of his atrocious purposes. What chance had I—fighting a man so utterly unscrupulous,
so strong-willed and remorseless, and endowed with a power so
tremendous and far-reaching as the possession of a chemical agent
capable of rendering himself imperceptible to mortal sight whenever it should please him to make use of it? How could I or anybody
bring such a man to justice? Why, even if I should foil his scheme
for my undoing, and were it possible, as well, to get the better of
him to the extent of satisfying myself beyond doubt as to his guilt,
what court on earth would believe the evidence I could bring forward? A tissue of absurdities; a network of hypotheses and chi-
meras! I should be laughed at as a madman, a foolish visionary; and
he would go scot free with undamaged reputation, free to work his
evil will upon an unconscious and defenceless world. Belleville's
advantage over me was so manifestly overwhelming that I confess
the prospect of entering into a trial of strength and cunning with him
daunted me. And yet, if I did not, Weldon's death would surely go
unavenged, and Miss Ottley's fate would be sealed. She would be
forced into a marriage—somehow or other—with a man she
loathed—the murderer of her dead lover. I felt so sure of this that
towards morning I resumed my packing. I did not go to bed at all.
After breakfast I went out and called at half a dozen newspaper

offices. I saw as many journalists, who all promised to paragraph my departure for the East. I then wrote a letter to the Society stating, guardedly, my intention of again visiting the Nile; and I caught the afternoon train to Dover. That night I slept at Calais. On the following day I went to Paris and put myself in the hands of a hairdresser and costumier, who carried on a peculiar business at Montmartre under the secret surveillance and government of the police. For a respectable consideration he effected a complete metamorphosis in my appearance. He speckled my black eyebrows with silver. He shaved off my moustache and beard and dyed my skin a jejeune saffron, my hair a bilious iron-brown. He forbade me to wear a starched collar. He taught me how to walk like an elderly man; and, finally, he provided me with a suit of clothes that fitted fairly well, but which could not be said to possess any other virtue. But the fellow was well worthy of his hire. When he had finished with me I could not recognise myself. The mirror showed me a gaunt piece of human wreckage. I was to the life a decayed gentleman; an unobtrusively rakish, elderly degenerate. I was remarkable in nothing except height, and even that singularity departed as I learned to stoop. In such guise I returned to London by way of Boulogne and Folkestone, and I took up residence immediately in a tenement-house in Soho, to which I had been recommended by my friend, the costumier. It was a curious place. It was populated by Frenchmen, Italians, and a sprinkling of Swiss, and a number of Russian political refugees. I found them a decent lot of law-abiding miserables. The majority were derelicts of fortune, who lived like parasites on the toil of some few hardworking, foolish artisans among them. And yet, despite their deplorable estate, they always had a cheerful word and a smile to spare for a stranger. They were a picturesque, interesting people, and I should have liked to study them under other circumstances. But placed as I was, I conceived it best to keep my room as much as possible, and I only went abroad to buy a paper and to eat and drink. On the fourth morning the expected summons came to hand. It was the first advertisement in the column. "D. Menchikoff. Fearless. Door-front. Twelve. Unfailing. Noiseless. Open. Mizpah." And this I interpreted to mean, "Fearlessly approach the front door at midnight this evening! You will find it open. Enter without noise! God be with you till we meet!"

CHAPTER TWENTY-FOUR

THE GIN IS SPRUNG

I SET OUT wearing rubber shoes and armed with a loaded revolver. This I concealed in my breast pocket. I timed myself so nicely that I arrived at Sir Robert Ottley's mansion on the fifth stroke of twelve. Forthwith I mounted the steps and softly tried the door. It was ajar. I pushed it back and entered, closing it noiselessly behind me. I locked it, too. The hall was unlighted and black as Erebus. I stood for a moment or two listening breathlessly. Then I thought I heard a sigh. "May!" I whispered.

I was answered by a sibilant soft "S-Sh!" Then a hand was laid upon my sleeve and I felt myself drawn forward. I gave myself up to be guided the more willingly that I hardly knew the place. We came to a staircase. My guide breathed "S-Sh" again, and muttered "stairs." We climbed them step by step. Heavens, how dark it was! Afterwards I was drawn like a shadow through a maze of thickly carpeted corridors. Finally, we stopped. The hand left my arm and I heard a door creak open. "Come!" whispered my guide. I stepped towards a dim, dim glow, and as I crossed the threshold, the door, shutting on my entrance, grazed my arm.

"At last!" the voice whispered.

It was a signal. Hardly was it uttered than a blaze of white light stabbed the darkness. I found myself in an immense apartment, blinking foolishly into the muzzle of a revolver presented at my forehead by Dr. Belleville. Our eyes met presently across the sights. His were smiling coldly.

"An excellent disguise, Dr. Pinsent; my sincere congratulations," he observed. "It is evident you have obeyed my instructions to the letter."

"Your instructions," I said.

"Ay. Mine."

"Then you—"

"The cipher was my idea entirely. Ah! but you must not blame Miss Ottley. She signed the first letter without understanding. Later, however, she would not write. She knew. I was obliged to use the typewriter, and in order to convince you of the authenticity of the letter I threw at your feet last Thursday night—my emissary followed you home and pretended to wish to wrest it from you. You fell into the snare. And now you are here, and no one knows, eh? No one knows?"

"You think so?" I asked. I was beginning to get back my wits.

But he only laughed. "It does not matter. The great thing is, you are here and in my power. That was all I wanted. Now, Ottley! Now!"

It was another signal. Something' hard and heavy crashed against my skull. For a second I fought for breath against a horrible feeling of sickness and impotence, then came blank night and nothingness. I had been sandbagged.

I recovered to find that my captors had strapped me hand and foot in a huge iron chair. I could not move an inch in any one direction, but otherwise my situation was tolerably comfortable. Belleville sat facing me some feet away. He was plucking thoughtfully at his big, black beard. There was no one else in the room. Perceiving I was awake, he arose and took from a table near him a glass of water, which he brought to me.

"It is not poisoned," he remarked. "I have considerable need of you for some time yet." He placed the glass to my lips then, and I drank with confidence. I felt better afterwards, but my head ached bravely still.

Belleville resumed his chair and again began to pluck at his beard. "No doubt your head aches," he observed. "I regret having been obliged to use you so discourteously, but we have had so much experience of your muscular vigour that to have risked a physical encounter would have been absurd. We might have been forced to kill you, and that would not have suited my plans."

"Indeed," said I. It cost me a painful effort to speak at all.

"I desire to be perfectly candid with you," said Belleville. "But before we get down to business it were as well to prove to you how completely at my mercy you are." He took, as he spoke, a revolver from his pocket and aimed carelessly at the opposite wall. "This apartment used to be a shooting gallery," he observed. "All the walls are padded." He then discharged the weapon six times in rapid succession. The bullets spattered on a plate of steel. The sound of the reports was simply deafening. A full minute passed before the echoes and reverberations ceased. All the while Belleville smiled at me. "No one heard but you and I," he said. "The futility, therefore, of wasting your breath in shouting for help will appeal to you."

I glanced about and found that all the walls I could see were windowless. The room was lighted by electricity. The door was thickly coated with padded cushioned leather. The floor was carpeted with one vast sheet of rubber. The place was fitted up as a chemical laboratory. I counted half a dozen glass tables littered with retorts and dynamos, testing tubes and other instruments. There were big glass cases filled with porcelain boxes and phials of drugs and large jars containing acids. And finally there was one object my eyes rested on with a little shock of recognition. This was the sarcophagus of Ptahmes. It was raised about three feet from the ground upon two steel trestles. The great sculptured lid was propped on end against a neighbouring wall. But although the coffin was open I could not see within it because the edge was almost on a level with my eyes.

"Are you satisfied?" asked Belleville presently. He had followed the direction of my glances with a sort of half-contemptuous, half-amused curiosity, reloading his revolver the while. The man evidently cherished an immense opinion of himself—but he was as cautious as a sage: witness the reloading of his weapon—despite the fact that I was as helpless as a trussed fowl.

"Yes. I am satisfied," I answered.

"And cool? What I mean is are you perfectly collected? Do you feel able to engage in conversation? Or are you too dazed—or perhaps too angry?"

"I can promise at least to listen and try to understand you."

He gave me a sardonic smile. "The under dog is a fool to be sarcastic," he said drily. "However, please yourself. Listen then! You are no doubt aware that it is one of my ambitions to marry Miss Ottley?"

"Yes."

"Captain Weldon stood some time since in my road."

"Yes."

"Peace to his ashes," smiled the Doctor. Then he frowned. "But to my astonishment I now find that the lady did not care for the gallant Captain."

"Indeed."

"Indeed and indeed." Belleville bit his lip. "But for you," he snarled.

I was silent.

"It is almost incredible, but it is true."

"She has confided in you?" I asked.

"As a preliminary step to defying me," replied Belleville. "It was rather silly of her, but perhaps she could not help herself. Women, even the wisest, are slaves to their emotions of the moment. I was willing to make all sorts of concessions, too. I even offered her your life."

"My life."

"I offered to permit you to live if she would marry me."

"And she?"

Belleville bared his teeth just as I have seen a jackal grin. "You know how women love to glorify the objects of their admiration," he said slowly. "In their opinion the men they—they love—are always the wisest, the strongest, the most astute and the best. I am free to admit, my dear Pinsent, that you are by no means a fool. You have no doubt a fairly keen intelligence—but Miss Ottley has placed you on an alabaster pedestal—pedestal do I say? A pinnacle! She has actually ventured to contrast your ability with mine to my disparagement. She rejected my offer with disdain and challenged me to measure wits with you. And when I accepted the challenge she calmly predicted that you would defeat and destroy me. It thus became my duty to show her how mistaken and fallible in truth is her estimate of me. Weldon's death taught her nothing, absolutely nothing. She protested that if I was really the *deus ex machina* it only proved me to be an ordinary sort of heartless murderer. Weldon's particular order of intellect never impressed her, it appears. But yours, in her eyes, is little short of divine. There was no help then but to dispose of you in such a way as to open her eyes. It is no boast to say that I could have killed you at any time of the day or night I pleased for weeks past. Had I done so, however, I should have been constrained so to arrange matters—as in Weldon's case—as to make your end appear natural; and I'm afraid Miss Ottley would on that account have been inclined to consider, for a second time, me a lucky prophet and you the second victim of an inscrutable Providence. That is her present attitude toward Weldon's final exit from the stage of life. I was obliged then so to arrange matters as to get you into my power, but, *bien entendu*, without the fanfare of trumpets. I flatter myself that I have managed very well. You may pretend the contrary if you choose, but you'll not convince me. I have had your every movement carefully followed, and I believe that outside of this house there is not a soul in England of your acquaintance who has a doubt but that you are on your way to Egypt. And I have neglected no precautions that could ever give rise to such a doubt. Immediately you quitted your lodgings in Soho this evening, my emissary entered your room by means of a master key and brought away your trunks. No one saw him, for he was invisible; and no one saw your trunks depart, for he made them invisible, too. They are at this moment in this house. You doubt me?"

"Yes," I cried. "I doubt you; produce them!"

"I am too comfortable to move," smiled Belleville. "But here is something I found at the bottom of one of them."

As he spoke he took from his breast pocket the mummy hand poor Weldon had given me. I could not suppress an exclamation. He had spoken truly then. Belleville tossed the hand upon a table. "I was rather glad to get it back," he said. "Not that it really mattered; but I wondered who had found it. Did Weldon still cling to it after he was dead?"

"You scoundrel!" I cried. "It was you— really then? You pushed him over the platform?"

He laughed. "In person, no, but by direction, yes." Then he became serious. "But let us avoid personalities, if you please. We each possess an ugly temper, I believe; and mine is sometimes uncontrollable. Do you agree?"

"Proceed!" said I.

He bowed ironically. "There is but little more to tell you now. You know almost all you need to know, and enough, I feel sure, to enable you to anticipate your fate."

"You intend to murder me, I suppose?"

"Exactly. But it depends on yourself whether you shall have a painless death or no. If you will do what I require you shall have the choice between aconite and morphia. If you refuse, well,"—he pursed up his lips—"you'll live longer, Pinsent; yes, you'll live longer—but frankly, old chap, you won't like it. I hate you, you know, and I am a surgeon, and you are there and I am here; I repeat, I hate you. And I am not only a surgeon, I am a skilful surgeon. I am, besides, a vivisectionist. That is one of my hobbies. And I'll keep you alive as long as possible. For let me yet again assure you I *hate—you—hate you, hate you!"*

There was no doubt of it. He hated me. The emotion was infectious. I hated him. I had before; but I now realised how much. After one long glance into his gloating eyes I lowered mine and asked in a voice I strove to render civil: "What is it you want me to do for you?"

"I want you to play the part of a friendly disembodied ghostly match-maker."

"I fail to understand you."

"Naturally. But listen. I intend to render you invisible. When that is done I shall bring Miss Ottley here. She knows your voice. You will speak to her. Do you see daylight now?"

"I begin."

"That is well. You will inform the lady that you are dead, but that your spirit is held in durance vile at my command. Like all other women, she is at heart deeply superstitious. She will believe what you say and she will conceive a prodigious respect for my power and ability. You will assure her that I control your fate and that you can only obtain deliverance from unimaginably awful tortures at the price of her consenting to become immediately my wife. Well?"

"A pretty plot," said I.

"I felt certain it would earn your admiration," he returned.

"I marvel at your candour!"

"My dear Pinsent," he said, smiling, "complete candour is the privilege of the all-powerful, and that am I—at least in your regard. I can perfectly afford to be perfectly frank with you, because I can compel you to serve me even should you decide to disobey me."

"Indeed, and how?"

"The thing is as simple as A, B, C. If you are so foolish as to refuse to play the part I have assigned, I shall render you three parts—instead of entirely invisible. I shall make your bonds, however, entirely invisible. You will then be put to certain electrical tortures of my invention, and I shall invite Miss Ottley to observe the spectacle of a soul in pain. I confess I should prefer you to behave like a sensible ghost and talk to her in the manner I have indicated; but you must admit that in the alternative she will, nevertheless, be forced to a conclusion flattering alike to my ambition and my pride."

"Is it possible that you are all the heartless scoundrel you pretend? Can you really find pleasure in the notion of winning the woman you are presumed to love—by a trick so infamous and despicable?"

"Yes, Pinsent, yes."

"You must be animated by a devil."

"On the contrary, my dear enemy, I am just an ordinary human being who has been seduced by the most extraordinary temptation that has ever been offered to a living being. A power has been placed at my disposal which puts me on a level with the immortal gods of ancient Greece. In deciding to make use of it, I have adopted their ideas of morality, almost, as it were, perforce. I now make a cult of my convenience, and a religion of the indulgence of my instincts. I intend henceforth to kill always what I hate, to possess what I love, to seize what I covet, and to enjoy what I desire. Miss Ottley dislikes and despises me. That has irritated my vanity to such an extent that it is necessary to my happiness that I should convert her dislike into subjection, her contempt into the unbounded reverence of fear. When she becomes my wife I shall be the master of her millions—her father is on the point of dissolution—and I shall be the tyrant of her person. I shall rule her with a rod of iron terror. That domination will give me a far greater joy than the vulgar pleasure of reciprocated passion. And not the least part of it will dwell in the reflection that you, my dear enemy, will have so largely and so unwillingly contributed to the gratification of my sweet will. Now you have all the facts before you. My cards are all exposed. It is for you to make up your mind what you will do. Don't decide immediately! There is no hurry. Think the matter over. As I am rather weary" (he yawned in my face), "I shall now leave you to your meditations till the morning. Good-night."

He rose, bowed to me with mock politeness and moved over to the door. A moment later he had gone, and with him the light vanished. I was left in the profoundest darkness, and my thoughts were nearly as colourless and sombre as the gloom in which I sat.

CHAPTER TWENTY-FIVE

THE MUMMY TALKS

THE SENSATION OF awakening informed me of the surprising fact that I had fallen asleep. I was rather proud under the circumstances that I had been able to do so. Probably I had slept for a long while, too, for the laboratory was lighted up, and it was evident that it had been carefully dusted in the interval. There was a sound of sweeping behind my chair, but strain as I would I could not turn my head to see who was my companion. "I say," I called out. "I am thirsty. Fetch me a glass of water, will you?"

The sweeping stopped. Presently steps approached my chair. They passed it, and next second I saw the giant Arab of the cave temple at Rakh, the wretch who had attempted to strangle me at my camp, and whom I had released from the sarcophagus of Ptahmes on the Nile. He stood before me, his extraordinary blood-coloured eyes staring at me with the glazed expressionless regard of an automaton. He was clad in a long, yellow shapeless garment like a smock, and his feet were shod in leather sandals. In one hand he held a broom. Very slowly he extended his other arm before my face, and I saw with a shock of aversion that the hand had gone. It had been severed from the wrist and nothing but a stump remained. Involuntarily I thought of the mummy hand which poor Weldon had given me. It still lay upon the table where Dr. Belleville had tossed it, full in my view. It was a left hand. The Arab's left hand had been lost. The connection was obvious. But—but—of course a mummy hand thousands of years old perhaps, could not have grown upon a still living, breathing man. Living! Breathing! The words repeated themselves as I gazed at the Arab. How like a mummy he appeared! His skin was of exactly the same colour as the mummy hand. It had the same shrivelled appearance, the same leather-like texture. And, good heavens! unless I dreamed he did not breathe! Not a movement of his body disclosed the smallest sign of respiration. I stared at him, appalled. His features were fixed and set rigidly. His mouth was closed. His nostrils were fallen in and glued together. How then could he breathe? And yet there was life in his gaunt frame; some animating spirit that controlled its mechanism, for slowly his handless arm fell back to his side, and he continued to regard me with a steadfast, unwinking stare. I examined his eyes and found that they were lidless. The lids had shrunken back and disappeared. A closer inspection showed that the eyes themselves owed all their lustre to reflected light. The cornea was in each orb nothing but a thin gelatinous-like film filled with tiny little crinkles that caught up and refracted passing rays from all directions. The whites were opaque black teguments, dry and dead. Behind the lenses was no sign of any pupil. There was nothing but an iris which seemed to be composed of dull red dust.

Living! Breathing! The Arab was a mummy! an animated corpse. Oh! Of course I dreamed. I must have dreamed. I have told myself that so many thousand times that it is a marvel the constant reiteration has not forced me to believe it. But I do not. Nor do I know what to believe. I am in as great a maze to understand now as I was then.

At first I conceived an almost intolerable horror of the thing before me. But finding that the Arab did not menace me, I gradually became accustomed to its most unpleasant and almost ghastly proximity. And after a time I felt so strong a fever of thirst that I forced myself to speak to it again.

I asked it for water. It did not move. I became convinced it heard but did not comprehend the language I employed. I spoke to it in French and German and in Arabic, but still it did not move. Finally I said to myself, "If it is a mummy, it will be an Egyptian and will understand the tongue of ancient Egypt." Then I gasped out such a term as I believed might have been used by a thirsty Theban asking for alleviation of his famine. The thing instantly moved off behind me. Presently I heard the sound of falling water, and a moment later a glass was pressed to my parched lips. I drained it thankfully, eyeing the while, with a feeling of deep, unconquerable repulsion, the sinewy black mummy hand that served me. I then thanked the Arab in the same tongue which had persuaded him to be my minister. He gazed at me a while and then moved to the table and looked at it. He appeared to be writing, but I could not be sure. I heard a curious, raucous scratching sound. Thus ten minutes sped by. Meanwhile, I shut my eyes and tried hard to persuade myself that I dreamed. Then a sound disturbed me. I opened my eyes with a start and saw that the Arab had returned to my side. He held a slate before me covered with hieroglyphics. Never had I greater occasion to bless my knowledge of that ancient language and to gratefully regard the patient years of labour I had spent acquiring it. But likewise never had I greater occasion to lament the imperfections of my knowledge and defects in my memory. I could understand a portion of the message—the greater part indeed—but still a part escaped me.

Briefly translated, the part I comprehended ran:

"It is not meet that Ptahmes—named Tahutimes—son of Mery, son of Hap, High Priest of Amen-Ra and the Hawk-headed Horus, should be a wicked unbeliever's slave . . . Death explains. . . .The spirit of a good man hurried hence accuses me unanswered at the. . . . throne. . . . For time un-ending. . . . Fanet. . . . King of all the Gods. . . . Thus only shall you escape the death that threatens. You shall swear to break my stele of ivory, to commit my papyri to the flames unread, to burn my body and scatter my ashes to the winds of Heaven. You shall swear by Amen-Ra, King of Earth and Heaven, to destroy. . . . the oppressor and your enemy. He has deciphered the inscriptions. He has mastered their meaning. He knows. He cannot be permitted to live lest I. . . . and he the enemy exalt himself and triumph over you and me . . . Swear then, and aid shall be accorded in your hour of need."

I gathered from this message that the ghost of Ptahmes inhabi-tated the mummy before me; that Belleville had possessed himself of some stupendous wizard power which enabled him to compel the soul and dust of Ptahmes to obey his infamous behests, but that Ptahmes was his most unwilling slave. I also gathered that Ptahmes promised me help if I would take an oath to kill Belleville, to de-stroy certain papyri and an ivory stele in Belleville's possession which I must promise not to attempt to read, and also to burn the mummified remains of Ptahmes, and so, I suppose, secure the rest of his troubled spirit. I did not pause to reflect on the wild unreality of the happenings my senses registered. They did not appear indeed unreal to me at all—then. On the contrary, I felt that I was con-fronted with a very grave and serious proposal, which if I decided to accept would be carried out to the letter as regards the assistance promised me, a circumstance that would oblige me as an honest man to keep my part of the contract. The question remained: Would I be justified in solemnly swearing to compass Belleville's death? Why not? Surely he deserved capital punishment if ever a man did.

By his own confession he had either murdered Frankfort Weldon or procured his murder; and he had cold-bloodedly assured me that he was relentlessly resolved to murder me. And there were other things to think of. He had given me positive proof of the possession of some unknown power over the laws of Nature which had enabled him already to commit crimes without incurring a shadow of legal suspicion. Were I then to effect my escape from him, it would be my duty as a citizen of the State to do all in my power to prevent him working further ill in the community. Yet I could not bring him to justice. I had no evidence to produce against him which the courts would not scorn and ridicule. The attempt to convict him of the murder he had confessed to me, would only result in branding me in all men's eyes as a lunatic. He would meanwhile be at liberty to go abroad to work his evil will upon the world. He would very soon revenge himself upon me, and destroy me in the same dia-bolically ingenious fashion, perhaps, in which he had killed poor Weldon. And Miss Ottley would then be at his mercy, with no man living to defend her. She might continue to resist him for a time, but in the end a man so unscrupulous and implacably determined would be sure to have his way. Able to make himself invisible—as I be-lieved he could—he might as a last resort rob her of her honour and so bend her proud spirit to his wish. It was this thought that finally determined me. I looked up and said quietly to the patient, waiting Arab: "Ptahmes, son of Mery, son of Hap, once High Priest of Amen-Ra, but now I know not what—I swear by the King of Earth and Heaven to destroy the stele and papyri unread if I shall find them, to burn your body and scatter the ashes, and to kill your enemy and mine."

The dark, fixed, corpse-like face of the Arab turned forthwith from me. He pressed the slate to his bosom with the stump of his left wrist and with the right hand rubbed out the hieroglyphic writing. He then glided over to the table and replaced the slate. I followed his movements with the most passionate attention, expecting him to return and immediately release me from my bonds. But he did no such thing. In the contrary, he moved slowly forward to the great sarcophagus and to my great astonishment I saw him climb over the edge and repose himself within the tomb. Presently he had entirely vanished from my sight. I could hardly credit my eyes. What was the meaning of his strange act? I waited for a few minutes, but he did not reappear. Then I called out his name aloud: "Ptahmes! Ptahmes!"

Nothing answered me.

I racked my brains to string together an imploring sentence in the ancient tongue of Egypt, and having fashioned one, I cried it forth in tones of passionate entreaty, by turns commanding and beseeching him to keep his pledge. And not once or twice, but a hundred times, did I address him in these ways. But I might as well have cried out to the stars. My efforts were all unavailing, and at length, wearied out with them, I desisted and abandoned my remaining energy to the bitter task of reactionary self-reviling. I caustically informed myself that my brain had gone wandering. Thus until I was hot all over with shame. Then in a more kindly spirit I cast about for excuses to salve my intellectual vanity. I ascribed the whole wild dream that I had dreamed to the blow my poor head had received last night. But all the while, deep at heart, I did not believe I had dreamed. I pretended to, in order to make sure that I still possessed a critical, scientific faculty. But I did not believe it really. I could not. And this fact is one more proof to me that faith in all its forms depends more upon feeling than intellectual conviction.

CHAPTER TWENTY-SIX

A Pleasant Chat With a Murderer

I AWOKE SO much refreshed and free from pain that I must have slept for many hours. Belleville was pinching my shoulder. His black-visaged face was curiously bilious-looking, and puffy purple hollows underhung his eyes.

"You didn't sleep thus on the banks of the Nile," he muttered, with a sick man's frown. "You were wakeful enough then. One would think you had been drugged."

"Indeed," said I. "But I had need to be wakeful then."

"Who set on the light," he demanded. "I swear I left you in dark. Who has been here?"

"Your Arab," I replied. "He swept out the room and gave me a drink. Then he climbed into the sarcophagus yonder, and unless he went away while I slept, there you'll find him."

The rascal looked perfectly astounded. "My Arab!" he repeated, staring sharply into my eyes. Then of a sudden he turned and simply rushed over to the big lead coffin. Stooping over the edge, he peeped into the interior and seemed to be shifting something with his hands. His back was all I saw, but it moved to and fro, and he strained on tiptoe. When he stood up his face was scarlet and his eyes were troubled. "Swept the room, you said, and gave you a drink?" he muttered half to himself. With that he took to examining the floor, crawling on hands and knees. His peregrinations took him behind me, and what he did there or found there I do not know; but he rapped out an oath and I heard him pacing up and down, swearing in an angry undertone. So five minutes passed, then he stalked into my view and showed me a very troubled and a very angry countenance.

"You asked my Arab for a drink?" he cried.

"I did," said I.

"In English?"

"What else?"

"Did he answer you?"

"In the kindliest fashion possible. He assuaged my thirst."

"Blast him!" cried Belleville, all of a tremble with rage. "The villain has been tricking me. Like enough I've loosed a force I'll yet have to reckon with."

"I don't comprehend," said I.

"Nor need you," he rapped back. "Shut your mouth till I address you or I'll cut your prying tongue out." The rascal was beside himself, that was evident. And since I was quite at his mercy I thought it best to do his bidding. He clapped a hand to his head and rushed once more to the sarcophagus. He glared over the edge for a minute, then turned and flung out his arms. "For two pins I'd do it now," he gasped. "Cut him to pieces and burn the parts. It's doubtful if I'll ever get more good out of him. But if I do that I'll kill the chance. And yet he's played me false already. Been laughing in his sleeve at me! But no—he can't have meant hurt or he'd have freed the prisoner. As easy that as fetch him a drink. No doubt he was asked. Yet he's not to be trusted now, that is evident. I'll have to gaol him, too. Let's see!"

He crossed the room and caught hold of the lid of the sarcophagus; but do what he could he was unable to shift it. I regarded his efforts with a deal of secret amusement. He emerged from the struggle panting and with disordered dress, and his temper in a molten glow. But he was not beaten. Leaving the lid alone, he wheeled a big lounge over to the sarcophagus and, tipping it on edge, heaved it up athwart the mouth. Then he piled everything of weight he could find atop of the lounge and soon he had built up a pyramid which would have taken a Hercules to shift, if shut up in the sarcophagus beneath. It was then that I began to feel I had been a notable fool in telling Belleville anything about the "Arab." But it was little use crying over spilt milk.

His labours over, the rascal sank into a chair before me, and began fanning his hot face with a piece of cardboard.

"Now for our business," he presently observed. "You've probably come to some decision, Pinsent. I wait to hear it."

"Well," I said, "the thing is in a nutshell. You've promised me nothing but a choice of deaths. I may be a fool, but I like life so well that I prefer a lingering sort to any other, however painless."

"You're a fool," he answered shortly, and pouted out his loose thick lips beyond his beard, so that he seemed to have the snout of a hairy pig. "You don't know what a pleasure it will be to me to torture you," he continued. "I'll make you suffer like the damned before you die."

"I don't doubt your will; it's your ability which is in question," I said, as coolly as I was able. "You may think you have me laid here very nicely by the heels, Dr. Belleville, and so you have in seeming. But you're not the only man who has a knowledge of the old magic arts of ancient Egypt. I tell you to your face that I possess a charm no whit less potent than the one you found the secret of in yonder tomb. And if you force me to use it, why, I shall use it. Now put that in your pipe and smoke it."

He stood up at once, greatly surprised, much incredulous, but also a little troubled and dubious, as I could see.

"You think you can bluff me?" he snarled. But I *had* bluffed him. I could read it in his eyes.

I answered him with nothing but a smile.

He assumed a sneer. His eyes glinted. He put his hand in his pocket and produced a revolver. He cocked the weapon and put it to my temple.

"Well, you've challenged me," he jeered. "In just one minute I'll blow your brains out. Your charm is now in question!"

For a few seconds a dark haze of blind terror shut off my power of vision. I felt the villain meant to do what he had threatened. His nerves had been shaken by what I had said to him about the Arab—though why, I could not fathom—and my challenge, although the merest bluff, had completed their disorder. He was in a spell of panic and it had swept his reason and his resolution to the winds. He intended to kill me in order to restore his own sense of security, and at once. And I was impotent to prevent him. He was counting aloud, "One, two, three, four." He had got up to fifteen before I even partially awoke out of my trance of craven fear. But in the next five seconds I had lived a whole series of lifetimes and I had received an inspiration born of wrath and hate and desperate necessity.

"Look in my eyes," I shrieked at him. "And listen if you want to live."

He looked at me. I put the strength of my existence into my gaze, and I felt a strange, wild thrill of exultation as I saw his eyes dilate encountering the glance I threw at him.

"My death means yours," I hissed. "My monitor stands over you. You'll be shrivelled as by lightning. We'll go together to the throne of God! Now shoot if you will and damn your soul for all eternity! Shoot—shoot!"

But Dr. Belleville did not shoot. His hand fell to his side. He staggered back, staring at me open-mouthed until the chair arrested him. I saw my advantage and pressed it home.

"Stop!" I shouted. "As you value your dirty life. Stop! Stand still and do not turn your head. One movement and we both die. I don't want to die for a dog like you."

He stood like a frozen image. Holding his glance with mine, I began to mutter in a sing-song way a string of meaningless Egyptian phrases. Then the more powerfully to impress the superstitious fool-scoundrel, all of a sudden I uttered a loud heart-rending groan and allowed my head to fall over on the strap that encircled and sustained my neck. But though I only affected to swoon, the frightful amount of will force and nervous energy I had expended in the crisis had induced a consequential lassitude so enthralling that I came very near to fainting in reality. And, indeed, it is quite likely that I lost my senses for a time. Soon, however, I felt water sprinkled on my face and slowly I raised my head. "A drink!" I gasped.

A glass was pressed to my lips. I drank thirstily and opened my eyes. Belleville, white-faced but composed now and gloomily frowning, was my minister.

"I make you my compliments," he said in cold, slow, even tones. "You have a quick wit and a nerve of iron. I am glad, because they saved me from a folly. You would cease to be of use to me dead, curse you, though I wish you carrion, and will make you worm food before I am much older."

"You'll not live to repent it," I replied. "I've bound your fate with mine by ties no mortal can unsolve."

"Enough of that rubbish," he retorted harshly. "You cannot haze me twice. You could not have at all if I had stopped to think or been quite well. But I'm liverish and out of sorts to-day—the result of staying up all night nursing Ottley."

"You'll see when the time comes—if you have the courage," I responded in an acrid tone. "You cannot scare me, Belleville, because you cannot harm me without hurting yourself—and in your deeps of heart, you rogue, you know it."

He burst out laughing, but there was a note of nervousness in his mocking mirth that pleased mg passing well.

"Pah!" he said at last. "Would you sit there trussed up like a chooky skewered for the table if you had the power you pretend?"

"Idiot!" I snapped. "Can electricity unbuckle straps without machinery? Yet it can splinter rocks without an effort and without assistance."

"Ah!" said he, "ah! So you pretend—"

"Try me!" I interrupted.

"Not I," cried he. "I've encountered so many wonders lately that I'm now beginning to regard what I of old considered the impossible as the most likely thing of all to happen. I don't believe you, Pinsent, but neither do I disbelieve you. Therefore, acting on the kindly hint you dropped, I'll take all sane precautions. Au revoir."

He marched to the door, passed out and disappeared. I chewed the bitter cud of thought for some hours. Meanwhile I grew desperately hungry, ay, and thirsty, too. There came a time when I would have given the last of my possessions for a beef-steak and a jug of water. And, oh! how tired I was of my position. The blood gradually ceased to circulate properly through all my parts. My hands became purple. My legs went to sleep. My limbs were on a rack of pins and needles and even breathing hurt me. I did my best by straining at the bonds at intervals to promote the arterial flow and stop the agony of muscular irritation. But it was a poor best, and I sank welcomely at length into a benumbed lethargic state near akin to stupor, from which I knew I could wake to anguish by the merest movement.

As near as I can guess twelve hours had uncoiled their lethal folds before my infernal captor returned to the laboratory. One instant I was sharply sensible and suffering most damnably. The rogue looked positively sick and he smelt like a gin palace. He had evidently drunk a deal of spirit, but he was not the least intoxicated. "It is over!" he cried and threw himself into a chair.

"What?" I questioned.

"Ottley is dead," said he, "and I am glad of it, all said and done, though I worked like a galley slave to keep him by me. He was a fine cloak for my doings, but he grew wearisome—the fractious old fool—at times. And I'm not sure I'd bring him back now—were I able."

"And Miss Ottley?"

"A pretty scene!" He shrugged his shoulders, then grimaced and whistled. "I'm her father's murderer, it seems!" He stretched out his arms and yawned. "But she's not responsible, poor thing—grief demented. The two consulting physicians heartily sympathised with me. They knew how I had worked, you see, and Sir Philip Lang himself suggested morphia. They've signed a paper giving me control of her—under their directions I'm trustee of the estate under the will besides. Lang thinks she may recover—ultimately, but it is evident that she must be confined. She raved of mummies, and spirits, and dead men come to life from the sleep of ages, and so forth. It impressed Lang, vastly. He tapped his sage old head and muttered 'Too much learning.' He has a fad that woman's brains are nurtured best on pap, and I had the tact to humour him. Oh! I'm a devilish clever fellow, Pinsent. What do you think?"

"There is little doubt of it," I said politely, very politely, indeed, for I wished to get as much information from him as I could and also something to eat and drink. "With your brains you might do anything. I suspect I have hitherto misjudged you. Still, I wonder that you are not an archbishop. It seems to me the Church would give you the proper cloak you need to exercise your talents in."

"Gad!" he cried. "There's point in that remark. But between ourselves, Pinsent, I aim at higher game than spiritual power."

"Temporal," I suggested.

"The highest," he answered, sitting up. "And what's to prevent me?" he asked defiantly. "No man's life is safe from me."

I was puzzled. "You'd not make yourself eligible for kingship by killing kings," I said.

"Kingship be damned," he sneered. "My father was an earl's bastard, but as for me, I'm a pure democrat. No, no, I'm going to abolish royalty. It has served its turn."

"But where do you come in?"

"The pleasure of the game is mine, the knowledge and the ecstasy of power unlimited to make and break."

"Oh! oh! my tiger, having tasted blood already, once at least, the thirst grows on you."

"Once at least—bah!" he jeered, grinning like a fiend.

"Pardon my ignorance," I entreated. "Who was your latest victim."

"Navarro," he answered, grinning still. "The scamp is a true clairvoyant and had to be shut up. He leaped from London Bridge the night you came here and stepped like a poor rabbit into the trap I laid for you."

"Well," said I, in tones husky with throat dryness and apparent admiration, "that makes two—Weldon and Navarro?"

"There is a third still," he answered, fairly snapping at the bait. "My old grandfather, the Earl of Havelock."

"And why did you murder him?"

"For his snobbish refusal to receive me as his kin ten years ago."

"Might one ask how?"

"It's a story to entertain," he answered, licking his lips. "He was over eighty, but he'd kept all his faculties, else there'd been no joy in killing him. A week since, I went to him invisible, entering the house with my blood cousin, now the Earl, soon after midnight

returning from a carousal. He did not see me, of course, and I took
care not to let him hear. But little care was needed, the degenerate
was filthy drunk. It was easy to find the old earl's room, the young
man got so sober passing it. The door was unlocked, too, so I had no
trouble first and last. I went over to the old chap's bed and looked at
him and laughed to see. He slept with his mouth wide and his
toothless gums were hideously funny. His teeth were in a glass of
H_2O beside the bed. I pulled his nose to waken him, having first
turned on the lights full. Then I played the ghost of my dead father.
'Your hour is come,' says I. 'I'm the spirit of your bastard son come
to warn you.' He shook all over, palsied with fear. 'No—no—no,'
he gasped, 'I'm not fit to die.' 'You're not fit to live,' I whispered,
stern as fate. 'How have you treated the son of your bastard son?
Have you been kind to him and helped him in the world?' 'Mercy,
mercy!' he whined. 'I know I have been remiss, but give one more
chance—another year—a week—a day—and I'll do my duty. I'll
bar the entail, I'll give him all.'

" 'Wretch!' I hissed—and sat me on his chest. It was heaven
sweet to hear his stifled moans. He did not struggle at all. And my
only regret was it was so soon over. He broke a vessel and smothered in his own blood. The papers announced next day that he had
died of the syncope of senility peacefully while sleeping. Ha, ha,
ha!"

I echoed the heartless villain's laugh, croaking out guffaws. The
sound irritated him. "Stop that raucous row!" he ordered,

"Then stop telling me funny stories, or else give me something
to drink!" I snapped.

He sprang afoot at once. "Lord!" he cried, "I'm not proposing to
starve you to death. Why the deuce did you not remind me? You've
been—let's see—sixty hours without food."

"Sixty!" I gasped. "Impossible."

"It's a fact," he said, and stalked out of the room. But he returned
within a few minutes carrying a tray set with cold meats and wine
which he set on a little table and wheeled before me. Then he freed
my right hand and stood over me with a revolver while I ate. But I
could not eat at once, for the good reason that my arm was para-
lyzed, and minutes passed before I could make use of it. Even then
it pained like a raw scald. But I suppressed a reference to its condition and at the earliest instant cleared the board in the fashion of a
famished wolf. Afterwards he bound me up again, standing behind
me to do it, out of respect for my strength, no doubt. Then he put up
his pistol and resumed his chair.

"Upon my soul, I enjoy a chat with you," he assured me. "You see, I have no one else to confide in"—here he grinned—"and there's a peculiar pleasure in unbosoming to a helpless enemy."

"The pleasure is mutual," I protested courteously. "No other man has given me such mental pabulum."

He closed one eye in a very vulgar manner. "Confess you expire with curiosity to hear more of my beautiful fiancée—the woman you love!"

"The more readily," I responded, "because I know you'll be delighted to taunt me with the satisfaction of that same curiosity."

"Ah!" said he. "You are a foeman worthy of my steel. My heart warms with hate for you; respectful hate." He took out a silver pocket flask of spirit and filled the cup.

At this he began to sip, eyeing me the while with secret delight at my carefully repressed impatience. But he was too anxious to torture me directly to keep me waiting long.

"She's in a drugged sleep this moment," he announced. "I'll keep her like that till after the funeral."

"That's unlike you," I remarked. "It's almost kind."

"Pish!" said he, "I can't afford to let her out of my control even for a moment."

"So?"

"So."

"But you will have to let her see her relatives, eh?"

"Fortunately she hasn't one blood relation in England. Her mother was an Australian, a Victorian farmer's daughter, and Ottley took good care not to marry the family. She has never even seen one of her mother's people."

"But her father's?"

"She is just as fortunately placed, from my point of view, in this regard. Ottley was the only son. And although I believe there is an old maiden aunt twice removed knocking round somewhere in Wales, I'm not afraid of her. She's bed-ridden and a pensioner. As I'm trustee of the estate she'll do what I tell her and stay where she is or I'll know the reason why."

"I'm sure you will," I agreed with pious fervour.

"The Fates seem to have deliberately conspired to assist me in every possible way," continued Belleville. "The only real woman friend Miss Ottley had, Lady Helen Hubbard, has gone to South America with her husband, and the only man friend who might have helped her sits in that chair. There is not another soul in England who has either the shadow of a right or interest to question my treatment. I'm her sole trustee and as well as that her legal guardian, for although she is over age she does not come into control of her fortune until she is twenty-seven unless she marries in the meanwhile."

"You propose, of course, that she shall marry you. When?"

"Oh, in a few days' time. It will naturally be a secret marriage in order to save scandal. But I'm determined it shall take place immediately."

"And afterwards—how will you treat her?" I had hard work to grind this question out.

Belleville gave a nasty laugh. "That depends on herself," he answered. "If she is a dutiful, docile wife she will have little cause to grumble."

"And—if not?"

"You know me and ask that?" he cried. Then he laughed again, stood up and shook himself. "I'm going to indulge in a nice comfortable sleep," he said. "You may not know it, Pinsent, but it's almost midnight. Take my advice and go to by-by, too! Pleasant dreams to you and au revoir." He went out gaping with yawns, but he turned out the lights as he went, and once more darkness enfolded me.

CHAPTER TWENTY-SEVEN

UNBOUND

IT IS NOT worth while describing the next few days. They were quite or almost colourless. Once each four and twenty hours, Belleville, taking sound precautions, released me for a short while from my prison chair to let me stretch my limbs and in the interests of keeping me alive for his own purposes. We had very little conversation, for he had fallen into a morose and gloomy mood, the result of an attack of insomnia. In answer to direct questions I learned that Sir Robert Ottley's funeral had passed without incident, but that Miss Ottley's violent grief had been succeeded by a long stupor. She was being nursed by a creature of Belleville's, an old Frenchwoman named Elise Lorraine in whom he evidently reposed a deal of confidence. Belleville spent most of his time at work in the laboratory, but what he did I could not see, for he conducted his labours behind my chair. On one occasion he gave way to a savage fit of passion, and without any cause whatever that I could perceive, he broke a number of glass implements upon the floor. Another time, having cut his hand in some experiment, he revenged himself by flogging me with a piece of whalebone until my flesh wherever he could reach it was covered with weals and blisters. He was not a nice man to live with and my hatred of him grew daily more intense. But perforce I was civil to him. On the eighth day he entered the room with a chalk-white face. I knew at once that something had happened; but I was not to learn what it was immediately. He disappeared forthwith behind my chair and for ten minutes stamped about swearing like a pagan. Then the lights went out of a sudden and he departed in the dark. He returned about four hours later, but I did not see him enter, although he put on the lights immediately. I heard him pass my chair; that was all. But a few seconds later a sharp and most acridly irritating odour filled the room, and soon afterwards he came forward and sank into his accustomed chair, opposite to mine. He looked positively ghastly. "To-morrow morning England will mourn the loss of her greatest physician," he announced in quivering tones. "Sir Philip Lang has just committed suicide."

"What!" I cried in deep astonishment. "Sir Philip Lang!"

He bared his teeth. "The world will think so," he snarled. "But in reality—but there, you shall judge. This afternoon without giving me notice the fool came to this house, forced his way into the sick room and had a long private conversation with May Ottley. I do not know to what conclusion he came, but she must have persuaded him of her sanity, for he ordered Elise to take her out for a walk; and if it had not been that Elise refused to obey him pending my arrival there would have been a pretty kettle of fish for me to fry. However, he won't trouble me again."

"You murdered him!" I gasped.

"Like an artist," said Belleville. "I stole upon him while he sat in his private sitting-room at supper and, standing opposite to him unseen, I reached out and poured some aconite into his wine. He was dead inside a quarter hour, and I took care that he made no outcry. The verdict should be suicide, I think. Don't you?"

With that he got up and left me.

That night while I slept he dosed me with chloroform, and while I was senseless he drew over my clothes a suit of rubber overalls. He also did whatever was necessary to render me invisible, and he gagged me with a piece of steel thrust under my tongue and secured around my throat and neck with fine wire that bit deep in the flesh. I awoke groaning with agony to find that I was stretched out on the naked framework of an iron bed.

Belleville stood over me grasping Miss Ottley by the hand. When I saw her I stopped groaning as if by instinct. I knew at once that she did not see anything except the bed. She looked well, but tragically sorrowful and wild. She was staring as it were through me.

"You see nothing," said Belleville's hollow voice, "but his spirit lies there for all that. It is in my power and cannot escape without I set it free. You know my price. It is for you to rule his fate, through me if so you wish.

"What!" he continued, "do you not believe—well, then, look now!"

Of a sudden he flashed a blue lighted lanthorn into my face and he did something else which sent a thousand stinging currents of electric anguish quivering along my nerves. I uttered a shriek, but the gag stifled it to a hissing wail, and then I fell to breathing groans. Hell can have no worse torments than that villain had devised for my undoing. Had my mouth been unfettered I should have besought the woman I adored for death at any price for rest of pain. As it was I prayed her with my eyes—and she saw and took a message.

"Let him go!" she sobbed, "and I will marry you. Oh, this is horrible!"

On instant the blue light faded out and a blessed heaven of diminished torture gave me peace.

Belleville took from his breast a naked dagger which he put into the girl's hand. "Strike, then!" he said. "Strike here," and he put his finger on my breast.

The devil proposed to make his innocent victim a murderess. I saw his purpose, and with every atom of my strength I groaned. It was the only warning I could send.

But I had played right into Belleville's hands.

"Hear him implore you!" cried Belleville.

"Oh! I can't, I can't," she wailed.

" 'Tis only a spirit—and it's the only way," he protested warmly.

Miss Ottley swung around suddenly and drove the dagger at his heart, but he had been expecting it. He caught her wrist and laughed. Then all my anguish recommenced. In the midst of it, made desperate, the girl leaned right across the bed and struck. The blade glanced down upon a rib and deeply pierced my side. Providence, surely, had directed the blow. She withdrew the dagger, then screamed aloud to see it dripping with blood. Belleville caught her in his arms and bore her roughly back. He bent her body on a table until she was as helpless as a dove, then took the blade and drew the horrid thing across her lips; so they were carmined with my blood.

"By this and this you'll remember you are mine," he said, and kissed her lips till his were bloody, too. Then the two stared deep into each other's eyes.

"I've killed his body; you, his soul," said Belleville. "We're well mated, you and I. There—I've no longer any fear you'll hurt yourself. You'll be henceforth too much afraid of him to die."

He let her go, and stood away from her. She swayed erect, then came forward till she stood beside me. I held my very breath for fear that she would hear. I don't know why.

"It is all a trick—a cruel, devilish trick. There's nothing there!" said the girl, her bosom heaving as she spoke.

Belleville laughed like a hyena. "Feel—if you dare!" he cried.

But she took him at his word. Her hands went out and, guided by a dark blotch which, as afterwards I learned she saw, she put them on my wound and drew them swiftly back ensanguined. Then horror settled on her like a black cloud on a mountain top. She turned about with one loud gasping sigh and sank down in a lifeless heap at Belleville's feet.

Soon afterwards I swooned, too, from pain and loss of blood. When I awoke my wound was neatly bandaged, and I was once more seated in my chair.

Belleville sat opposite smoking a cigar. He was dressed very smartly in a frock suit and a tall hat was set jauntily on his brow. He wore a geranium in his buttonhole. His face was wreathed in smiles. A bottle of champagne was set before him on a table and he sipped at a glass with an air of triumphant good-humour.

I found that I could speak; my gag had been removed.

"Water!" I implored him.

He started, then pressed forward with his glass. "Where the devil is your mouth?" he said.

He could not see me, that was plain.

"Here!" said I. "Water."

"It is my wedding morn—and you shall toast me in wine or go thirsting," he rapped out.

Then he found my lips and I drank life into my veins. I have never tasted draught one-half so glorious.

"I was married less than an hour ago," he said, "at a registrar's office. She's no longer Miss Ottley, Pinsent."

I was silent.

"Do you hear me, man?" he demanded.

"I hear," I answered.

He nodded his head and smiled. "I suppose you are wondering why you're still alive, eh?"

"You'll die when I die," I muttered wearily. "You are afraid to kill me, that is why."

"Bosh!" he flashed back. "I have a better reason far. To-morrow she will be my wife indeed—a maid no longer—Pinsent. It was worth keeping you alive to gloat on that."

"Oh! I see."

"But you don't see everything, Pinsent. She insists upon seeing your body to-day in order to be sure that you are dead."

"Ah!"

"She still has a lingering doubt that I have tricked her, and she has sworn on the cross that unless I produce your corpse for her inspection she will take her own life rather than—you can guess what, Pinsent."

"Yes—I can guess."

"So you see the time draws nigh for you to die."

"God only knows."

The villain frowned. "But before you go you must do something for me."

"And that?"

"You must write her a letter telling her that your only hope of soul resurrection and salvation lies in her obeying me. She now considers me a dangerous magician, but I want her to regard me as a sort of deity."

"I will not do it, Belleville. You ought to know me better by this."

"I think you will," said he. "That is if you really care for her. You see it will save her a lot of—let's call it inconvenience. With such a weapon as your message I can rule her kindly. But rule her in any case I shall. If you deny me I'll gag you this moment so you can't make a sound, then I'll bring her here and beat her as I would a dog. How will you like that?"

"I'll write the letter," I said huskily.

A few minutes later the thing was done, and I had signed my name to the atrocious expressions of his demand. To transcribe them I am too ashamed.

"What now?" I asked.

"The last scene in the last act," said he, as he put the letter in his pocket. "I may tell you that I intend always to keep your body by me—for her to look at—if she ever shows a mind to mutiny."

"In spirits?" I questioned.

"The embalming oil of the princes of old Egypt. I found the receipt in Ptahmes' tomb," he answered. "I propose to convert you into a mummy."

With that he took off his hat and coat, rolled up his sleeves and put on a huge oil-skin apron. "I'll not kill you till the last moment necessary," he observed. "In fact, you'll be half-mummy before you die; I have a curiosity to discover if the process of substitution is painful. I rather think it must be."

He moved over as he spoke to the sarcophagus and began to shift the objects that sealed up the mouth. It took him some minutes to do so, and as he put down the couch, last of all, one of the castors crashed upon his toe. He cursed the misfortune like a madman and danced about the floor on one foot like a dervish, winding up by striking me brutally with closed fist on the lips. That gave him back his self-control.

"I'll teach you to laugh at me," he growled. Then he returned to his work and stooping over the great coffin he hauled out the lifeless mummy that had rested there so long. For an instant I glimpsed the strange dead features of the dust of Ptahmes which so strikingly resembled the effigy carven on the lid of the sarcophagus and also the Arab who had twice in Egypt attempted to destroy me. Then Belleville carelessly threw the thing upon the couch; and traversed the room to where stood three glass jars filled with a dark viscous fluid. One by one he rolled these on end across the floor till all three stood beside the coffin. Afterwards he disappeared behind my chair, returning soon, his head covered with a long breathing mask. I watched him—one may guess with what passionate attention. He unscrewed the stopper of the nearest jar, seized the thing bodily in his arms and poured out the contents into the sarcophagus. A curious cloud-like steam arose that hazed the prospect, but soon it dissipated. The air was filled with the perfume I had first smelt in the cave temple of the Hill of Rakh. But it was not altogether overpowering. It made my pulses throb and brought a great rush of blood to my head and hands and feet much as would the scent of amyl nitrate. But it did not take away my senses. Belleville, protected by his mask, was in no way affected. He quickly unstoppered the second jar, and added its contents to the first. Then he turned and approached me, taking off his helmet as he came. The action apprised me that the wonderful perfume had almost died away. There was now a healthy and stimulating odour in the room that resembled boiling tar. Evidently the two jars had contained different chemicals. A loud, seething, bubbling sound was plainly to be heard; it came from the sarcophagus.

Belleville sat down and wiped his forehead with a handkerchief. "We must give the stuff ten minutes to mix," he said and, taking out his watch, he glanced at the time. "It's twenty past eleven," he remarked. "You'll begin to mummify at the half hour precisely, Pinsent, so if you are a religious man you'd best compose your soul in prayer."

I am not ashamed to say that I followed his advice. I closed my eyes and asked the Omnipotent for remission of my sins. And since it seemed to me that my hour had come, I resolutely put aside my detestation of the monster who designed to murder me, and I even asked for his forgiveness, too. Then a great, deep, splendid peace mantled over me, and for the first time in my life I truly realised the littleness of man's existence and the majesty of resignation. It was almost worth while to go through all I had been compelled to endure to experience at the end that mood of grand, calm dignity. I felt almost sublimely detached from my surroundings. I opened my eyes at last and said with perfect calm:

"I am ready, Belleville."

He stood up and stretched out his arms, yawning widely. Then of a sudden everything was dark.

"What in Hell—?" shouted Belleville. I heard him rush forward cursing angrily, then he stumbled and fell headlong to the floor amidst a crash of glass. In the same instant unseen hands fumbled over me. My bonds suddenly relaxed and I was free. I stood up, stiff but quivering in every nerve. There followed a rasping sound, a match flickered into light, and I saw Belleville rising from the ruins of a broken jar. He held the lucifer above his head, and it showed standing at an angle between us the tall frame of the Arab of the cave temple at Rakh.

Belleville ripped out an oath. There came a blinding flash of light and the deafening report of a revolver. I staggered from the chair to the wall and leaned against it, helpless as a babe. The echoes were still thundering in rolling waves of brain-dazing sound from wall to wall when the pitch blackness of the room was again relieved by the glare of electricity. Belleville had succeeded in turning on the lights. He stood by the door peering all about him. For a moment I thought all was up. I was free, certainly, but my muscles were so cramped and tautened that I could hardly move a finger. I was not fit to contend against a breath of wind, let alone a burly ruffian like the Doctor. But the next instant I remembered I was still invisible. I could not see my own hand held before me, and I had immediate proof that he was unable to perceive me.

"Where are you, Pinsent? are you hurt?" he cried.

I did not answer, but, following his glance, I looked at the couch and there I saw what utterly astounded me. The mummy of Ptahmes lay upon the couch in exactly the same attitude as when Belleville had flung it there aside from the sarcophagus. Who, then, or what, had set me free? I examined the apartment eagerly, but saw nothing living save Belleville, who with cocked revolver thrust out before him now stepped forward cautiously into the room, waving his arms about him as he walked, and muttering, as he walked, through clenched teeth a string of angry blasphemies.

CHAPTER TWENTY-EIGHT

THE STRUGGLE IN THE CHAMBER

THE ADVANTAGE I possessed was dangerously minimised by my physical incapacity, but I hoped, given time, to get back some measure of strength. The great thing was to preserve my liberty until I had acquired force enough to use it. I speedily realised that I could not remain where I was, for Bellville was making towards me and reflection would soon teach him that weakness would compel me to seek a prop for my support. But I feared to move lest the sound should betray my whereabouts. For the same reason I almost feared to breathe. I thought to myself, "Oh, that he would fire again so that I could move elsewhere under cover of the noise."

Once or twice he seemed to look me in the eye. He made a zigzag to my chair. There he paused and listened. I ceased to breathe. Only six feet separated us. But impatience consumed him. "Tell me where you are!" he growled, "or by the Lord when I catch you I'll tear you limb from limb." I breathed while he spoke and ceased when he stopped.

"You can't escape me!" he snarled. "I've only to light my blue lamp and I'll find you in a minute. But if you put me to that trouble and make me waste my precious oil besides, well, look out, that's all!"

I clenched and unclenched my hands; the use of them was coming back to me.

"Very well," said Belleville. He passed my chair and stalked to the other end of the room, where he opened a cabinet. I moved slowly and painfully to the very centre of the room. Then I stood stock still. Belleville, returning, paused within a foot of me. He carried a bull's-eye lanthorn. This he put upon the table, and presently he struck a match. A moment later a round shaft of intense blue radiance shot across the room and marked a moon-shaped sphere on the wall. It began to flit along the wall, up and down from the very floor to the height of a man's chest, until it touched the corner. Then it flashed back twice over the same path, and afterwards attacked the next wall. Sooner or later it would be bound to encounter and, perhaps, discover me. But Belleville was only a few feet off. Perhaps if I sank down the shaft would pass over me without touching. At least I could try. Suppressing a shriek of agony, I crouched upon my hands and knees. Then came another thought. Slowly and laboriously I began to crawl nearer and nearer to my enemy. The blue shaft was now shooting right over my head. I crept behind him and, breathing noiselessly, stood up. If I had possessed a tithe of my strength I might have reached out and caught his neck and strangled him with ease. But I dared not risk it. All on a sudden he uttered an oath. The lamp had gone out. "Damn the thing!" he growled. Putting down his revolver on the table, he opened the lamp and peered in at the smoking wick. We were now face to face and his cocked weapon lay within eighteen inches of my hand. I tried my fingers and found that they were reasonably supple. The blood was streaming through the puffy veins and vesicles. The operation hurt horribly; in fact, I was one mass of crude, raw, painful man flesh. But now I was full of hope and despite the muscular torments of returning animation I felt that my vigour was returning. Belleville snuffed the wick and struck a match along the table. The head came off. He took another and rubbed it on the sole of his shoe, stooping slightly to do so. As he moved I reached out and twined my fingers round the hilt of his revolver. But I had not the strength to lift it up. I cannot paint the agony of that experience. I exerted every atom of my will, but my hand was like a putty puppet. Tantalus never suffered torture half as keen. Withdrawing my hand, I put the fingers in my mouth and sucked the still half-lifeless digits. Meanwhile, the lamp flickered alight; Belleville took up his revolver and resumed his task. I watched him hungrily. The blue shaft once more began to play and stab the walls. It darted hither and thither, like an incandescent elf, dancing up and down and round and round, and into every hole and cranny of the room. But it did not find me out, because moving round and round the table as Belleville moved I always kept behind him. But this could not last for ever, and, indeed, the end came too soon. Belleville uttered suddenly a savage curse and swung round full upon me. Perhaps I had made some sound that had betrayed me to his nerve-strained senses. I do not know. He cried, "Ha! at last," and fired point blank. The bullet whistled past my temple. The smoke of the discharge flamed blue in the rays of the lanthorn. I fell upon the table and thrust it like a ram with all my force against my adversary. He fired again and once more missed, but ere he could repeat his tactics the table struck him and the lanthorn fell. He staggered back and the lanthorn rolled underneath the table. I pushed the table forward and kicked the lanthorn with my foot. It went out. Belleville, recovering his equilibrium, stood like an image peering straight at me and listening. Yet he did not see me: and for the moment I was safe, for the table was between us. But the man had brains. Judging swiftly where I was most likely to be, he gave an unexpected spring and vaulted clear across the obstacle. I had just time to step back ere he landed. He swung his arms about like flails, but failing immediately to find me, his ugly temper must needs flare up in curses. It was just what I needed to cover the sound of my movements. I evaded him and returned to the table, and then he knew not where I was. In a few moments he realised his folly and, once more relapsing into silence, he took up his lamp. But the oil had either been wasted or was exhausted. The wick refused to catch. He groaned out a blasphemous oath on this discovery, and rushed down to the cabinet, from which first he had procured the lanthorn. I followed him as swiftly as I could, having care to make no sound, and while he was filling the lamp with oil from a beautifully carven vase of solid gold Egyptian ware of the fifteenth dynasty, I once more put my hand upon the hilt of his revolver, which he had momentarily laid upon the edge of the cabinet. But this time I found I could hold and use it, too. Shadow-like, I caught it up and put my finger on the trigger. Then I backed away a yard or two and leaned upon a case of glass and steel.

"Belleville!" said I.

He started as though an adder had stung him, then seeing his pistol gone, he let both vase and lanthorn fall in his dismay and swung on heel to face my voice.

"It's my turn now," I muttered. "Hands above your head—up, man, up—higher—higher!" He saw the muzzle pointing at his breast and sullenly obeyed. I made him walk backwards to the chair that formerly had prisoned me and sit in it. And then, the steel pressed to his ear to keep him still, I managed, with one hand, to pass a strap around his throat and buckle it. Afterwards I similarly bound his wrists and ankles. When all was done I was so sore spent, so hideously full of weary pain, that I lay upon the floor and sank immediately into a troubled sleep. Belleville woke me with his struggles to get free. Somehow or other he had pryed himself on tiptoe backward, and the heavy chair, overbalancing, had dragged him over in its fall. That I had not heard, but the weight of iron and his own body was all curiously pressed upon one forearm, and the pain of it set him groaning like a wounded bull. The strangest thing of all was that this arm was free. Somehow or other he had writhed it loose. After I had tied it up again I sat down to think what I should do. I was not, however, in the mood to sit in judgment on him then, for although much stronger from my sleep, the exertion hurt, and every pang I suffered was too powerful an advocate of vengeance to let me try the rascal soberly. I needed food and drink. Not finding any in the room, I tried the door and after some short search, made out its fastening—a simple but clever slip of prodigious strength. I found the key to it in Belleville's pocket. He was madly anxious to be made acquainted with his fate, but I turned a deaf ear to all his questions, and slipping out of the room, I slammed the door on his solicitations. I found myself in a long, blind passage, lighted with a single jet, with another padded door set in its farthest end. This opened to the same key as the first. It gave me egress on a second passage, which led by three right angles to a big velvet-draped arch and a bifurcated maze of broad-balconied corridors. Here I saw the natural light of day for the first time in more than a week. Ah! how I revelled in it. I stopped before an open window and peered forth on a walled courtyard and the blank, tall wall of a neighbouring mansion beyond. Street sounds percolated to my ears. It was like coming back to life from the grave. Drawing back from the window, after some deep, delicious moments, I looked to find my body and my hands and feet. But I could not see aught but vague, delusive shadows, though the sunbeams glistened on me. The phenomenon filled me with a new sense of marvel and uncertainty. I had to pinch myself to make sure I was not a disembodied phantom—such stuff as dreams are made of. Yet I was real enough to touch, thank Heaven. Reassured, I made for the nearest door and softly tried it. Within was a man's bedroom—Belleville's, perhaps. It was untenanted. The next apartment was a sitting-room. It was also untenanted, but it contained a table, cover-spread for two. With a sigh of joy, I entered and hurried to the table. Under the first cover was a cold partridge pie. I did not touch the others, but, Lord, how I enjoyed that pie! I might have been a wolf—and then champagne! Later, seduced by an open cigar-box on the mantel, I threw myself upon a lounge and lit a weed. In ten minutes I was my own man again, and almost comfortable, for the torments, that had racked my wretched muscles on reawakening from their tethered lethargy, were disappearing fast. But I was not permitted longer rest. Warned by a tap on the door, I had barely time to toss my cigar into the grate, when the door opened and a short, squat negro stepped into the room. He carried a salver of sweetmeats to the table; he stopped short and uttered a guttural exclamation of surprise. Next instant he was joined by a companion, but no negro, an Arab, a tall, thin Arab, who was the living counterpart of the mummified corpse of Ptahmes I had left in the laboratory, and of the mysterious scoundrel who had attempted my life in the cave temple at Rakh, and at my camp on the banks of the Nile. I was so utterly astounded that I wonder I did not shout out my amazement.

The negro spoke in Arabic. "By Allah, he has eaten and alone," he cried. "Now tell me, Ptahmes, how a man shall serve a master with so little feeling for his servants."

The Arab stalked solemnly over to the table and eyed the ruined pie.

"He hungered. He ate. May his shadow increase," he drawled.

"For my part," retorted the Nubian, with an ill-natured scowl, "his shadow may wither and I shall not grieve. It is impossible to please him."

"His gold is good and hard and yellow and much," said the Arab, in a sort of sing-song.

"Add to that ill-got," replied the negro, "and I shall be an echo to your speech. Natamkin tells me that the lady weeps still, though no more a prisoner, and he took her forth into his whirling Babel town this morning. He has put a spell on her to deprive her of her gold."

"What matter if he shares it with his slaves?" demanded the Arab.

"I fear him," said the Nubian.

"I also," drawled the Arab. "But guard your idle tongue Uromi! He may be listening to us now."

The negro shuddered and made as if to hastily depart. But the Arab laughed, and he stopped looking both angry and ashamed.

"Allah!" he exclaimed, "you laugh, but you may have spoken true."

"Ugh!" said the Arab, "he has bigger fish to fry—the white man you enticed into the room of wonders dies to-day."

"You—know that, Ptahmes!"

"Ay—I am to help him to embalm the body. Now I think of it, I wonder he has eaten. I was to stir the pot while he made merry with the lady over wine—the unbelieving dog. At one of the clock he ordered me to go to him. 'Tis almost time."

"Will you not fear to stay alone in that great room of magic, Ptahmes?"

"Like enough, Uromi, but I shall think me of the pay and work with tight-shut eyes till he returns."

"What has he promised you?"

"Five pieces of gold, Uromi. Do you covet them?"

"I would not cross the threshold of that room for ten times five."

"You have a chicken's heart, Uromi."

"And you a miser's gizzard."

The Arab uttered a sardonic laugh. "Get to your woman's work!" he sneered. "And clear those things away! You had better tell Natamkin to serve the lady in her room!"

"And you—oh, great Lord!" growled the Nubian, with elephantine sarcasm.

The Arab, however, did not trouble himself to answer. With a mien of princely dignity he stalked in silence to the door and vanished.

I said to myself, "There, without doubt, goes the man who, in the nick of time, released me from my bonds. He is my friend." The reflection gave me substantial satisfaction, for much against my will I had hitherto been compelled to ascribe my salvation to a supernatural agency. But now all was changed. Without doubt the Arab had been secretly watching over me, and when the time came he turned out the lights, rushed into the laboratory and unfastened my straps. Afterwards, he had adroitly managed to escape before Belleville could turn on the lights again. No doubt, too, this Arab was the man of my dream, who had bargained with me to kill Belleville when I got free, to destroy the mummy of Ptahmes, the Priest of Amen-Ra— and his papyri and steles. Why he should have driven such a bargain I could not fathom. And why, moreover, he should have taken the trouble to impersonate the mummy and pretend he could not speak, I was also at a loss to understand. Suddenly I remembered that the animated mummy of my dream had conversed with me in the tongue of Ancient Egypt per medium of a slate and had seemed not to understand modern Arabic. Also, his left hand had been removed—and this Arab enjoyed the undiminished use of his. My head whirled at the contemplation of these essential contradictions. Were they one and the same man or not? Was it possible that Belleville's Arab servant could be a professor of the language of Sesostris? And I recollected, too, how closely I had scrutinised the ghostly mummy's face and realised its utter deadness. The mystery, after all, was not to be as easily solved as my first warm flush of fancy had conceived. Realising this, I put it out of mind and arose to address myself to the practical affair that lay before me. The Nubian was in the act of quitting the room, laden with a heavy tray of dishes. I followed him out into the corridor and leisurely made back to the laboratory. I met nobody en route, but once inside the blind passage, which opened on my old prison chamber, I became aware that something had gone wrong. The air was heavy with the mysterious scent of the sarcophagus. Moreover, the door of the laboratory which I had been careful to shut close was now ajar. Instinctively, I slipped the key I had just used on the outer door, into my mouth and hurried softly up the passage. There a bewildering surprise awaited me. The laboratory was apparently untenanted by living beings. The mummy of Ptahmes still lay upon the couch. The straps which had fastened Belleville to the chair were all unfastened and Belleville himself had disappeared. Yet there were noises in the room, noises of footfalls and the tinkling of glass. Presently I saw a large glass phial move quietly from a marble slab and stand poised in air. A second later the stopper, which had been laid beside it, sprang up, too, and settled neatly in the phial's mouth. Then the bottle leaped up high into the air and settled, with mysterious precision, on a shelf. I stared at these wonders half-understanding, half-dazed. But soon I comprehended all. Belleville's voice speaking in Arabic came to me through the hush.

"That will do, I think. There only remains for us to steal upon him now and take him by surprise. Serve me well in this, Ptahmes, and I shall treble your reward."

"The man is of iron strength, master," answered the Arab's voice. "It is true that we are two to one and he is unsuspicious, but I should like well to have a knife."

"Nonsense," retorted Belleville. "I cannot make steel invisible. We must needs trust to the sandbags. Now lead on to the lady's room and take care from this moment that you make no sound."

On this I left the doorway and, slipping into the opposite corner, pressed flat against the wall. Presently the door creaked open and I heard the noise of breathing. I followed it as gently as a shadow, halting sharply when I could not hear it or it grew too near. I was weaponless—for I had left Belleville's revolver in the laboratory ere for the first time leaving it. But still, I dared not arm myself, for to have done so would have given my adversaries, sooner or later, a certain clue to my position; and my only hope of worsting them now consisted in preserving my absolute invisibility and at the same time knowing where, in the general sense, they were. My first great difficulty arose in the passage of the outer door. I dared not slip out with them, and since they locked it after them, I was forced to wait some time before I deemed it safe to open it again. Thus, when I reached the outer passage there was absolutely nothing left to guide my steps. However, I hurried to the arch and thence looked forth along the bifurcated corridor. Seeing and hearing nothing, I sank to the floor, and like an Indian pressed my ear against the boards. One far-off panel a little later creaked distinctly. Wood, though carpeted, is a fine sound conductor. This gave me the direction. Hot foot I followed it. But soon I came to a corner and beyond a short, wide cul-de-sac, with three closed doors. Here I stopped with straining ears and listened with a beating heart and bated breath. The con-spirators were there, beyond the scope of doubt; and presently I knew the door they wished to pass. I saw the handle turn and heard a sigh. "Locked," murmured a voice in English—then in Arabic it breathed. "Keep closely by me, Ptahmes, hold my coat!" Three sharp raps followed on the panels. A voice that thrilled me, asked within the room, "Who is there?"

A voice, the cleverly twisted voice of Belleville, answered in a sharp falsetto from without, "It is I, my dear young lady, Sir Philip Lang."

The door was immediately opened and I saw the sad face of my sweetheart.

"Sir Philip!" she cried—then, seeing no one, she stopped, dis-mayed. Of a sudden she uttered a shriek and fell back into the room, back, back, clasping her hands to her neck and struggling to cry out. I guessed the reason instantly—Belleville had seized her by the throat. I sprang to her assistance, but paused again—by a miracle, in time—just across the threshold. Miss Ottley—I shall not, cannot call her Mrs. Belleville, though, indeed, she was—went spinning across the room, free, I saw. I slipped along the wall beside the lintel and waited, holding breath. What next? The door slammed and the bolt shot in answer to my question. Then came a long si-lence. Miss Ottley stood beside the farthest wall, supporting herself on the back of a saddle-bag chair, a picture of horror and fear per-sonified. I would have given all the world for liberty to soothe her fears, to take her in my arms and comfort her. But it was not to be. Everything depended on my cunning and my silence. Tearing my glances from her ashen face, I looked around the room. It was her bedroom. The bed occupied one corner. Beside the canopy was an open window through which the light streamed in, striking full upon the door. Against another wall stood a Duchesse toilet table and a huge bemirrored clothes chest of carven ivory and ebony. The floor was covered with a thick pile carpet of dark crimson hue. The window curtains were of purple velvet. The bed's canopy of crimson silk. The walls were painted black and gold. It was, indeed, a mourning chamber.

"Who is it—who is it?" gasped the white-faced, black-robed mourner. I glanced at her again and saw that one hand was pressed tightly to her side.

No answer coming, she repeated her demand with more composure. Then a curious thing happened. A board creaked, and looking swiftly at the floor, I saw the imprint of a foot marked in the pile. It vanished and the pile sprang up again resiliently, but, twenty inches farther onward towards the girl, a second sole-shaped hollow formed itself and there remained. An instant's flashing search disclosed three others. I now knew for certain the position of my enemies, and with a wild heart-throb of joy I nerved myself for action. The shape of the footmarks showed me that both men faced the girl, and that they were standing about a yard apart. With two noiseless strides, I stepped behind the rearmost. Then I stooped and seized a pair of hard, lean thighs and heaved a body up and sent it hurling through the air above the second set of footprints. "I've got you again, you dog!" I cried; then stepped back swift and noiseless to my former place. The trick was perfectly successful. Silent, save for their heavy breathing and the trembling of their feet, the rascals writhed and stamped about the room, locked, doubtless, in a close embrace, although I could not see them. As for me, I slipped presently to a chair, caught it up, and guided by a sound, I brought it crashing down upon the head of one of them. There followed a heavy groan, then a dagger blade flashed out of nothingness and once, twice, thrice, it rose and fell. Murder was being done before my eyes, but I had only half a mind to stay it, and indeed, before I could the knife had vanished into mist again, and all to be seen was a dark flow of scarlet fluid that welled in air and sank upon the carpet.

I waited spellbound. Which was alive—which was dead?

Belleville's voice put the question at rest suddenly. "Well done, Ptahmes," he gasped in Arabic. "He had me throttled when you struck. You shall have fifty pounds for this day's work."

"Thanks, good master." I returned and edged towards his voice. But at that moment Miss Ottley fell in a swoon, and death could hardly have availed to keep me from her side. With a bound I was across the room, and in another second she was in my arms.

Belleville must have seen, but thinking me the Arab, instead of chiding, he commended me. "Carry her to the laboratory," he commanded. "I'll follow with this carrion. We must dispose of it. Nay, wait. I'll go first. Damn him, how he bleeds!" he added in English. Then a little later, "He is wonderfully light for so tall and strong a man."

By then he must have had the Arab's body in his arms. I heard heavy footfalls stamping to the door. Carrying my burden, I followed them. The door opened and we both passed out. I hated the thought of taking my sweetheart to that room of horror, but I could not bear to leave her where she had been so terrified, to recover by herself. And in the next place I did not dare to let Belleville even for a moment out of my reach. He would soon be bound to discover his mistake and then the fight would be renewed with the advantage all on his side, since he was armed with a weapon, which, it was evident, he could conceal till the time came for using it. Prudence demanded that I should seize and disarm Belleville before his suspicions became excited. Prudence also demanded that I should leave my sweetheart somewhere on the journey. But I could not bring myself to do the latter, her face so near to mine, her breath upon my lips. That is why I went to the laboratory, and why I took her with me.

CHAPTER TWENTY-NINE

SAVED BY FIRE

BELLEVILLE'S FIRST ACT, after tossing the Arab's corpse upon the floor and bolting the laboratory door, was to rush over to the couch and remove therefrom the mummy of Ptahmes. This he placed with careful haste upon a marble slab, and he commanded me, in Arabic, meanwhile, to carry the lady to the couch. I obeyed him in silence. He then ordered me to take up the body of the Englishman, Pinsent, and bring it to the sarcophagus. This gave me an opportunity to examine the Arab. I did so, and found him quite dead. Belleville's dagger had twice pierced his heart. I then raised the corpse and carried it to the great lead coffin. "What next, master?" I asked in guttural Arabic.

Belleville's voice answered from behind me. "Lift the carrion up! That is well. Now let it slip into the bath! Gently, Ptahmes, gently—or the stuff will splash. Here—I will help you."

"Where?" I demanded. I was trying to locate him.

"Wait," he replied—then "Here!" His voice sounded from across the sarcophagus.

A second later his hand brushed one of mine and passed. "I'll take the shoulders," he said. "You take the feet! Be careful, man—gently, gently!"

It was maddening to be so near and yet so far. But there was nothing for it except to follow his directions. I, therefore, grasped the corpse firmly by the ankles, when the greater weight of it had been transferred, and then I watched the great blood clot upon its chest—the only visible sign of its existence—sink down, down to the liquid contents of the coffin. Soon it rested there like a crimson lily on the surface of a pond. I let my fingers loose their hold and the unseen limbs of the corpse subsided on the liquid with an oily swish. The whole corpse seemed to be floating. Belleville realised this as soon as I. "Wait here!" he said to me—then added in English, speaking to himself, "Where the deuce did I put that glass rod? Ah! I remember." Then I heard the thud of his retreating steps, and a

174

little later I saw waveringly approaching me from across the room, apparently of its own volition, a long, glass, solid bar, about four feet long and an inch thick. I was overjoyed at the sight, for my hands were free, Belleville could not see me, and the glass rod informed me exactly of his whereabouts. Quick as thought, I slipped around the sarcophagus and, making a little detour, got behind the murderer. He went straight to the coffin and plunged the rod within it. Doubtless he was using it to submerge the corpse. I heard a hissing, bubbling sound, and Belleville saying, "Watch me closely, Ptahmes—for this is what you must do."

I crept upon him until I could hear his breathing quite distinctly, although he was not greatly exerting himself. Then came the time to act. "My God!" he suddenly exclaimed—"not Pinsent— Ptahmes —what's this?"

The glass rod was still. It stood bolt upright in the sarcophagus, and so rigidly motionless that I guessed Belleville's weight was leaning on it. I gave a swift glance into the coffin and almost shrieked with surprise. The liquid had made the dead Arab visible again, and his death-mask grinned up at us with a fixed and blood-curdling stare. On instant I opened my arms wide and threw them round my unseen enemy. He uttered a howl of rage and terror and turned within my grasp to fight me, biting and clawing like a savage beast. But very soon I mastered him. Disregarding his ani-mal-like efforts, I seized him by the throat and beat his skull upon the edge of the sarcophagus until he had quite ceased to struggle. Then, anxious, of all things, to make sure of him by seeing him, I heaved him up and allowed him to slide headforemost down into the bath beside the Arab he had murdered in mistake for me. I reasoned that since the liquid there had made the Arab visible, it should produce a like effect on Belleville. But I was utterly un-prepared for the result. The stuff must have been an acid of tre-mendous power. It awakened the senseless wretch to almost instant tortured consciousness. A series of dreadful shrieks filled the room with strange detonating echoes. Belleville was no sooner in the coffin than out of it and visible in part. His face and hands were plainly to be seen. They came out white and dripping wet, but a few seconds' contact with the air turned them red as blood. I seized the glass rod to defend myself, expecting an attack. But there was no need to use it. The shrieking wretch staggered down the room to the first dispensing cabinet. He tore the door open and clutched at a big phial, the contents of which he poured upon his hands and splashed upon his face, wailing all the while like a lost soul in the depths of

Hell. Happily he did not keep this up for long. The drug that he applied to his hurts, whatever it was, must have salved them, for in a moment or two his heart-rending outcries subsided to a deep, low sobbing. Even that, however, was more than I could stand. I wanted Belleville dead, but I could not endure the sight and sound of his agony—agony that I, unwittingly, had caused.

"Belleville," I called out, "can I help you?"

He gasped and caught his breath, turning his face towards me. To my surprise it was no longer scarlet. It had caught the hue of leather, and the eyes were mantling purple at the whites.

"I did not know the stuff was acid," I continued. "If there is anything I can do to soothe your suffering, I shall and gladly."

"You dog!" said he. "You've ruined me and now you are gloating over your handiwork."

With that, he put his hand in his bosom and began to steal in my direction. I remembered his concealed dagger and called out, "Be warned, Belleville—I can see you. Your dagger will not help you."

"Oh! Oh! Oh!" he groaned, and stopped short.

"Hugh Pinsent's voice—oh, Heaven!" cried Miss Ottley —behind me. She had awakened from her swoon.

I swung on heel and watched her rise. "Hugh!" she sighed. "Hugh—where are you, dear?" Then she saw Belleville, and the hideous apparition he presented, a black pain-tortured face hovering in mid-air, with two dark, ghostly hands outstretched before it, froze her blood. Mercifully, she swooned again and fell back senseless on the lounge. Belleville recommenced his moaning, and began walking up and down wringing his hands. I stood silent, lost in thought and wondering what I ought to do. Belleville told me. He stopped on a sudden and called my name twice, "Pinsent, Pinsent."

"Here!" said I.

"I am at your mercy now," he muttered, in a broken voice. "I'm blind."

"What!" I cried.

"Ay," said he, "and my facial extremities are dying fast—pah! my nose is already dead; look." He put up one hand to his face and before my eyes broke off his nose and tossed it on the floor. It snapped like a piece of tinder, leaving a black, ugly stump.

Next he plucked the dagger from his breast—or rather, from where his bosom seemed to be—and cast it on the floor. I was speechless with horror and surprise.

"Now that you have naught to fear from me," he groaned, "if you have a heart in your breast you will help to end my pain."

"Anything, anything—only tell me how!" I cried, advancing towards him as I spoke. But hearing me approaching, he shouted out for me to stop. "Don't come near me!" he wailed. "Don't touch me—or I shall try to murder you—I'll not be able to prevent myself—and I want to undo some of the ill I've done before I die."

I halted. "But what then shall I do?" I asked.

"Light the asbestos fire. You'll find matches in the table drawer. I am perishing of cold, that is the only thing that will soothe the anguish I am going through. Oh! be quick, be quick!"

I flew to obey him, and in a moment I had set the stove ablaze. Belleville found his way to it as if by instinct, and stooping down, he pressed his awful-looking face against the bars, groaning in a way that made my very flesh creep. "Yes—yes, I'm blind," he kept muttering, between his moans. "And very soon I shall be dead. I must atone. I must atone."

"Belleville," I said at last—I forced myself to say it, for his face had grown ink-black, "are you not wasting precious time? Is there not something I can get to counteract the acid? It appears to—"

"Hush!" he interrupted. "There is nothing. It is eating into my brain. Besides, I am blind and do not wish to live. But let me think. This pain—I cannot use my wits—it dazes me! Ah! now! I must. I must. How can I die with all—Pinsent! Pinsent!"

His voice was a piercing scream.

"Yes—yes," I answered. I was shaking like a reed.

"Is there not a big jar of yellow spirit near the coffin somewhere?"

"Yes."

"Then, for God's sake, lead me to it."

I caught him by the hand and guided him forthwith to the jar.

"Take out the stopper," he entreated. I did so and thereupon he plunged his hands into the vessel and began to lave his neck and face, sobbing raucously the while. The odour of the stuff, however, was so nauseous to me that I stepped back in order to escape it.

Belleville seemed to know at once. "Pinsent!" he cried, "where are you?"

"Here," said I.

"Go and wake her, my wife!" he muttered suddenly. "I have something to tell you both before I go. I am dying fast."

I hastened to do his bidding, but before I reached Miss Ottley's side I was arrested by a loud thudding crash. Turning swiftly, I saw that Belleville had overturned the jar. Its contents had already flooded the floor. He hovered over with a lighted vesta in one of his black hands.

"What are you doing?" I demanded.

He stooped floorwards with the match and instantly a mighty flame shot up that licked the very roof. "Revenge!" he shrieked. "Revenge! I've fooled you, Pinsent, fooled you. Now we all shall die together. Look!" With that, he steeped both hands in the burning fluid and, flitting like a salamander through the flames, he made for the sarcophagus. I could not have stayed him had I wished, for there was a sea of fire between us. But in good truth I was too dazed for the while, at least, to move a muscle. Reaching the great lead tomb, the dreadful flaming object that had once been Belleville thrust his lambent hands into the coffin. There followed an explosion of appalling fury. A mass of brilliant, white, combustible shot up with a mighty roar from the sarcophagus to the ceiling. It pierced the padded lining like a thunderbolt and flashed into the room above. But on its impact with the ceiling it also splashed a rain of fire about the great laboratory. In two seconds the whole place ran with flames. By a miracle I was not touched. But it was not so with Miss Ottley. Her skirt was ablaze. I rushed forward and tore the thing off in strips before it burnt her—then seizing her in my arms, I made like a madman to the door. A hideous burning object lay before it shrieking sulphurous curses. It was Belleville. But he had come to the end of his strength and he could not stay me. The catch yielded to my hand and I dashed into the passage half blinded with fire and smoke, but safe. I did not rest until I had reached the staircase. Miss Ottley was then awake. She struggled in my arms, so I set her down and faced her. But she did not see me. Her dress was smouldering in places. She seemed utterly bewildered. A woman ran up to her and began to put out the burning patches with her hands. The house was in an uproar. Servants—they were all either Arabs or Nubians—ran hither and thither shouting and screaming in a panic. The woman, evidently a nurse, who attended to Miss Ottley, was the only white person to be seen. She was evidently terrified, but she did not lose her head. She kept asking Miss Ottley in French to explain what had happened. Nobody seemed aware that the house was on fire. They had all been merely alarmed by the noises they had heard. Miss Ottley in the middle of it all began to weep. She was thoroughly upset and ill, and I perceived at once that she was on the verge of a mental and physical collapse. In the circumstances, I judged it best to remain a silent onlooker of events and not to take any action unless there arose a real necessity. It was plain that I was still in-

visible. And as for the house being on fire, I deemed it utterly de-
sirable that it should burn down to the last shaving and thus fittingly
entomb in its destruction the ghastly tragedy of the laboratory. The
issue tallied largely with my wishes. The fire was seen first from the
street. There followed a veritable pandemonium. The coloured
servants fled like cowards for their lives, and in an incredibly short
space of time the house was in the hands of firemen and police.
Miss Ottley was taken by the nurse out into the street and there
questioned by a sergeant. But she was quite unable to answer his
insistent queries satisfactorily. All she could say was that she had
been a long time ill. She had fainted in her room that afternoon, and
Dr. Belleville or someone had carried her to the laboratory. When
she woke up she had heard a frightful noise. She supposed it was
one of the Doctor's experiments. She thought she had fainted again,
but she remembered nothing more until she found herself with her
dress on fire at the foot of the staircase. She could not explain how
she got there. The sergeant was civil enough to her, but the fool, in
his fussy officiousness, overlooked her weak condition, and the girl
broke down and utterly collapsed before he realised his quite unnecessary cruelty. The worst of it was that the French nurse had
disappeared during the colloquy. There was, therefore, no woman at
hand to attend to my poor sweetheart. Fortunately, however, a
physician appeared opportunely on the scene, and at his direction
she was immediately conveyed to a hospital. After she had gone, I
did not tarry very long. Choosing a place where the cordoned crowd
was thinnest, I slipped back through the park railings, over which I
climbed and dropped into the park, feeling the weight of my invisibility acutely. From this vantage point I watched the conflagra-
tion for a while. The house was manifestly doomed. Indeed, the
efforts of the firemen were entirely directed to save adjoining
buildings. A hundred jets of water played upon the walls of these in
thin continuous streams. Men about me were talking the matter over
as if it personally appealed to them. They mostly viewed it with a
sort of half-secret satisfaction. The misfortunes of millionaires do
not excite much sympathy in the hearts of the mob.

One man glibly quoted, "Lay not up unto yourselves treasures in
this world!" on the occasion of a grimy fireman bringing out a
magnificent but half-destroyed silver-framed canvas of Velasquez.
But the crowd cheered the fireman for his pluck all the same. At
length I realised that I was very tired, and hungry, too, so I slunk off
and made my way to Dixon Hubbard's rooms. They were locked, of
course, and I had not the key. I had left it with the porter of the

building. But I could not go to him and ask him to give it up to an apparently fleshless voice. Wondering what to do, I crept into the passage, sat down in a corner underneath the stairs and waited for an inspiration. Waiting there, I fell asleep.

CHAPTER THIRTY

THE LAST

I AWOKE IN the grey light of dawn, stiff with cold and aching in every limb. Arising, I left my hiding-place and went into the vestibule. The night porter sat on a stool in his little office toasting his toes before the stove and reading one of the morning papers. I stepped up to the door at once. Hearing my footsteps, he looked around. "Good-morning, Michael," I said, as well as my chattering teeth would let me. "Do you want all that fire?" I had forgotten that I was completely invisible. The fellow sprang to his feet with a start and stared at me aghast. "What's the matter with you?" I demanded, testily.

" 'Ere—you keep off. I've done nothing to 'arm you!" he whined, and he backed before my advance against the wall of the office, the very picture of abject terror. His appearance recalled me to my senses. But it was too late to cry over spilt milk. I thought it better to make a confidant of the man if he would let me.

"Don't be frightened, Michael; there is no need. I'm not a ghost, feel my hands!" I said.

But panic seized the fellow. He uttered a wild shriek and fled for his life into the passage. I could hardly help laughing, but I saw a chance in the contretemps to end my immediate difficulty—so I went straight to the desk, and fortunately found it open. In Hubbard's pigeon-hole was the key I wanted. I took it out, caught up a *Times* and hurried up the stairs. In another moment I was safe in Hubbard's room with the door locked against intrusion. My first care was to set the asbestos ablaze and warm myself. Then I opened the paper and found at once the news I sought under great cross headlines in the main sheet. Miss Ottley's house had been completely gutted by fire. Some of the walls still stood, but with the exception of a few pictures, the whole of the valuable art furniture and the late Sir Robert Ottley's splendid collection of Egyptian coins, manuscripts and curios had been destroyed. It was supposed that Dr. Belleville had perished in the flames, but no sign of his remains had been discovered. The fire, as far as it was possible to ascertain, had arisen from an accident due to the unsuccessful conduct of a chemical experiment. It was well known in scientific circles, said the journal, that the Doctor had been engaged in a series of experiments, the object of which had been kept a close secret, but a city firm of manufacturing chemists had recently supplied him with large quantities of a certain highly inflammable liquid compound possessing radio activities which had been prepared at enormous cost, under his directions. The manager of the firm, on being interviewed, stated that in his opinion, this compound was principally responsible for the tragic disaster. There was always a danger in handling it of spontaneous combustion, it appeared, and if it once took fire, by no means could it be extinguished except by the shutting off of all supplies of oxygen. Failing this, it would burn to the last with the most explosive energy. According to Miss Ottley's statement, when first interrogated by an officer from Scotland Yard, she had been in the laboratory with Dr. Belleville at the time of the catastrophe. She had lately been very ill and it seems she had fainted. It was extremely probable that the Doctor, in his anxiety to revive her, had neglected his usual caution and had done some careless thing which had led to his destruction. Probably he had been killed outright by the first explosion. It was, however, a matter of general relief that Miss Ottley had managed to escape, and that there had been no further sacrifice of life. Everyone would sympathise with the unfortunate young lady in her sad position. Only a few weeks ago the gallant young officer to whom she had been engaged to be married, had come to an untimely end in a railway accident on the very eve of his wedding day. Then, a little later, the dark angel had deprived her of a loving and beloved father, the great millionaire archæologist, whose recent operations on 'Change had startled the world, and made of him the richest man in the United Kingdom. And now, she had lost by death the kind and learned guardian to whom her late father had entrusted her future and the management of her enormous fortune. Nobody would be surprised to learn that this great accumulation of calamities had reduced the fate-stricken young lady to a state of utter physical prostration. She had been taken yesterday evening, after her rescue from the burning mansion, to the Albert Hospital, but she had subsequently been removed to the Walsingham Hotel, where the management had placed a suite of rooms at her disposal. She was there being treated under the care of Drs. Fiaschi and Mason, the well-known heart and nerve specialists. These gentlemen express themselves hopeful of her ultimate recovery, but they do not conceal the fact that she is at present in a very low condition, and it is significant that the road in front of the hotel was, in the small hours of the morning, thickly overspread with tan.

This last paragraph, as may easily be conceived, filled me with anxiety. I resolved to go at once to the Walsingham Hotel and find out exactly how she was for myself. But, fortunately, in moving towards the door to put my purpose into execution, I had to pass the mirror-backed door of a clothes press. I did not pass it then. I stopped, spellbound. I was no longer invisible. That is to say, my face and hands were not—although my body was. The mirror showed me a head floating apparently in mid-air and a pair of hands hanging mysteriously from nothing. My eyes were curiously goggled with a thin, gelatinous-like film, with a glassy surface that was bound about my head. This I tore off forthwith and curiously examined. It was actually composed of gelatine. Tossing it aside, I ran my fingers over my clothing and discovered, from the sense of touch, that I was clad to the neck in one unbroken combination suit of rubber overalls, which included footgear. I soon made out the secret of its fastening, and tearing it open, I stepped forth into the light of day and perfect visibility, to find that I still had on all the clothes I had worn when Dr. Belleville trapped me, except my boots. The overalls, however, remained visible, or rather partially so, for their inner surface viewed from the opening was discernible. I put them carefully aside for future investigation and proceeded to make a toilet. My first care was a hot bath. The hall porter, whom I had frightened so desperately a little while before, answered my ring. He was astounded to see me, but I did not choose to make him any explanations, and he was too overcome to ask me for any. A little later I was luxuriating in a steaming bath, which removed the last vestige of my Parisian disguise. Most of the paint, however, had worn off before, so it was the easier to become myself again. But not quite my old, familiar self. My experiences had permanently aged me. There were lines upon my face that I was stranger to, and with which I made reluctant acquaintance. And my hair was liberally streaked with grey. I had put on ten years, at least. I felt old, too, that was the worst of it—old, ill and thick-blooded and infinitely world-weary. I felt a hunger for the desert and big open spaces; a need to hasten from the grinding, selfish life of cities, with their secret crimes and gilded vices and dull-herded groping after sordid happiness. But I did not wish to go alone. At a little after eight o'clock I entered the Walsingham and demanded to see Miss

Ottley's head nurse. She was at breakfast, but the waiter told me that Miss Ottley had spent a good night and was still asleep, so I was content to wait. Afterwards, I had to lie to the nurse in order to be permitted to see the invalid. I told her that I was Miss Ottley's nearest living relative, and I suppressed the fact of my medical qualifications. The woman, otherwise, would have referred me to the physicians, who had employed her, and I should have been put off for hours. As it was, it required all my powers of persuasion to induce her to admit me to the sick room. But I prevailed on her at last, with a show of stern authority, and a curt intimation that her position depended on my complaisance. The falsehood is not one that I feel any shame at, for I knew what an effect my appearance would make in the patient, and I was determined, at all costs, to be with her at the moment of her waking. I shall pass over the preliminary period that I spent beside her bed. It is too full of sorrow to recall with anything but misery. The poor girl was as frail and wan as any spirit. They had cut off all her glorious hair, and the hand I kissed, which lay so weakly on the coverlid, was whiter than a snowflake, and almost as destitute of vigour. She slept as gently as a weary babe, and it was hard at first to believe thoroughly she lived. But at length she sighed and her great eyes slowly opened and looked up questioningly into mine. She thought that she was dead and that my ghost had sought her out. "Hugh!" she whispered, and a soft smile lighted her face and made it infinitely lovely, though so wan. "I knew that I should find you, dear," she sighed. "And so I could not help but pray to die. Will God punish us for that?"

But I kissed her on the lips—the first long kiss of love that I had known—or she—and she came back warm with quickened hope and will to live within my arms. And all was well with us.

There is little more to tell. As soon as she was strong again we married quietly, and now we live in a place where crowded cities are unknown—far from old England's shores. I never again saw Belleville's Arab servant, who so marvellously resembled the old High Priest of Amen-Ra; nor his companion, the Nubian, Uromi. They disappeared after the fire, and not all the efforts of the police could trace their hiding-place. The invisible suit of overalls is still in my possession—but it had lost its old mysterious properties, and although I expended months of patient labour to explore its secret, it was all in vain. To this day I cannot tell who released me from the chair in which Belleville had bound me in the murderer's laboratory. And I am still unable to explain the many other little mysteries that so involved us in the period of our contention with the wretch, the fatal termination of whose wicked scheming I have set forth in these pages. The greater part of Sir Robert Ottley's fortune has been given to the poor. The rest we settled on my wife's sole living blood relation, the old bed-ridden aunt, whom she has never seen. We both felt that we should be doing well to dispose of riches that—to an extent, at least—must have been acquired by arts of sinister significance. Still, we have never wanted, and we are not likely to. My profession yields us a comfortable living in these grand but sparsely settled wilds. And, although we sometimes think regretfully upon the delight we once experienced in searching out the lettered past of long-dead centuries, we have other interests now to fill our lives and banish vain regrets. We have our growing children to attend to and provide for. We are of real service to the people who surround us, for my wife is the schoolmistress of the district, and I am the only surgeon in a radius of one hundred miles. Then, we have our books and our long evenings together in the splendid twilight of the endless plains. We have given up the past for the future. And we are happy in our labour and our love.

THE END

Some contemporary reviews of

The Living Mummy

Herald, (Melbourne, Australia), Thursday, 8 December 1910

It is regrettable that Mr. Ambrose Pratt should so frequently exercise his skilful pen in the realm of sensational fiction, but when that is said it has to be admitted that his melodramatic stories are interesting, and sometimes exciting. He has gone to Egypt, the land of mystery, for the plot of his new book, though the scenes of the most blood-curdling incidents are laid in London. The "Living Mummy" is used for criminal purposes by his discoverer and his colleague. The horrors in the closing chapters are rather sickening.

Advertiser, Adelaide, Saturday, 7 January, 1911

With power to make himself and others (with their will or not) invisible, is there any limit to the mischief a villain like Dr. Belleville might do? Apparently not, judging from "The Living Mummy." Getting in tow with Sir Robert Ottley, a great Egyptologist, he acquires a good deal of occult knowledge concerning the old shepherd kings of the Nile, and with the mummy of one he makes great play. The revivified corpse obeys his summons much as did the genii of Aladdin's lamp, and at his bidding commits no end of murders. Belleville's aim is to marry Helen Ottley, and he makes away with all who stand in his path. His mummified servant, attired in the mantle of invisibility, grapples with the victim, and either kills him with his invisible hands or puts him in the way of being killed, as was the case with poor Weldon, whom Belleville erroneously suspects as a rival. He is seen to struggle on the edge of the platform, and then to fall under the wheels of an approaching train. The horrified onlookers not seeing his assailant suppose that he has gone mad or has had a fit. In the end Belleville meets the tragic death he has so long deserved, and the hero appropriates Helen. Not for years have we read a romance with so many thrills in each chapter.

Western Mail (Perth, WA), Saturday, 31 December 1910

In many of its details this novel of Mr. Pratt's is of the gruesome sort. Its creepiness is suggestive of Rider Haggard's "She." Its weirdness recalls the days of witchcraft. There is a love affair which was no doubt intended as a sweetener of the whole, but its effect is small in competition with resurrected Egyptian mummies and Arabian ghosts.

It may at once be said that the novel is powerfully written. The skill to plot and the art to describe are both shown to be possessed by the author in a high degree. The atmosphere of the story, so long as the author sojourns in Egypt, seems perfect. It is just possible that when the scene is removed to England the atmosphere is rather too Egyptian for even a modicum of probability to assert itself. Despite that, the tale is a clever one and will appeal to readers who enjoy intricate plots, daring deeds, and a mystery—like life itself—that is never solved.

The narrator of the tale and Sir Robert Ottley were Egyptologists, both sojourning in Egypt at the same time; the one deciphering inscriptions, the other in search of a mummy:—

It was hard work in my tent. I had almost completed translating the inscription of a small stele of Amen-Hotep III., dated B.C. 1382, which with my own efforts I had discovered, and I was feeling wonderfully self-satisfied in consequence, when of a sudden I heard a great commotion without. Almost immediately the tent flap was lifted, and Migdal Abu's black face appeared. He looked vastly excited for an Arab, and he rolled his eyes horribly. "What do you want?" I demanded irritably. "Did I not tell you I was not to be disturbed?"

Sir Robert Ottley, his daughter May, and a dozen of Arabs had arrived. The men who were to be inveterate rivals met for the first time.

It appears Sir Robert had been disappointed in not recovering the mummy of Ptahmes, and, in conjunction with a Dr. Belleville, he began to make mummies. He had discovered in a tomb an essential oil with wonderful possibilities for mummy making. Sir Robert took a severe illness, and the relater of the tale—Dr. Pinsent— nursed him back to life. While in Sir Robert's camp Dr. Pinsent became aware of the oil discovery, and his life from that moment was in danger. Sir Robert experimented on an Arab with the oil, and was able to secure suspended animation for an indefinite period. Then comes an account of Dr. Pinsent's capture of the launch and punt with the mummy, the mummy's escape and Pinsent's escape, and the scene is changed to London, where the deeds are still more diabolical. It harmonises with the plan of the story to have the assistance of spiritualistic mediums in London to try [to] unravel many of the incidents. A medium accurately describes the mummy:—

> It is apparently the body of a man of latter middle age. It is of great proportions. It is almost seven feet in length. But the body is very lank and shrunken and ill-nourished. The nose is long and hooked like the beak of an eagle. The eyes are closed. The mouth is shriveled and almost shapeless. The chin is long and pointed. The skin is dark brown, almost black. On the feet are fastened rubber shoes, on the soles of which are particles of dried mud.

All this results from Sir Robert's discovery in the tomb of Ptahmes:—

> This secret is one which teaches its possessors how to control the forces of Nature, in a manner any imagination can only guess at. They have learned how to override the laws of light, not only rendering opaque objects transparent, but positively invisible.

Register, Adelaide, Saturday, 10 December 1910

Black Magic

Is Mr. Pratt also among the Americans? It may happen to an Australian journalist, to have his book printed in U.S.A.; but why should he write of "my first pipe in three days," of "cooling off," and of "well people"? Why should he make his English characters say "sweet as pie," or "going blind on my say-so"? The only reference to this country is dragged in thus:— "It's another of those spook mediums of his. He would shelter Hill, or even that Australian wife-murderer Deeming, if they said they were mediums." For the rest, the story is of a familiar type—excavation in Egypt, with adventures thrown in, a mysterious 'find,' an uncanny Presence moving in London, a brilliant, unscrupulous man of science. "My dear enemy, I am just an ordinary human being who has been seduced by the most extraordinary temptation that has ever been offered to a human being. A power has been placed at my disposal which puts me on a level with the immortal gods of Ancient Greece. In deciding to make use of it I have adopted their ideas of morality almost, as it were, perforce. I intend henceforth to kill always what I hate, to possess what I love, to seize what I covet, and to enjoy what I desire." And so to a grimly sensational climax in a laboratory, with half-understood supernatural forces playing their part in the physical struggle of hero and miscreant. The heroine promised at first to have something uncommon. The man who loved her called her "impenetrable, a female anachronism. She belonged of right to the age of iron." But when the struggle began she became merely the usual feminine pawn in the game. The story is brisk and always readable, and it has some odd, striking illustrations in colours.

RAMBLE HOUSE's

HARRY STEPHEN KEELER WEBWORK MYSTERIES

(RH) indicates the title is available ONLY in the RAMBLE HOUSE edition

Keeler Related Works

A To Izzard: A Harry Stephen Keeler Companion by Fender Tucker—Articles and stories about Harry, by Harry, and in his style. Included is a compleat bibliography.

Wild About Harry: Reviews of Keeler Novels—Edited by Richard Polt & Fender Tucker—22 reviews of works by Harry Stephen Keeler from *Keeler News*. A perfect introduction to the author.

The Keeler Keyhole Collection: Annotated newsletter rants from Harry Stephen Keeler, edited by Francis M. Nevins. Over 400 pages of incredibly personal Keeleriana.

Fakealoo—Pastiches of the style of Harry Stephen Keeler by selected demented members of the HSK Society. Updated every year with the new winner.

Strands of the Web: Short Stories of Harry Stephen Keeler—29 stories, just about all that Keeler wrote, are edited and introduced by Fred Cleaver.

RAMBLE HOUSE's LOON SANCTUARY

A Clear Path to Cross—Sharon Knowles short mystery stories by Ed Lynskey.

A Corpse Walks in Brooklyn and Other Stories—Volume 5 in the Day Keene in the Detective Pulps series.

A Fair Californian—Novel by Olive Harper about a young woman's quest for gold — a quest that turns into something completely unexpected.

A Jimmy Starr Omnibus—Three 40s novels by Jimmy Starr.

A Niche in Time and Other Stories—Classic SF by William F. Temple.

A Shot Rang Out—Three decades of reviews and articles by today's Anthony Boucher, Jon Breen. An essential book for any mystery lover's library.

A Snark Selection—Lewis Carroll's *The Hunting of the Snark* with two Snarkian chapters by Harry Stephen Keeler—Illustrated by Gavin L. O'Keefe.

A Young Man's Heart—A forgotten early classic by Cornell Woolrich.

Alexander Laing Novels—*The Motives of Nicholas Holtz* and *Dr. Scarlett*, stories of medical mayhem and intrigue from the 30s.

An Angel in the Street—Modern hardboiled noir by Peter Genovese.

Automaton—Brilliant treatise on robotics: 1928-style! By H. Stafford Hatfield.

Away From the Here and Now—Clare Winger Harris stories, collected by Richard A. Lupoff

Beast or Man?—A 1930 novel of racism and horror by Sean M'Guire. Introduced by John Pelan.

Black Hogan Strikes Again—Australia's Peter Renwick pens a tale of the 30s outback.

Black River Falls—Suspense from the master, Ed Gorman.

Blondy's Boy Friend—A snappy 1930 story by Philip Wylie, writing as Leatrice Homesley.

Blood in a Snap—The *Finnegan's Wake* of the 21st century, by Jim Weiler.

Blood Moon—The first of the Robert Payne series by Ed Gorman.

Bogart '48—Hollywood action with Bogie by John Stanley and Kenn Davis

Butterfly Man—1930s novel by Lew Levenson about a dancer who must come to terms with his homosexuality.

Calling Lou Largo!—Two Lou Largo novels by William Ard.

Cathedral of Horror—First volume of collected stories by weird fiction writer Arthur J. Burks.

Chalk Face—Curious supernatural murder thriller by Waldo Frank.

Circus-Show—Joseph Delmont's 1931 epic tale of circus life and murder.

Cornucopia of Crime—Francis M. Nevins assembled this huge collection of his writings about crime literature and the people who write it. Essential for any serious mystery library.

Corpse Without Flesh—Strange novel of forensics by George Bruce

Crimson Clown Novels—By Johnston McCulley, author of the Zorro novels, *The Crimson Clown* and *The Crimson Clown Again*.

Dago Red—22 tales of dark suspense by Bill Pronzini.

Dark Sanctuary—Weird Menace story by H. B. Gregory.

David Hume Novels—*Corpses Never Argue, Cemetery First Stop, Make Way for the Mourners, Eternity Here I Come*. 1930s British hardboiled fiction with an attitude.

David&Son: Peregrine Parentus and other tales—Collection of tales and memoirs by Avram Davidson and Ethan Davidson, some published for the first time. Introduced by Grania Davidson Davis.

Dead Man Talks Too Much—Hollywood boozer by Weed Dickenson.

Death in a Bowl—1930's murder mystery by Raoul Whitfield.

Death March of the Dancing Dolls and Other Stories—Volume Three in the Day Keene in the Detective Pulps series. Introduced by Bill Crider.

Deep Space and other Stories—A collection of SF gems by Richard A. Lupoff.

Detective Duff Unravels It—Episodic mysteries by Harvey O'Higgins.

Devil's Planet—Locked room mystery set on the planet Mars, by Manly Wade Wellman.

Dime Novels: Ramble House's 10-Cent Books—*Knife in the Dark* by Robert Leslie Bellem, *Hot Lead* and *Song of Death* by Ed Earl Repp, *A Hashish House in New York* by H.H. Kane, and five more.

Doctor Arnoldi—Tiffany Thayer's story of the death of death.

Don Diablo: Book of a Lost Film—Two-volume treatment of a western by Paul Landres, with diagrams. Intro by Francis M. Nevins.

Dope and Swastikas—Two strange novels from 1922 by Edmund Snell

Dope Tales #1—Two dope-riddled classics; *Dope Runners* by Gerald Grantham and *Death Takes the Joystick* by Phillip Condé.

Dope Tales #2—Two more narco-classics; *The Invisible Hand* by Rex Dark and *The Smokers of Hashish* by Norman Berrow.

Dope Tales #3—Two enchanting novels of opium by the master, Sax Rohmer. *Dope* and *The Yellow Claw*.

Double Hot & Double Sex—Two combos of '60s softcore sex novels by Morris Hershman.

Dr. Odin—Douglas Newton's 1933 racial potboiler comes back to life.

E. Charles Vivian—*Evidence in Blue, Accessory After* and *The Lady of the Terraces*.

E.C.R. Lorac—*Black Beadle, The Case in the Clinic, The Devil and the C.I.D.* and *Slippery Staircase*.

E. R. Punshon novels—*Information Received, Crossword Mystery, Dictator's Way, Diabolic Candelabra, Music Tells All, Helen Passes By, The House of Godwinsson, The Golden Dagger, The Attending Truth, Strange Ending, Brought to Light, Dark is the Clue, Triple Quest,* and *Six Were Present*: featuring Bobby Owen.

Ed "Strangler" Lewis: Facts within a Myth—Authoritative illustrated biography of the famous American wrestler Ed Lewis, by noted historian Steve Yohe.

Evangelical Cockroach—Jack Woodford writes about writing.

Fatal Accident—1936 murder-by-automobile mystery by Cecil M. Wills.

Fighting Mad—Todd Robbins' 1922 novel about boxing and life

Five Million in Cash—Gangster thriller by Tiffany Thayer writing as O. B. King.

Food for the Fungus Lady—Collection of weird stories by Ralston Shields, edited and introduced by John Pelan.

Francis M. Nevins—Three omnibus volumes of novels: *Publish and Perish / Corrupt and Ensnare, Into the Same River Twice / Beneficiaries' Requiem* and *The 120-Hour Clock / The Ninety Million Dollar Mouse.*

Freaks and Fantasies—Eerie tales by Tod Robbins, collaborator of Tod Browning on the film FREAKS.

Gadsby—A lipogram (a novel without the letter E). Ernest Vincent Wright's last work, published in 1939 right before his death.

Gelett Burgess Novels—*The Master of Mysteries, The White Cat, Two O'Clock Courage, Ladies in Boxes, Find the Woman, The Heart Line, The Picaroons* and *Lady Mechante*. Recently added is A Gelett Burgess Sampler, edited by Alfred Jan. All are introduced by Richard A. Lupoff.

Geronimo—S. M. Barrett's 1905 autobiography of a noble American.

Gordon Eklund—*Second Creation, Retro Man* and *Stalking the Sun*: three volumes of the author's best short stories.

Go Forth and Multiply—Anthology of science fiction tales of repopulation, edited by Gordon Van Gelder.

Hake Talbot Novels—*Rim of the Pit, The Hangman's Handyman.* Classic locked room mysteries, with mapback covers by Gavin O'Keefe.

Hands Out of Hell and Other Stories—John H. Knox's eerie hallucinations

Hell is a City—William Ard's masterpiece.

Hollywood Dreams—A novel of Tinsel Town and the Depression by Richard O'Brien.

Homicide House—#6 in the Day Keene in the Detective Pulps series.

Hostesses in Hell and Other Stories—Russell Gray's most graphic stories

House of the Restless Dead—Strange and ominous tales by Hugh B. Cave.

Inclination to Murder—1966 thriller by New Zealand's Harriet Hunter.

Invaders from the Dark—Classic werewolf tale from Greye La Spina.

J. Poindexter, Colored—Classic satirical black novel by Irvin S. Cobb.

Jack Mann Novels—Strange murder in the English countryside. *Gees' First Case, Nightmare Farm, Grey Shapes, The Ninth Life, The Glass Too Many, Her Ways Are Death, The Kleinert Case* and *Maker of Shadows.*

Jake Hardy—A lusty western tale from Wesley Tallant.

James Corbett—*Vampire of the Skies, The Ghost Plane, Murder Begets Murder* and *The Air Killer* – strange thriller novels from this singular British author.

Jim Harmon Double Novels—*Vixen Hollow/Celluloid Scandal, The Man Who Made Maniacs/Silent Siren, Ape Rape/Wanton Witch, Sex Burns Like Fire/Twist Session, Sudden Lust/Passion Strip, Sin Unlimited/Harlot Master, Twilight Girls/Sex Institution.* Written in the early 60s and never reprinted until now.

Joel Townsley Rogers Novels and Short Stories—By the author of *The Red Right Hand: Once In a Red Moon, Lady With the Dice, The Stopped Clock, Never Leave My Bed.* Also two short story collections: *Night of Horror* and *Killing Time.*

John Carstairs, Space Detective—Arboreal Sci-fi by Frank Belknap Long

John G. Brandon—*The Case of the Withered Hand, Finger-Prints Never Lie,* and *Death on Delivery*: crime thrillers by Australian author John G. Brandon.

John S. Glasby—Two collections of Glasby's Lovecraftian stories: *The Brooding City* and *Beyond the Rim*. Introduced by John Pelan.

Joseph Shallit Novels—*The Case of the Billion Dollar Body, Lady Don't Die on My Doorstep, Kiss the Killer, Yell Bloody Murder, Take Your Last Look.* One of America's best 50's authors and a favorite of author Bill Pronzini.

Keller Memento—45 short stories of the amazing and weird by Dr. David Keller.

Killer's Caress—Cary Moran's 1936 hardboiled thriller.

Knight Asrael and Other Stories—Collection of fourteen fantasy tales by Una Ashworth Taylor

Knowing the Unknowable: Putting Psi to Work—Damien Broderick, PhD puts forward the valid case for evidence of Psi.

Lady of the Yellow Death and Other Stories—More stories by Wyatt Blassingame.

Laughing Death—1932 Yellow Peril thriller by Walter C. Brown.

League of the Grateful Dead and Other Stories—Volume One in the Day Keene in the Detective Pulps series.

Library of Death—Ghastly tale by Ronald S. L. Harding, introduced by John Pelan

Lords of the Earth—A novel of meddling dabblers in the occult invoking the ancient powers of Atlantis. J.M.A. Mills' sequel to *The Tomb of the Dark Ones.*

Mad-Doctor Merciful—Collin Brooks' unsettling novel of medical experimentation with supernatural forces.

Malcolm Jameson Novels and Short Stories—*Astonishing! Astounding!, Tarnished Bomb, The Alien Envoy and Other Stories* and *The Chariots of San Fernando and Other Stories.* All introduced and edited by John Pelan or Richard A. Lupoff.

Man Out of Hell and Other Stories—Volume II of the John H. Knox weird pulps collection.

Marblehead: A Novel of H.P. Lovecraft—A long-lost masterpiece from Richard A. Lupoff. This is the "director's cut", the long version that has never been published before.

Mark of the Laughing Death and Other Stories—Shockers from the pulps by Francis James, introduced by John Pelan.

Mark Hansom Novels—*Master of Souls, The Ghost of Gaston Revere, The Madman, The Shadow on the House, Sorcerer's Chessmen & The Wizard of Berner's Abbey.*

Max Afford Novels—*Owl of Darkness, Death's Mannikins, Blood on His Hands, The Dead Are Blind, The Sheep and the Wolves, Sinners in Paradise* and *Two Locked Room Mysteries and a Ripping Yarn* by one of Australia's finest mystery novelists.

Miles Burton novels — *A Smell of Smoke, Death Leaves No Card, Situation Vacant* and *Death Paints a Picture.*

Mistress of Terror—Fourth volume of the collected weird tales of Wyatt Blassingame.

Molly and her Man of War— Romantic novel with a difference, by Arabella Kenealy.

Money Brawl—Two books about the writing business by Jack Woodford and H. Bedford-Jones. Introduced by Richard A. Lupoff.

More Secret Adventures of Sherlock Holmes—Gary Lovisi's second collection of tales about the unknown sides of the great detective.

Muddled Mind: Complete Works of Ed Wood, Jr.—David Hayes and Hayden Davis deconstruct the life and works of the mad, but canny, genius.

Murder among the Nudists—1934 mystery by Peter Hunt, featuring a naked Detective-Inspector going undercover in a nudist colony.

Murder in Black and White—1931 classic tennis whodunit by Evelyn Elder.

Murder in Shawnee—Two novels of the Alleghenies by John Douglas: *Shawnee Alley Fire* and *Haunts*.

Murder in Suffolk—A 1938 murder mystery novel by the mysterious 'A. Fielding.'

My Deadly Angel—1955 Cold War drama by John Chelton.

My First Time: The One Experience You Never Forget—Michael Birchwood—64 true first-person narratives of how they lost it.

My Touch Brings Death—Second volume of collected stories by Russell Gray.

Mysterious Martin, the Master of Murder—Two versions of a strange 1912 novel by Tod Robbins about a man who writes books that can kill.

Norman Berrow Novels—*The Bishop's Sword, Ghost House, Don't Go Out After Dark, Claws of the Cougar, The Smokers of Hashish, The Secret Dancer, Don't Jump Mr. Boland!, The Footprints of Satan, Fingers for Ransom, The Three Tiers of Fantasy, The Spaniard's Thumb, The Eleventh Plague, Words Have Wings, One Thrilling Night, The Lady's in Danger, It Howls at Night, The Terror in the Fog, Oil Under the Window, Murder in the Melody, The Singing Room.* This is the complete Norman Berrow library of locked-room mysteries, several of which are masterpieces.

Old Faithful and Other Stories—SF classic tales by Raymond Z. Gallun

Old Times' Sake—Short stories by James Reasoner from Mike Shayne Magazine.

One Dreadful Night—A classic mystery by Ronald S. L. Harding

Pair O' Jacks—A mystery novel and a diatribe about publishing by Jack Woodford

Pawns of Destiny—Psychological drama by Kay Seaton.

Perfect .38—Two early Timothy Dane novels by William Ard. More to come.

Prince Pax—Devilish intrigue by George Sylvester Viereck and Philip Eldridge

Prose Bowl—Futuristic satire of a world where hack writing has replaced football as our national obsession, by Bill Pronzini and Barry N. Malzberg.

Ralph Trevor—*Murder in Silk, Easy for the Crook, Front Page Murder, The Deputy Avenger, The Phantom Raider* and *Invitation to Murder.*

Red Light—The history of legal prostitution in Shreveport Louisiana by Eric Brock. Includes wonderful photos of the houses and the ladies.

Researching American-Made Toy Soldiers—A 276-page collection of a lifetime of articles by toy soldier expert Richard O'Brien.

Reunion in Hell—Volume One of the John H. Knox series of weird stories from the pulps. Introduced by horror expert John Pelan.

Ripped from the Headlines!—The Jack the Ripper story as told in the newspaper articles in the *New York* and *London Times.*

Rough Cut & New, Improved Murder—Ed Gorman's first two novels.

R. R. Ryan Novels — *Freak Museum, The Subjugated Beast, Death of a Sadist, Echo of a Curse, Devil's Shelter* and *No Escape*. Introduced by John Pelan.

Roland Daniel Novels — *Ruby of a Thousand Dreams, The Girl in the Dark,* and *A Roland Daniel Double: The Signal and The Return of Wu Fang.*

Ruled By Radio — 1925 futuristic novel by Robert L. Hadfield & Frank E. Farncombe.

Rupert Penny Novels — *Policeman's Holiday, Policeman's Evidence, Lucky Policeman, Policeman in Armour, Sealed Room Murder, Sweet Poison, The Talkative Policeman, She had to Have Gas* and *Cut and Run* (by Martin Tanner.) Rupert Penny is the pseudonym of Australian Charles Thornett, a master of the locked room, impossible crime plot.

Sacred Locomotive Flies — Richard A. Lupoff's psychedelic SF story.

Sam — Early gay novel by Lonnie Coleman.

Sand's Game — Spectacular hardboiled noir from Ennis Willie, edited by Lynn Myers and Stephen Mertz, with contributions from Max Allan Collins, Bill Crider, Wayne Dundee, Bill Pronzini, Gary Lovisi and James Reasoner.

Sand's War — More violent fiction from the typewriter of Ennis Willie

Satan's Den Exposed — True crime in Truth or Consequences New Mexico — Award-winning journalism by the *Desert Journal.*

Satan's Secret and Selected Stories — Barnard Stacey's only novel with a selection of his best short stories.

Satans of Saturn — Novellas from the pulps by Otis Adelbert Kline and E. H. Price

Satan's Sin House and Other Stories — Horrific gore by Wayne Rogers

Second Creation — The first volume of selected short stories by Gordon Eklund.

Secrets of a Teenage Superhero — Graphic lit by Jonathan Sweet

Sex Slave — Potboiler of lust in the days of Cleopatra by Dion Leclerq, 1966.

Slammer Days — Two full-length prison memoirs: *Men into Beasts* (1952) by George Sylvester Viereck and *Home Away From Home* (1962) by Jack Woodford.

Star Griffin — Michael Kurland's 1987 masterpiece of SF drollery is back.

Stakeout on Millennium Drive — Award-winning Indianapolis Noir by Ian Woollen.

Strands of the Web: Short Stories of Harry Stephen Keeler — Edited and Introduced by Fred Cleaver.

Summer Camp for Corpses and Other Stories — Weird Menace tales from Arthur Leo Zagat; introduced by John Pelan.

Suzy — A collection of comic strips by Richard O'Brien and Bob Vojtko from 1970.

Tail of the Lizard King / Kaliwood — Two novellas by Adam Mudman Bezecny paying homage to the sleaze genre.

Tales of the Macabre and Ordinary — Modern twisted horror by Chris Mikul, author of the *Bizarrism* series.

Tales of Terror and Torment Vols. #1 & #2 — John Pelan selects and introduces these samplers of weird menace tales from the pulps.

Tenebrae — Ernest G. Henham's 1898 horror tale brought back.

The Alice Books — Lewis Carroll's classics *Alice's Adventures in Wonderland* and *Through the Looking-Glass* together in one volume, with new illustrations by O'Keefe.

The Amorous Intrigues & Adventures of Aaron Burr — by Anonymous. Hot historical action about the man who almost became Emperor of Mexico.

The Anthony Boucher Chronicles — edited by Francis M. Nevins. Book reviews by Anthony Boucher written for the *San Francisco Chronicle,* 1942 – 1947. Essential and fascinating reading by the best book reviewer there ever was.

The Barclay Catalogs — Two essential books about toy soldier collecting by Richard O'Brien

The Basil Wells Omnibus — A collection of Wells' stories by Richard A. Lupoff

The Beautiful Dead and Other Stories — Dreadful tales from Donald Dale

The Best of 10-Story Book — edited by Chris Mikul, over 35 stories from the literary magazine Harry Stephen Keeler edited.

The Bitch Wall — Novel about American soldiers in the Vietnam War, based on Dennis Lane's experiences.

The Black Dark Murders — Vintage 50s college murder yarn by Milt Ozaki, writing as Robert O. Saber.

The Book of Time — The classic novel by H.G. Wells is joined by sequels by Wells himself and three stories by Richard A. Lupoff. Illustrated by Gavin L. O'Keefe.

The Broken Fang and Other Experiences of a Specialist in Spooks — Eerie mystery tales by Uel Key.

The Strange Case of the Antlered Man — A mystery of superstition by Edwy Searles Brooks.

The Case of the Bearded Bride — #4 in the Day Keene in the Detective Pulps series.

The Case of the Little Green Men — Mack Reynolds wrote this love song to sci-fi fans back in 1951 and it's now back in print.

The Charlie Chaplin Murder Mystery — A 2004 tribute by noted film scholar, Wes D. Gehring.

The Cloudbuilders and Other Stories — SF tales from Colin Kapp.

The Collected Writings — Collection of science fiction stories, memoirs and poetry by Carol Carr. Introduction by Karen Haber.

The Compleat Calhoon — All of Fender Tucker's works: Includes *Totah Six-Pack, Weed, Women and Song* and *Tales from the Tower,* plus a CD of all of his songs.

The Compleat Ova Hamlet — Parodies of SF authors by Richard A. Lupoff. This is a brand new edition with more stories and more illustrations by Trina Robbins.

The Contested Earth and Other SF Stories — A never-before published space opera and seven short stories by Jim Harmon.

The Corpse Factory — More horror stories by Arthur Leo Zagat.

The Crackpot and Other Twisted Tales of Greedy Fans and Collectors — The first retrospective collection of the whacky stories of John E. Stockman. Edited by Dwight R. Decker.

The Crimson Butterfly — Early novel by Edmund Snell involving superstition and aberrant Lepidoptera in Borneo.

The Crimson Query — A 1929 thriller from Arlton Eadie. A perfect way to get introduced.

The Daymakers, City of the Tiger & Perchance to Wake — Three volumes of stories taken from the influential British science fiction magazine *Science Fantasy*. Compiled by John Boston & Damien Broderick.

The Devil Drives — An odd prison and lost treasure novel from 1932 by Virgil Markham.

The Devil of Pei-Ling — Herbert Asbury's 1929 tale of the occult.

The Devil's Mistress — A 1915 Scottish gothic tale by J. W. Brodie-Innes, a member of Aleister Crowley's Golden Dawn.

The Devil's Nightclub and Other Stories — John Pelan introduces some gruesome tales by Nat Schachner.

The Disentanglers — Episodic intrigue at the turn of last century by Andrew Lang

The Dog Poker Code — A spoof of *The Da Vinci Code* by D. B. Smithee.

The Dumpling — Political murder from 1907 by Coulson Kernahan.

The End of It All and Other Stories — Ed Gorman selected his favorite short stories for this huge collection.

The Evil of Li-Sin — A Gerald Verner double, combining *The Menace of Li-Sin* and *The Vengeance of Li-Sin*, together with an introduction by John Pelan and an afterword and bibliography by Chris Verner.

The Fangs of Suet Pudding — A 1944 novel of the German invasion by Adams Farr

The Finger of Destiny and Other Stories — Edmund Snell's superb collection of weird stories of Borneo.

The Gold Star Line — Seaboard adventure from L.T. Reade and Robert Eustace.

The Great Orme Terror — Horror stories by Garnett Radcliffe from the pulps

The Hairbreadth Escapes of Major Mendax — Francis Blake Crofton's 1889 boys' book.

The House That Time Forgot and Other Stories — Insane pulpitude by Robert F. Young

The House of the Vampire — 1907 poetic thriller by George S. Viereck.

The Illustrious Corpse — Murder hijinx from Tiffany Thayer

The Incredible Adventures of Rowland Hern — Intriguing 1928 impossible crimes by Nicholas Olde.

The John Dickson Carr Companion — Comprehensive reference work compiled by James E. Keirans. Indispensable resource for the Carr *aficionado*.

The Julius Caesar Murder Case — A 1935 retelling of the assassination by Wallace Irwin that's more fun than Shakespeare's version.

The Kid Was a Killer — Caryl Chessman's only novel, based on his own experiences.

The Koky Comics — A collection of all of the 1978-1981 Sunday and daily comic strips by Richard O'Brien and Mort Gerberg, in two volumes.

The Lady of the Fjords — Barnard Balogh's novel of Norse gods and heroes, reincarnation, and a love affair transcending mortality.

The Living Mummy — Gruesome 1910 horror novel by Ambrose Pratt involving evil mysteries resurrected from Ancient Egypt.

The Lord of Terror — 1925 mystery with master-criminal, Fantômas.

The Man who was Murdered Twice — Intriguing murder mystery by Robert H. Leitfred.

The Melamare Mystery — A classic 1929 Arsene Lupin mystery by Maurice Leblanc

The Man Who Was Secrett — Epic SF stories from John Brunner

The Man Without a Planet — Science fiction tales by Richard Wilson

The N. R. De Mexico Novels — Robert Bragg, the real N.R. de Mexico, presents *Marijuana Girl, Madman on a Drum, Private Chauffeur* in one volume.

The Night Remembers — A 1991 Jack Walsh mystery from Ed Gorman.

The One After Snelling — Kickass modern noir from Richard O'Brien.

The Organ Reader — A huge compilation of just about everything published in the 1971-1972 radical bay-area newspaper, *THE ORGAN*. A coffee table book that points out the shallowness of the coffee table mindset.

The Place of Hairy Death — Collected weird horror tales by Anthony M. Rud.

The Poker Club — Three in one! Ed Gorman's ground-breaking novel, the short story it was based upon, and the screenplay of the film made from it.

The Private Journal & Diary of John H. Surratt — The memoirs of the man who conspired to assassinate President Lincoln.

The Ramble House Coloring Book — Twenty illustrations to color in, each adapted from one of Gavin L. O'Keefe's cover designs.

The Ramble House Mapbacks — Recently revised book by Gavin L. O'Keefe with color pictures of all the Ramble House books with mapbacks.

The Secret Adventures of Sherlock Holmes — Three Sherlockian pastiches by the Brooklyn author/publisher, Gary Lovisi.

The Secret of the Morgue — Frederick G. Eberhard's 1932 mystery involving murder and forensic science with an undercurrent of the malaise that's driven by Prohibition.

The Sign of the Scorpion — A 1935 Edmund Snell tale of oriental evil.

The Silent Terror of Chu-Sheng — Yellow Peril suspense novel by Eugene Thomas.

The Singular Problem of the Stygian House-Boat — Two classic tales by John Kendrick Bangs about the denizens of Hades.

The Smiling Corpse — Philip Wylie and Bernard Bergman's odd 1935 novel.

The Sorcery Club — Classic supernatural novel by Elliott O'Donnell.

The Spider: Satan's Murder Machines — A thesis about Iron Man.

The Stench of Death: An Odoriferous Omnibus by Jack Moskovitz — Two complete novels and two novellas from 60's sleaze author, Jack Moskovitz.

The Story Writer and Other Stories — Classic SF from Richard Wilson

The Strange Thirteen — Richard B. Gamon's odd stories about Raj India.

The Technique of the Mystery Story — Carolyn Wells' tips about writing.

The Tell-Tale Soul — Two novellas by Bram Stoker Award-winning author Christopher Conlon. Introduction by John Pelan.

The Threat of Nostalgia — A collection of his most obscure stories by Jon Breen

The Time Armada — Fox B. Holden's 1953 SF gem.

The Tomb of the Dark Ones — Adventure in Egypt where ancient forces are roused from æons of slumber. A J. M. A. Mills novel from 1937.

The Tongueless Horror and Other Stories — Volume One of the series of short stories from the weird pulps by Wyatt Blassingame.

The Town from Planet Five — From Richard Wilson, two SF classics, *And Then the Town Took Off* and *The Girls from Planet 5*

The Tracer of Lost Persons — From 1906, an episodic novel that became a hit radio series in the 30s. Introduced by Richard A. Lupoff.

The Trail of the Cloven Hoof — Diabolical horror from 1935 by Arlton Eadie. Introduced by John Pelan.

The Triune Man — Mindscrambling science fiction from Richard A. Lupoff.

The Unholy Goddess and Other Stories — Wyatt Blassingame's first DTP compilation

The Universal Holmes — Richard A. Lupoff's 2007 collection of five Holmesian pastiches and a recipe for giant rat stew.

The Werewolf vs the Vampire Woman — Hard to believe ultraviolence by either Arthur M. Scarm or Arthur M. Scram.

The Whistling Ancestors — A 1936 classic of weirdness by Richard E. Goddard and introduced by John Pelan.

The White Owl — A vintage thriller from Edmund Snell

The White Peril in the Far East — Sidney Lewis Gulick's 1905 indictment of the West and assurance that Japan would never attack the U.S.

The Wonderful Wizard of Oz — by L. Frank Baum and illustrated by Gavin L. O'Keefe.

The Yu-Chi Stone — Novel of intrigue and superstition set in Borneo, by Edmund Snell.

They Called the Shots — Collection of authoritative articles by Francis M. Nevins exploring the action movie directors of the late silents through to the late 1960s.

Time Line — Ramble House artist Gavin O'Keefe selects his most evocative art inspired by the twisted literature he reads and designs.

Tiresias — Psychotic modern horror novel by Jonathan M. Sweet.

Tortures and Towers — Two novellas of terror by Dexter Dayle.

Totah Six-Pack — Fender Tucker's six tales about Farmington in one sleek volume.

Tree of Life, Book of Death — Grania Davis' book of her life.

Trail of the Spirit Warrior — Roger Haley's saga of life in the Indian Territories.

Twelve Who Were Damned — Collection of weird menace tales by Paul Ernst.

Two Kinds of Bad — Two 50s novels by William Ard about Danny Fontaine

Two Suns of Morcali and Other Stories — Evelyn E. Smith's SF tour-de-force

Two-Timers — Time travel double: *The Man Who Mastered Time* by Ray Cummings and *Time Column* and *Taa the Terrible* by Malcolm Jameson. Introduced by Richard A. Lupoff.

Ultra-Boiled — 23 gut-wrenching tales by our Man in Brooklyn, Gary Lovisi.

Up Front From Behind — A 2011 satire of Wall Street by James B. Kobak.

Victims & Villains — Intriguing Sherlockiana from Derham Groves.

Wade Wright Novels — *Echo of Fear, Death At Nostalgia Street, It Leads to Murder* and *Shadows' Edge*, a double book featuring *Shadows Don't Bleed* and *The Sharp Edge*.

Walter S. Masterman Novels — *The Green Toad, The Flying Beast, The Yellow Mistletoe, The Wrong Verdict, The Perjured Alibi, The Border Line, The Bloodhounds Bay, The Curse of Cantire, The Baddington Horror* and *Death Turns Traitor.* Masterman wrote horror and mystery novels, some introduced by John Pelan.

We Are the Dead and Other Stories — Volume Two in the Day Keene in the Detective Pulps series, introduced by Ed Gorman. When done, there may be 11 in the series.

Welsh Rarebit Tales — Charming stories from 1902 by Harle Oren Cummins

West Texas War and Other Western Stories — Western hijinks by Gary Lovisi.

What Was That?—Ghostly murder mystery from 1920 by Katharine Haviland Taylor.

What If? Volume 3 — Richard A. Lupoff introduces SF short stories that should have won a Hugo, but didn't.

When the Bat Man Thirsts and Other Stories — Weird tales from Frederick C. Davis.

When the Dead Walk — Gary Lovisi takes us into the zombie-infested South.

Whip Dodge: Man Hunter — Wesley Tallant's saga of a bounty hunter of the old West.

Win, Place and Die! — The first new mystery by Milt Ozaki in decades. The ultimate novel of 70s Reno.

Writer, Volumes 1, 2 & 3 — A *magnus opus* from Richard A. Lupoff summing up his life as writer.

You'll Die Laughing — Bruce Elliott's 1945 novel of murder at a practical joker's English countryside manor.

You're Not Alone: 30 Science Fiction Stories from *Cosmos Magazine*, edited by Damien Broderick.

RAMBLE HOUSE
www.ramblehouse.com
flyingspiderster@gmail.com
10329 Sheephead Drive, Vancleave MS 39565 USA

I *always look for* the 'RAMBLE HOUSE' *when I want a* PLEASANT BOOK*!*

Your troubles are at an end when you choose a Ramble House novel. No more doubts! No more disappointments! A Ramble House novel will give you hours of happy reading. Next time, just say to your librarian, "A Ramble House, please!"

www.ingramcontent.com/pod-product-compliance
Lightning Source LLC
Chambersburg PA
CBHW031111260626
47172CB00001B/306